THE

PLUNDER

ROOM

THE

PLUNDER

ROOM

John Jeter

THOMAS DUNNE BOOKS
ST. MARTIN'S PRESS ✹ NEW YORK

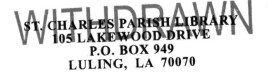

THOMAS DUNNE BOOKS.
An imprint of St. Martin's Press.

(continued on page 295)

www.thomasdunnebooks.com
www.stmartins.com

LIBRARY OF CONGRESS CATALOGING-IN-PUBLICATION DATA

Jeter, John.
    The plunder room / John Jeter. — 1st ed.
      p. cm.
    ISBN-13: 978-0-312-38065-6 (alk. paper)
    ISBN-10: 0-312-38065-8 (alk. paper)
    1. Honor—Fiction. 2. Conduct of life—Fiction. 3. South Carolina—Fiction. 4. Domestic fiction. I. Title.
    PS3610.E8779p55 2009
    813'.6—dc22

                           2008029910

First Edition: January 2009

10 9 8 7 6 5 4 3 2 1

For Katherine and Jack,

my parents,

with love

It is a grand mistake to think of being great without goodness, and I pronounce it as certain that there was never a truly great man that was not at the same time truly virtuous.

—BENJAMIN FRANKLIN

Part One

THE

NEXT

MOURNING

CHAPTER ONE

MY GRANDFATHER tries to pull me closer. I can barely hear his whisper, and my wheelchair won't let me get any nearer, so I maneuver as best I can to lean into his deathbed. His breath is redolent of the blood and decay he must have smelled during the war in Europe, his infantrymen dying around him. I gather he's trying to tell me about the great Southern commandment he's never broken.

"Honor . . ." he says through the same soft breaths he took as a baby, "all . . . we have . . ." He looks up at me with those eyes as blue as the heavens to which he's going; perhaps he already sees his beloved wife waiting for him. "Our legacy . . . Randol."

I squeeze his crumpled hand as he lies in the bed where my grandmother Pearl Clementine died nearly two dozen years before. Losing PeeCee devastated Grandfather even more than . . . well, he rarely spoke of the war, but he'd been in love twice as long as he'd been in the military.

Grandfather cherished his United States Army, no doubt about that. To hear Grandfather tell it, in the few stories he *did* tell, the army was an entirely different outfit in his day. The Grand Old Army, they called it then. Grandfather would have given his life for his army, even before his country; to Grandfather, they were more than the sum of the parts in ways I can't imagine or understand today. And in the South, why, the army, especially in those days, was an institution revered as highly as the Church herself.

The old colonel's silver hair flows to his T-shirt collar; he always wore his hair a tad longer than most officers, but then he's also kept more of it than nearly all who live to ninety-three.

"It's . . ." He licks his sandpaper lips and grips my hand. His skin is wrapped on him as taut, white, and thin as the wrapper on a Vietnamese spring roll; you can almost see through the old man. His grand walrus mustache, though, still bounces with every struggling word. "Like virginity." He manages a chuckle. "Once you lose . . . your honor, it's gone . . . forever."

He knows he's almost gone, too. Grandfather wheezes an exhausted cough. I believe he's ready to go, yet I feel as if I am keeping him somehow, keeping him from PeeCee. He may even be thinking about a good, heavenly romp right about now, randy rascal that he always was with her. Still, after a life lived as long and remarkably as his, how could you be late for your own Judgment Day?

"I don't . . . a key." His slow glance drifts toward his mahogany chest of drawers. "That will get you . . . the Plunder . . ."

No telling how many dead Nazis live up there. Grandfather kept them in trunks, U.S. Army footlockers half the size of coffins. He'd stuffed his entire history in the boxes and left them in one of the four bedrooms upstairs. The Plunder Room, we call it.

"Everything"—he tries to shake his head and forms something of a frown, a rare kind of cloud in the otherwise temperate sky of his face—"in there . . . is yours." He wheezes again. He must be in pain, but he would never betray that, never has. "I don't trust them with . . . don't trust . . ."

He closes his eyes in one last bit of mortal distress. "You . . . I trust . . . Jupe, no . . ." A tear appears at the corner of his left eye. "Jupe will pay . . . but everything . . . you . . . need . . . to know is in the Plund . . . love . . . above all, honor . . ."

After so many years hearing that word, it finally explodes on me with definitive impact, like Captain George S. James's ball on Fort Sumter: Even in his report to Confederate General P. T. Beauregard that April 1861, a Brigadier General Cooper wrote that James had "the honor of firing the first shell" on the fort. In the South, family honor is like the suit you wear from visitation through the funeral—you don't take it off, and if you do, folks not only notice, especially in a town as small as New Cumbria, South Carolina, but they also figure you're out to destroy the dignity of your family's line forever, backward and forward. And you have to live with that and, worse, die with it. That's pretty much what Rhett Butler was trying to get through to Scarlett's hormones amid all the damned Yankees' dishonorable flames.

My mind stops wandering through the Old South when my grandfather reaches toward the ceiling, the sky, calls to the Lord, and breathes his last.

So my grandfather, Colonel Edward Randol Duncan—a graduate of West Point, whose motto is "Duty, Honor, Country," and whose name I carry, in part—has passed our Southern family's most cherished mantle on to me, along with a key and perhaps a secret or two.

Three days later, I'm shivering at Grandfather's graveside. I look around our family's cemetery, dating back to the 1680s, for possible accomplices to help me in my new mandate, the mission given to me by my grandfather. Last night, hundreds of guests poured through my grandfather's home, paying their respects and filling themselves with fried chicken, artichoke pickle, finger sandwiches, and sweet tea. Through it all, I sat in my wheelchair, eyes glazed like the honey ham, while I accepted condolences and tried to figure out how I could get myself to the Plunder Room. I might as well have contemplated climbing Mount Hood as the antebellum home's grand staircase.

But today, at Grandfather's funeral, the bugler playing taps in the woods behind us brings my attention back to the service. Amid the mournful brass dirge, the real sobbing starts. My son, Eddie, seated in a plastic folding chair behind me, sniffles a little. On my own cheeks, a tear freezes halfway down, and another falls into my lifeless lap.

The afternoon happens to be perfect burial weather. The forty or so mourners around Grandfather's flag-draped casket are huddled in a fine, cold mist. The Piedmont autumn would have reminded Grandfather of the Ardennes or Germany. He would have loved this.

Eddie leans into my ear and hisses.

I turn back and whisper, "The hell . . . ?"

Eddie points his eyes toward the tree line opposite the family chapel.

My father, Edward Jupiter Duncan, is tilting into a loblolly pine, one of hundreds on the sixty-five-acre tree farm he has just inherited from his father. Jupe is likely throwing up from last night's drinking, but it's also possible that after yesterday's six-hour visitation and all that fried chicken, coleslaw, and potato salad and all those cheese straws and tea biscuits, he might not be feeling too well; they don't call them *deviled* eggs for nothing. Never mind the vodka Jupe kept pouring into his red Solo cup.

But Jupe isn't . . . throwing up.

"It's not like I can go fetch the idiot, Eddie," I hiss back.

"What do you want *me* to do?" Eddie snaps.

I can't very well move, trapped as I am in the front row. My chair feels so big among all these feeble little seats. Besides, the chaplain is just about to lean over and hand me the American flag that had flown over the U.S. Capitol for fifteen minutes and only moments before had been draped on Grandfather's coffin by the snappy color guard from Fort Jackson.

Jupe is leaning into his trees and damned if he isn't . . .

"On behalf of the president of the United States, a grateful nation, and a proud United States Army," says the chaplain, a Major Henderson, according to his name tag and the insignia on his dress blues, "this flag is presented as a token of our appreciation for the honorable and faithful service rendered by your grandfather, Colonel Edward Randol Duncan, United States Army, retired, to his country and his army."

My father is taking a leak on those loblolly pines, the cash cow that his father left him, not to mention on the proud legacy that Grandfather conveyed to me in those treasured moments before he died. That was just a few days ago, in the dim light from an old Oriental lamp with red tassels, amid the smell of his Old Spice cologne and the odor of decay. The silence of that big house knew nothing but love and honor, dignity and respect—Southern mores my grandfather had never outright taught me but believed I would learn by watching. After Grandfather's final breath, I sat in silence at his bedside for a few moments and prayed for the repose of his soul. Then I rolled over to his chest of drawers. Among black woolen socks and a couple of jewelry boxes containing silver tuxedo-blouse studs, I found an old brass key no longer than a nickel. When we were kids, even though we *knew* the room was haunted, my half brother, Jerod, and I would look through the

Plunder Room's keyhole, as big around as your pinky. All we could see were Grandfather's footlockers. As far as Jerod and I knew, the room contained nothing but trunks and ghosts. Grandfather entrusted the room and what's inside to only me. I have no idea what lock this little key fits, though my guess is that it opens some other place that holds the larger key to the Plunder Room.

I take the flag and whisper to the chaplain, "Thank you," then turn my chair for hasty good-byes to the miserable mourners and promise that I will see them all back at my grandparents' house in New Cumbria.

Eddie has already corralled Jupe into the front seat of Grandfather's old Crown Victoria, which I'd retrofitted for my paraplegia. I'd first had to convince Grandfather to quit driving, when he was ninety-two. After heaving my wheelchair into the backseat, I push myself behind the wheel and Jupe over to the passenger side. He manages to slide into a slouch. Eddie doesn't say a word; in fact, seeing as how it's gotten a little easier to handicap people since *I've* become handicapped, I'd wager my son is stoned.

Gazing through the curtain of mist on the windshield, I growl at Jupe. "Hey, Dipshit."

"Is that any way to talk to your father?" he moans and slurs, or maybe the other way around.

"Is peeing on your inheritance, missing most of your father's funeral, and showing gross disregard for his memory, his son and grandson, his friends, his entire *country*—is that any way to treat *your* father?"

"He's dead. Not a whole lot he can do about that."

"You're something else, Jupe—"

"Try calling me 'Dad,' Randol, like most sons do. I never did appreciate your grandfather naming me after his favorite horse. *You* could show a little more respect."

I pull out of the cemetery and begin the eight-mile drive

from Little Brook back to New Cumbria. "I could show a little more respect, but . . ." He's already passed out. Through the rearview mirror I watch Eddie, who has long since taken off his sharp regimental tie and blue blazer. "Where did things go wrong?" I whisper, almost to Eddie, but mostly to the ghost of my grandfather.

"Huh?" is all I get from the backseat.

"I don't know. Your granddad here, the complete malfunction that he is, coming from the hero that he did?" I get a little choked up, and for the second time today my eyes sting. "I just really don't want you to turn out like him."

I shoot a look at Jupe, then back at Eddie, then through the dismal film, but the wipers can't seem to sweep away the misery.

It's almost eight-thirty and the guests have finally gone home, depleted of stories and sobs. Volusia still putters in the kitchen at the far back of the house. Eddie has gone to bed. Jupe and I sit in the front parlor—the China Room, Grandmother called it. She decorated it chock-a-block with mother-of-pearl screens, two faux Ming vases and braided money trees, a pair of cast-iron incense burners as big as basketballs that weigh more than bowling balls, and a one-hundred-percent genuine rickshaw that Grandfather bought her during his tour in Tientsin from 1935 to 1937. The rickshaw stretches full across the back of the room under the southwest window, framed by towering bamboo plants. Its crimson seat cushion shines like a siren's succulent lips. The rickshaw has broken many a child's heart, at least two generations who would have given anything to play on it. More often than I care to remember, I have heard the story of Jupe's "borrowing" the contraption for a big date one night long ago.

As much as I love my grandparents' home, I would be all too happy to give up what is rightfully my father's to my father; the house and everything in it belong to Jupe now. Back in my wandering days, whenever I returned to New Cumbria, I tossed my bags into the servants' quarters between Grandfather's quarter-acre vegetable garden and the woods at the edge of the rear property line. Grandfather called the squat whitewashed bivouac the SQ, as opposed to the HQ, his own home, the big house, his headquarters.

In the SQ, Eddie and I have made a nice little pad for ourselves. The four-room wood-frame cabin isn't quite a bungalow, but it's hardly a shack. Let's put it this way: Before the accident, I was far more comfortable bringing a woman back to Randol's Rec Room than to Grandfather's Garrison, if only because of the privacy. Plus, I didn't have to explain where my grandparents' world of antiques came from. Since the accident, though, I have shuffled between the SQ and the house, mostly to spend time with my grandfather. Thankfully, I could leave the heavy nursing care to Volusia, who has worked here as long as I can remember and appears to be leaving no time soon, despite her employer's passing. I can't do everything myself.

As I watch Jupe snooze in the China Room, it occurs to me that he probably wants to live in this forgotten old mill town about as badly as he wants a colonoscopy; at his age, he needs one. When Jupe was a boy, he couldn't wait to get out of New Cumbria, so why would he want to return now? Besides, he has his "business interests" in Wrenton, and he'd never be willing to drive the hour plus each way more than one day a week. Of course, I can't imagine Jupe and Eddie and me living on the same property. I could least of all imagine what Volusia would have to say about that. The fact is, Jupe will live wherever he wants, the hardheaded son of a bitch. Since I left home at sixteen, he has lived, according to him, in Shanghai (I find that hard to believe), the Bahamas (ditto), New Orleans (in his dreams), Manhattan, Saigon (which, as far as I can figure, did most of the damage that had ever been done to my father), and, for three months, a prison in Tegucigalpa, Honduras, where I had to go fetch him when I was thirty-five.

Tonight Jupe's silver-blond hair drapes over the collar of his navy blue blazer, whose shiny veneer blares its age. Masking tape holds the right stem of his wire-rimmed spectacles in place. His magnified eyes, which used to be robin's-egg blue, wander loose in a clouded sky of red, white, and just plain tired. His skin, a mottled mixture of gray, yellow, and tan, doesn't sag; he doesn't have enough for that. At sixty-eight, my father looks a little like one of those guys my grandfather liberated from the guys whose souvenirs are packed in the Plunder Room.

"You look like hell, Jupe."

"I look like hell?" He looks up at me. "It's been a long day. Sad, too. Don't you think you'll be sad when you lose your old man?"

"I don't think I'll pee in his trees."

"Volusia still here? I could use a cup of the South's best coffee."

I look at my watch. She's put in too many hours. "Are you planning on living here?"

He slouches deeper into the cherrywood davenport, bigger than the backseat of a 1957 Buick. The sofa was also shipped over from China. You can curl a man Jupe's size into the shape of a cinnamon roll and he will fit onto just one cushion, that's how big the seats are. Chinese silk of red, ivory, blue, and green still dazzles after all these years, hand-embroidered with dragons, orchids, and vines. And comfortable? You can sink into one of those big round silk pillows and be lost for days. To anyone who pays enough attention, Jupe would probably claim that he lived in one in 1973.

I snap my fingers at him. "Hey, are you wasted? Hungover? Gone to another planet? Mourning the enormity of your father's loss to this family and to this nation? Not paying any attention to me or your surroundings—that's just so completely self-absorbed—"

He looks up, almost startled. "For pity's sake, Randol, would you just shut the fuck up?"

"Dad. Please. I asked a simple question."

"Actually, you asked four. You were about to ask five."

"So?"

"That's six."

"You are such a child," I mutter, rolling toward the kitchen, where I hear Volusia winding up her endless day.

You can't tell that two hundred or so guests shuffled, ate, drank, and greeted one another through the house all day. Volusia and her hand-picked staff had, in less than an hour, spit-and-polished the downstairs so that it looks as if nobody even *lives* here, much less ever visited. Still, I know Eddie and I will have enough fried chicken and trimmings to last weeks.

Volusia meets me in the darkness of the pantry, which actually is a hallway between the dining room and the kitchen, with shelves on both sides to hold the silver, china, and dry goods.

"I thought I heard you roll your lazy ass toward the galley. What you want, Mister Randol?"

"Would you mind bringing my father and me some coffee—absolutely no alcohol in his, please—and mine . . . you know how I like it."

"Do I look like your Step'n Fetchit?"

"Do I look like your paycheck?"

She smiles at me. Volusia is one handsome woman; "high

yellow" Grandmother's friends used to call her. At fifty-two, Volusia still could be a model. No wonder Grandfather enjoyed her company so much.

"She has one of those asses, like a shelf you can put your cocktails on," Grandfather once remarked to Jupe when I happened to hear them out on the porch.

"You didn't ever—"

The fact that Jupe even wondered, let alone asked Grandfather, such a thing made me want to run out to Grandfather—because I *could* run then—and ask why he didn't shoot his son on the spot.

Volusia is already ahead of me with two cups and saucers of my grandmother's finest china, a glass of cold tap water, and a paper towel.

"What's the water for, V?" I ask.

She tosses it into my father's face, careful not to hit the Chinese silk, and quick with the paper towel to mop up what little water did hit the cushions.

"What the f—"

"You watch your mouth in this household, Mister Edward Jupiter." She pulls a small bar of soap from her white "domestic" smock and rams it between his dentures. She gets all the little soaps she could ever want from a niece who works at the new Hyatt in downtown Wrenton; I guess you never know when you'll need to stuff one in somebody's foul mouth. Good enough reason to watch your tongue at all times in my grandparents' house.

"Now, didn't your son just aks you a question, Mister Jupiter?"

Jupe spits out the soap, grabs Volusia's paper towel, swabs his mouth, spits into it, and fills his mouth with hot coffee.

"I really wish you wouldn't do that, Volusia," he says, wide awake now, pretty much for the first time tonight.

She has long since left the room.

"Well?" I ask. "She's clearly waiting for an answer."

"I haven't decided yet."

"Just so you know, it doesn't matter to me either way." I study him. "On second thought . . ." I pause, shake my head so he doesn't notice. "Want some more coffee?"

"Since when does Volusia do your bidding for you, Randol?"

"Funny how folks tend to like you when you spend time with them, Dad, and, well, when you pay them."

"I pay my people," he says, on the defensive and almost sitting upright, also for the first time today.

"'Indignant' looks as good on you as a mustard stain on a seersucker suit, ol' man." I have as much interest in talking about my father's business dealings, whatever they are, as I do in discussing whether he may have ever lived in Bora Bora with a swimsuit model.

"Listen, Dad—"

"It makes me feel better to hear you call me that." He finishes his coffee and licks his lips, then rests his head against the cool Chinese silk.

"Grandfather and Grandmother's room, the whole place, in fact, is yours now. You're welcome to it. Stay here. I can always stay where I am, in the servants' quarters. Or I can move into the HQ, the big house. It's no problem."

"Mighty generous of you, son." He pops out his dentures and wipes off the soap film and starts gumming his lips the way old men do. I always thought that was funny-looking, sort of like a large-mouth bass trying to say something important.

The telephone rings in its explosion of a bell. In his waning years, my grandfather installed a ringer box over the recliner where he would sit and read; the only time he watched TV was to see my ex-wife, Elsbeth, on CNN, or to take in the occasional program on the History Channel or watch *Nova*, the PBS science show. I remember the first time Grandfather met Elsbeth, after we were married, after my grandmother died. That was when I realized I couldn't determine whether Grandfather was a first-class flirt or a world-class charmer or whether you could be both and get away with it. "Really, sir, I'm an anchor, so I just dictate the news," she said with humility that rang as fake as margarine on a butter plate. "I fought dictators the best part of my life," Grandfather said, giggling, then turned to me with that twinkle in his blue eyes. "You're screwed, m'boy."

Jupe nearly jumps off the couch. "Goddamn phone rings like a prison alarm."

"All too familiar, Jupe, I know, but do you really want another oral cleansing? Volusia takes special exception to the name-in-vain stuff."

Seeing as how Jupe isn't about to move and Volusia takes little interest in answering Grandfather's phone, I reach across my grandfather's recliner as best I can and pick up the handset.

"Duncan."

"Narrows it down. Do you know how many Duncans live around there?"

"I'll be damned." I look at my father, trying to hide my astonishment, even though I won't tell him Jerod is on the other end. "Where are you?"

"Doesn't that maid—what's-her-name, Volvo, right?—still carry around those little soaps, in case you curse like that?"

"Seriously. Where are you? Are you here in New Cumbria? Coming home? Grandfather's funeral was today. Everyone asked about you."

"I have no idea where I am." I hear an impish laugh in the background and hope against hope that he's alone.

"Describe your location to me."

"It's an airport."

"Are you alone?"

"Is Dad there?" he asks.

"After a fashion."

"We're in Wrenton, so I'll see you in about an hour, hour and a half."

"We?"

"I'll rent a car, drive down to Grandfather's, and we'll catch up then."

Click.

I will, in fact, be damned.

Jupe jolts up as if Grandfather had just told him to. "Who was that?"

I roll back toward the kitchen, making certain this time that Volusia really can hear me; I know all the creaks in the floor in the living room, across the formal dining room, and through the pantry, and I hit every single one with determined alacrity.

She meets me before I reach the pantry, where I tell her of Jerod's impending arrival. Her laughter detonates the darkness.

"That little son of a bitch," she says. "He's coming home."

"He's bringing someone."

"Uh-uh, not here, he's not. Ain't going to be no unhitched hos in your grandparents' house, no. I don't care if it *is* over their dead bodies. He's welcome to put her up in the Bait Shack"—that's what they call the New Cumbria Motor Lodge off U.S. 36 By-pass three miles west of town—"and *he* can stay here if he wants, but them two aren't staying under the same hallowed roof. That'd be over *my* dead body."

Jerod had managed to miss the biggest death of his life. Everybody in town would love to give him hell about that, but everybody loves Jerod too much to give him hell about much of anything. So I have to wonder why he's bothering to come home now at all.

"Volusia?" I ask, pulling her into the kitchen so that my father won't hear, not that he could or would care even if he did. "I need to ask you a huge favor."

"You know I'd do most anything for you, Mister Randol; you almost the only one who could be considered sane in this man's outfit."

That's what my grandfather occasionally called his tiny army of descendants. Hearing those words, I miss him now more bitterly, more painfully, than ever.

"Never mind."

Perhaps she knows what I'm thinking, that I'd like her to find some help—maybe some guys from the nursing home down the street—to pull me upstairs, but it's late, almost ten o'clock. Besides, the only way I could get back downstairs would be on my backside, through inglorious thumps of gravity. I almost burst out laughing at the thought, catheter and bag flying every which way. Volusia looks at me as if I've finally lost my mind.

She's exhausted, with still too many things to worry about before getting home: what to do about Jupe, still scrunched in the sofa; how to handle Jerod and his latest bimbo in the event they try to stay in the house together; and how much she's getting paid for her extraordinary hours. And missing Grandfather with steely disconsolation. Her day has been too long.

Right now we have to get Jupe into my grandparents' bedroom, where, by rights, he can live to the end of his days, which, also by rights, could be tomorrow. And I have to wait up for Jerod.

"I could ask you to help get Dad into bed for me."

"I'd sooner wheel you into hell for an ice-cream cone."

"Mind staying here for a sec?" I roll into my grandfather's room and open his mahogany dresser, where I keep his checkbook, then back into the kitchen. In the callous fluorescent light over the breakfast table, I write Volusia a check for a hundred dollars, which seems generous for her work. "Beats the forty-six dollars a month my grandfather used to pay his cook in China."

Without so much as looking at it, she folds the check and slides it into the white blouse of her uniform. "Assuming you paid me what I think you did, adjusted for inflation, the Oriental fella made only a little bit better than six bucks a day less than me. Somethin' to think about, I reckon."

Volusia turns to leave through the back door, beaming a victory smile at me. Over her shoulder, she adds: "Old Chinese proverb, Mister Randol: 'Wealth is but dung, useful only when spread.'"

Returning to the China Room, I find that my father is passed out again. He's curled up on the Chinese silk of the big old davenport. It's up to me to get my father into bed on my own.

"Get up." I'd love to kick him, like mashing shoe leather into a hobo. "Rise and shine," I say, a little louder this time, using the expression Grandfather used on me the year I lived with my grandparents when Dad served in Vietnam. I used to take a long time to wake up then, too, but I was usually faking it.

"Hey!" I scream. If I had the sure aim that Volusia does with water, I'd use it, but I would splash it all over the couch and destroy the fabric. I can't understand how the silk has survived all these years without so much as a stain. I suppose my grandfather's beloved Pearl Clementine, our beloved PeeCee, was the plastic seat-covering of their lives, protecting the finer things in life, while Grandfather was the force field that never let anything evil or ugly get anywhere near his wife and home.

The thought occurs to me now that somewhere along the way, Jupe left his father's orbit, and both men allowed that to happen as happily as Grandfather let his tomato vines grow. The trouble is that Grandfather never really did understand his only son, his only child, let alone know how Jupe made his way in the world. Apparently, Grandfather didn't *want* to know, either. But now that Grandfather's dead and Jupe's out of his mind, I wonder if it doesn't make sense for at least one of us to get to the bottom of the family business, as it were, bring everything out into the open, put everything on the table.

Not that I have all the time in the world.

"Hey! One last time, you can't sleep here. You've got to—"

Jupe shakes his head, then runs his hands through his thick hair, so much like Grandfather's. The resemblance between father and son had always been alarming. If Jupe wore a walrus mustache like Grandfather's—a big, bushy broom of upper-lip hair that, incidentally, never changed color from the original sandy blond—he would look just like his old man.

"Calling me names like 'Dipshit.' For Pete's sake, son. Show a little respect."

"Either get up and go to bed, Dad-o, or get out."

"Says who and what army?"

"Want me to call Volusia back in to kick your ass clear back to Wrenton?"

"The mouth on you, boy."

"Grandfather's gone, lest you didn't notice because you were too busy pissing in the woods, so if you're not man enough to take over what's left of this family, and you can't handle the responsibilities of running this household, then Volusia had best not catch you in here tomorrow morning."

"You just said I was entitled to this house."

"You can't sleep on the couch."

"Why not? It's my house now." His eyes are slits. "Who was that who called a second ago?"

I don't want him to know that Jerod, his favorite son, is on his way here. "Wrong number. Don't worry about it."

"You always have actual conversations with folks who dial wrong numbers?" He rubs his eyes and raises his eyebrows. He begins to wake up now. The full-blown charm and manipulation will follow. Nobody survives those.

"Listen, Dad, it's late. We're both exhausted. I'm wrung out, too beat to talk. Eddie's already asleep down in the SQ. He's got school tomorrow, and you've got to work, or whatever the hell it is you do. I've got a lot of stuff to do around here, and I'm not in any mood—"

He actually waves his hands at me in his version of surrender. I guess I've talked him into giving up or giving out. "Great. G'night. I'm heading to the guest quarters, whatever. I'd be too creeped out to sleep in the old Bird's bedroom. It'd be too much like he was still in there."

Jupe shuffles off to the guest room, where many a history-maker has slept: General William Westmoreland, one of the state's most famous warriors, who led American armies in Vietnam; at least two South Carolina governors; the U.S. Senate's oldest living member; three motion-picture stars, including one starlet and another who, little did Grandfather know, was gay; and several writers. Of the latter, I would have loved more than anything to meet her in person, one of the South's most curious, lovable, and enduring scribes, not to mention my personal favorite: Nelle Harper Lee.

"Night, Dad."

After the bedroom's glass doorknob clicks, I hear him cough once.

For a few minutes, I wait by the front door for my brother. Every now and then, I look back over my shoulder and up the grand staircase, thinking about how to get to the Plunder Room.

CHAPTER TWO

VOICES TOO SPIRITED for so early in the morning rico-
chet off the Gravoises' house next door. Words fire down the hill,
shoot through the thin walls of the servants quarters, pierce the
whitewashed cracks of the house, and skitter across the gray plank
floor: "Here," "no," "she," "can't," and "Jerod" pepper my room
and wake me up.

The exchange has the same effect as countless movie scenes:
A shaggy guy looking hungover jerks his head up at his alarm
clock as if he's never seen it before. He stares at the red numbers
staring back at his red eyes. The guy clubs the clock until it's
smashed to bits, or he throws it against the wall, where it smashes
to bits.

My alarm clock reads six fifty-nine, but the clock's not the issue. The issue is that it's Friday, the day after my grandfather's funeral, and voices, one belonging to a man and one clearly Volusia's,

are outside on Grandfather's porch having a grand time antago-
nizing each other on a cold February morning.

Why would Volusia be here, anyway, after her sixteen-hour
day yesterday? And besides, with Grandfather permanently out of
the home she has been paid all these years to keep, she's overdue
for a nice, long vacation.

Rolling out of bed, I drag myself into my wheelchair. The
cold chrome delivers an electric shock in my little house's chill.
Eddie still sleeps in the next bedroom, where he's curled under a
foot-thick pile of Grandmother's quilts. The navy-blue sweat suit
I'd slept in is decent enough for company, I suppose, but from the
sound of things on the porch, this isn't *polite* company.

By four A.M., I couldn't wait up for Jerod anymore. What
could have taken him so long to get from Wrenton to New Cumbria? Why would he be showing up now, at dawn, more than
seven hours after he called?

Rolling up the driveway, I see that Jupe's black BMW is
gone, replaced by an equally black sport-utility vehicle. I push
myself alongside the veranda's balustrade until I reach the ramp,
which Grandfather had had installed for me after my accident. I
pull myself up the long wooden incline and turn right onto the
porch, still unnoticed, toward the banter.

"For the last time, Jerod Duncan, I'll give you till the count
of three to get your little friend—"

"And for the last time, Volusia, all I'm asking you is, please,
just this once, just for me and . . ."

"And" happens to be standing next to him.

And if she isn't *the* most gorgeous woman I have ever laid
eyes on, then she's one of the most remarkable women in history.
If Helen of Troy had the face that could launch a thousand ships,
the one on Grandfather's porch could disarm the armada. Until

now, I had thought my grandmother held the monopoly on mortal beauty.

Here stands a woman I can hardly bring myself to look at: her perfect teeth could be Steinway keys; her azure eyes dance like Fred and Ginger; her natural sandy blond hair falls in a carefree cascade over her slight shoulders; and her body . . . the only view I get is my brother's brown Orvis parka halfway down ivory Italian-linen trousers, complete with de rigueur wrinkles. My father, if here, would have claimed that he once lived in the pants' fashionable furrows for a few weeks at one time or another.

For an instant, I lose myself in something my grandfather used to say about beauty. Volusia, on the other hand, has little trouble switching her glare between Jerod and this magnificent feminine experience. Instead, she turns on me, as if I've arrived just in time to referee a cockfight.

"Who's he?" asks Aphrodite incarnate, the one person on Earth whom I would suddenly give my life for, my son having just lost the highest ground of my spiritual real estate.

Jerod turns away from Volusia and says, "Annie, this is my brother, Randol. Randol, Annie. My . . . girlfriend."

I nod with as much ease as Jerod handles his introduction.

Volusia turns to me as if she expects me to say something. "Cat got your tongue?" she mumbles.

"Jerod, um"—I glance at Annie—"could you excuse us for just a second, please? I thought y'all would be here, I dunno, several hours ago. I, um—"

"I know, we got a little—"

"I found them all tangled up together here in the hammock, Mister Randol," Volusia says, pointing to the Pawley's Island hammock that Grandmother put up on this side of the porch before I was born. "I can't believe they didn't get rope burn."

I can't believe she just said that.

"I can't believe y'all didn't freeze your asses off." I can't believe *I* just said *that.* "Excuse me, Jerod, for a second. Volusia?" I motion for Volusia to approach my chair.

"Listen," I whisper into her ear. "First off, what are you doing here? You worked forever yesterday. Grandfather's dead now, so it's not like you really even need to *be*—"

"I'm not about to let the venerable Duncan household become Hades to y'all's three-headed hound of hell, with you an' Eddie and now Mister Jerod moving in, especially not with raw meat the likes of this"—she tosses her head back toward Annie—"within sniffing distance."

"Okay, but, listen for just a sec. It's cold out here. She's not spending the night—"

"Looks like to me she jus' did."

"On the porch!" I hiss. "I can't believe they didn't get frostbite. Of all the idiotic—"

"The shame! Wun't surprise me, Mister Randol, if, now that your God-fearing grandparents, looking down from both the right *and* left hand of God awmighty, wouldn't just go ahead and authorize Him to burn this Sodom and Gomorrah right down to the ground. All's I need is enough fair warning so I can get myself—"

"Volusia, enough already. If you want to be a real good Christian, the best way would be to welcome my prodigal brother in, along with his"—I swallow—"Mary Magdalene, warm them up, and offer them something to eat, some of your extremely good and extremely hot coffee, and we'll discuss the issue later."

"Your father's going to have a fit." Volusia pulls herself together and doesn't so much welcome the guests into the house as she yanks the front door open and walks in before they do.

My father's going to have a fit. The notion's too funny, but laughing now would be bad form, and if I learned anything from my grandparents, manners would top the list.

"So. Jerod." I let him grab the handles of my chair. His lady friend lingers behind him; I'd always meant to put a rearview mirror on my chair. "Welcome home."

"Sorry I'm late." His voice sounds husky from exhaustion, dry from the cold.

"Late—hell, you missed the entire funeral, the entire wake. All that's left is to talk about Grandfather's will, and you already know what's in that for you—nothing." I try to crank my head over my shoulder to look at him and catch a glimpse of Annie. "And I imagine you'll want to see Jupe—"

"Dad?"

"Jupe, Dad, whatever. You should have seen him yesterday, Jerod. Did he show his ass or what." I look up at Jerod's striking two-day beard and whistle.

Jerod smiles at nothing. He's no more paying attention to me than he's paying late fees on an overdue library book.

Jerod could always afford a certain level of oblivion because when most of us hold a pair, he draws a full house. At the same time, he also seems to be the only man in the world who doesn't realize, doesn't understand, simply doesn't *get*, that Lady Luck has always been accessible to him like a booty call, a one-night stand whenever he feels he needs her. Or maybe that's it; maybe he *does* get it, and for reasons that have always mystified me, Lady Luck's perfectly okay with the arrangement. The thing is, Jerod's not the only one I know who's been getting away with that his entire life; he learned from the best. And on top of the charm and charisma he inherited from my father, Jerod managed to hold on to the one thing Jupe squandered years ago—his Romanesque good looks.

This is how good-looking Jerod is: "Real soldiers," Grandfather used to say, "are capable of crying in the face of real beauty." When my brother was born, my grandfather, then Major Edward

Randol Duncan, wept. (Grandfather would not have shed a single tear upon seeing Annie this morning, but only because no *woman* could ever eclipse the delicate and graceful exquisiteness of my grandmother PeeCee. "She's a looker," Grandfather would have said about Annie, "but I've seen mares equally handsome that get my jodhpurs in a bigger stir.") Jerod's thick wavy black hair parts in the middle and frames beguiling gray-blue eyes, big and innocent as a toddler's. He is tall and thin, like elegant stationery on my grandmother's Victorian writing desk. He and I couldn't be any more different: I am squat and reminiscent of various produce. Granted, I was much leaner when I had legs, but when you have a face like an eggplant, topped with thinning strands of silvery hair like corn silk, you don't usually make people weep over your good looks.

In the grand foyer of my grandparents' house, he stands, I sit; we stall. Volusia has returned to the kitchen, and we're in no hurry to return to her earshot. Annie wanders around, looking at the rooms as if she is in a museum. To the left is the China Room, to the right the formal living room. The foyer's ceiling, with the hand-carved crown molding, rises fifteen feet. From that hangs a 1930s French crystal chandelier with more than two hundred pieces of smooth round rock crystal. The Oriental rug's silken threads under my wheels betray myriad funerals, retirements, debutante parties, and other society functions since the end of the last century. Annie's beauty, which floats like the specter of some bygone socialite past my grandmother's portrait, would have impressed PeeCee, though I wish I had Pearl Clementine's genteel ability to size up anyone with instant, dead-on precision.

Jerod pays her no attention. "Where *is* Dad, by the way?"

"Beats me. I noticed his car is gone. Hungover for sure. Dead, maybe. Could be in jail—again."

"He told me—" Jerod stops. His voice is firm, almost angry,

perhaps slighted by his father's refusal to be here for his favorite son's return.

"I guess he caught just enough shut-eye to leave before you got here."

"Yeah, that's what Volusia said. She saw his car was gone, didn't recognize *my* car, and found me and"—his eyes roll toward Annie—"well, you heard the rest."

"I imagine he's gone back to Wrenton. Good for him." I had long since decided against telling Jerod that I hadn't told Jupe about his call.

He wheels me into the China Room while Annie studies the oil portrait of PeeCee above the fireplace in the living room. Annie appears as transfixed as the woman in the frame. Grandmother once told me that she could determine a person's integrity with their first eye contact, and that she could stare honesty out of anyone. When he was a boy, Jerod was wise enough to make sure PeeCee never found him.

"I need your help with something," Jerod finally admits.

"Not with women, it appears."

"Never," he says with a smile devoid of arrogance yet full of charm. He's the only person I know who can manage the combination.

"*You* need *my* help with something." I can't help but laugh.

"Yes, Randol, I do."

"If it's a health-related issue, I have an organ or two available, but if you look through the shop window, you can probably tell the merchandise isn't all that great. If it's business, forget about it. I'm as interested in knowing your business affairs as I am in knowing"—I glance toward Annie—"about Jupe's. I quit working for him after the . . . incident. Jupe's affairs made me queasy, anyway."

Jerod fails to hide a sneer.

He doesn't slouch into the sofa the way our father did last night. Instead, he leans with regal comfort into the silken cushions, as if they'd been designed for his comfort. He crosses his legs. Even his beige-and-blue argyle socks are fashionable inside the Cole Haan penny loafers the color of a fudge sundae.

"Alrighty, then." Jerod sighs and laces his fingers behind his head.

"What's that supposed to mean?"

"Well, it means that since you're obviously not going to help me—"

"With your business, that's all I said. Besides, I'm not a businessman. You don't want me getting near anything that smacks of business." I don't bother telling him that I now write music reviews for a Webzine called seriousmusic.com. Not that he would care or read anything I've written.

"Or helping with little else, presumably." He folds his hands in his lap and takes his turn looking at Annie, who now begins, at her own peril, to move toward the kitchen, whence the perfumes of Volusia's sumptuous breakfast float: coffee, scrambled eggs, smoked bacon, biscuits handmade with lard and real butter, grits—you can even smell the fruit compote, with fresh, hand-grated coconut.

"I'm just looking for one favor; a single, itty-bitty little favor." He runs a hand through his hair. Makes you want to cry. "Annie."

"What *about* Annie?"

"She needs a job."

"Here?" I could just about stand up I'm that flabbergasted.

"Somewhere." His hand flutters like a lost bird. "Around here."

"Not in New Cumbria."

"I thought she'd have her best shot at getting a job—"

"Jerod, she could get hired anywhere in the world. She could be the *entire* Dallas Cowboys Cheerleaders squad. Or, if you want something more highbrow and less misogynist, she could anchor all three news networks. Just not CNN; that job's taken." I wink at him.

"She wants to get away from the big city for a while. Y'know, enjoy small-town life. Spend some time in the South. Different pace and all."

That rings as true as the Liberty Bell. "What's she do?" My curiosity gives way to general distrust of my half brother. "Model? Actress? Brain surgeon?"

I think of Toby Lawson, who is, in fact, New Cumbria's neurosurgeon and the father of Eddie's best friend, Tyler. I smile at the notion of Jerod's young siren working alongside Dr. Lawson, who should be practicing at the Mayo Clinic, anywhere else but New Cumbria, South Carolina. If anyone can size up anyone else in this hamlet, it's Toby Lawson. Volusia can, too, but she lacks the circumspection that in hospitals they call bedside manner, and in polite society we call discretion.

Volusia's white soles squeak across the heart-pine floor. She hands us each a cup of coffee, the steam curling like a genie that I hope might give us three wishes apiece—one and a half, anyway, not to get greedy: I half wish that my half brother will get the hell *back* out of town and take his trouble with him.

"Breakfast almost ready," Volusia reports, as if the aroma hasn't already announced that, "and I'm 'bout ready to have Miss Universe out this house, certainly out my kitchen."

"Is she bothering you, Volusia?" Jerod's innocence sounds as compelling as the charm that drives it. "Because if she is . . ."

Volusia turns away on a rubber-soled scream. "She can't stay here."

"Here." His face manages to stay put. He'd fought this fight once already this morning. He's ready to fight it again.

She turns back and glares at him. "Here. In this house or in New Cumbria."

"What makes you think she—we—can't live in New Cumbria?" He looks at me as if she has just informed him that we have to put down a beloved bird dog. "Randol?"

Of course, he could've said, *Bite me, Volusia, we can live any-freaking-where we want to live; this is a free country.* But when you've got the charisma of Jerod Barrows Duncan, whose middle name hearkens to antebellum family gentility, you should use it.

He shoots me a smirk that I pray Volusia doesn't see, because he thinks he knows what I'm thinking. Scandal would erupt within and without New Cumbria if a strange woman, especially an unmarried one and one allegedly courting a Duncan, were to move into the late Colonel and Mrs. Duncan's household. More-over, if Jerod, in fact, did move Annie into the house without first putting a wedding band on her finger, I wouldn't put it past PeeCee to ask God to raise Grandfather from the dead so he could throw them both out of the house, by force of arms, if nec-essary.

Without a word, as seems to be the way this family works, the problem apparently has solved itself. Jerod sighs, and I take another sip of coffee through a smile and wink at Volusia, who chuckles and spins back to the kitchen, where, presumably, Annie lurks without supervision.

"Okay. Jerod. What's she do?"

"She's a teacher. High school."

"From?"

"Connecticut. Good family, all that. Super-smart. Knows com-puters inside out."

"So she teaches computers?"

He shakes his head. "She just *knows* them; she teaches everything else. Mostly history. If that's not irony." I wasn't aware that he even knew the word *irony*, and I'm certain he doesn't know what it means now. What my brother's missing is the irony that he's finally seeing some pride in someone other than himself.

So the ensuing pause suggests we switch to Jerod's favorite subject. "Okay, so. What is *your* plan, then?"

"I thought you weren't interested."

"Oh, well, curiosity got the best of me."

"You know how curiosity puts civets in stir-fries," Jerod says, trying to sound smarter than he is and failing.

I sip my coffee, keeping my eyes on him and waiting for him to divulge something meaningful that won't rearrange my life.

He finally says, "I have a few loose ends to tie up."

"Loose ends."

"Business matters."

"Business matters."

He sips his coffee, too, but shakes his head. "It's nothing like that."

"Like what?"

"Like what you think."

"I don't think anything you think I think, but if it is what I think it is, which is something involving Dad, I have no idea what Dad does. Not only that, I'm not interested in what Dad does, and the less I know, the happier I am, and the happier, it appears, New Cumbria seems to be." I rest the saucer on my lap. As hot as it could be, I still wouldn't feel it. "Which, by the way, brings me to yesterday. Collectively, the entire town of New Cumbria, South Carolina, was miffed, mystified, and disappointed by your absence at Grandfather's funeral."

Jerod hangs his head in the most ridiculous display of phony shame I've ever seen. "I'm sorry," he whispers. He appears to be fighting back tears, which are so far from real that he would need tweezers to squeeze them from his tear ducts.

"Listen, okay. Breakfast is being laid up," I say, rolling toward the dining room. "So give me the skinny, but be fast because I'm hungry and my bullshit-ometer is about to explode. First, why did you get here so late? Which begs the second question: Why did you come home at all, if you couldn't even bother to get here on time? Third, and very briefly, why do you think it's okay to bring Helen of Troy to New Cumbria while you run around taking care of 'loose ends'? And, finally, other than thinking that I can help the most beautiful woman I have ever laid eyes on get a job—what in heaven's name do you *want* with me, Jerod?"

Jerod stands speechless for the first time since I changed the little guy's diapers after his mother, Caroline Weingarten, left my father when I was eight years old.

"Boys!" Volusia calls from the kitchen. Seeing as how we have a guest, breakfast will be served in the formal dining room. "First plate's coming out. By the time the third plate's out, if y'all aren't at the table, I'm takin' 'em back and th'owin' everything out." She will, too; I've seen her do it.

Jerod opens up like a fire hose: "Okay, I got here late because everything hit the fan with my . . . company, which is an import-export business, I guess you'd call it, which deals in exotic oils—frankincense and myrrh, to be exact—because Christian merchandising and retailing is a seven-billion-dollar business and I started out selling little Jesus nails, charm bracelets, y'know . . ."

Charm bracelets. Now, *that's* fitting. My brother speaks with the urgency of an auctioneer and the lilt of a Realtor.

"But Islamic fundamentalists started going bat-shit in Somalia, which isn't the only place you can get *Boswellia* and *Commiphora*, but it is—"

"Could you translate from drugstore Latin?"

"The B word is frankincense, the other is myrrh. We had Air Force hotshots who liked to fly errands for us, AWOL soldiers from I-don't-know-how-many countries, Christian mercenaries running around Djibouti and Mogadishu, missionaries in Somali villages—all these people collecting all this high-end tree sap for us, which we paid them for handsomely, I might add. I mean, this stuff was the real deal, like that yellow stuff you put in Spanish food—"

"Saffron."

"Right." He snaps his fingers. "That stuff's, what? Thirty-five, thirty-six bucks an ounce, almost like pot."

"Nice, Jerod. Try to keep your conversational tone a little lower than conversational—"

"Boys!" Volusia snaps. "I said now!"

Jerod turns me toward the dining room. "We had the goods, the real goods, I'm telling you, and we were doing great there for a while. We had a manufacturer in New Jersey that boiled the sap into a clear liquid and put it into those diffusers you plug into any wall outlet. And wherever you plug this stuff in—your dining room, living room, your bedroom—I swear to God, literally, it starts smelling like you're right there with the Three Wise Men and the baby Jesus in ancient Nazareth."

"Fragrance du Manger? There's an idea," I say. He smacks the back of my head, then I remember seeing the stuff on shelves. "That's that Essence of Essenes, right? The 'Jesus juice' they sell in the dollar stores everywhere?"

"Right! That's my product."

"Bad name, seriously. 'Essence of Essenes.' Sounds good, but historically inappropriate. Uncool, even."

"Trouble was, my sources started drying up for the genuine article, so we switched to a chemical re-creation. We couldn't see changing the ingredients on the label, but consumers—and the Feds—took notice. Things headed south. So I did, too."

I wave him to a stop. I've heard enough about business. It's time to move on to Annie and the favor he wants me to do for her.

Jerod knows full well that I'm the last Duncan standing, so to speak, who knows everyone in New Cumbria with any pull, position, and power. My grandfather never let a small-town perquisite like that go to his head, but if he could ever help anybody, he figured a well-placed call or two wasn't hard to make.

"Boys." Volusia watches as I take my place at the head of the vast oak table where Grandfather always held court during dinner, the biggest meal of the day, from noon to one o'clock. Annie sits to my right.

"Dear Lord," I pray in rote, "thank You for this meal and she who prepared it. Let us use this food to Your service. Amen."

Volusia disappears through the swinging door back into the kitchen. Jerod digs in.

"Why doesn't Volusia join us?" Annie asks. "She made so much, and it all looks so delicious!"

Jerod and I trade smiles at her stunning naïveté. You can't laugh at a simple, sweet comment like that.

After a pause that's gentle without being awkward, she twirls her fork through her runny scrambled eggs, just the way I like them, and looks at me with a curious smile. "You remind me a little of Lyman Ward, only a lot less cranky."

I almost drop my silverware. Here she is, hardly thirty years old, best guess, and she lobs the name of a character from a book older than she is, Wallace Stegner's 1971 classic, *Angle of Repose*.

I glance at her. "I'm not dying of bone disease."

"From what Jerod tells me, you're as immersed in family lore as Lyman was in his." I would be a lot more interested in family lore if I could get rid of my family and get up to the Plunder Room, but this house is starting to feel like a homeless shelter for beautiful people.

I finally work up the nerve to look this woman square in the eye and realize I don't have my grandmother's gift. "What is it you do?" I ask.

"I'm a teacher by training. High school. Jerod yanked me away." She smiles, but her inflection echoes hollow and distant, the way people sound when they're not on solid ground. That's understandable, but I also hear an underlying edge, as if she's determined to work her newfound refugee status to some compelling advantage. "Never mind that I wanted to get away from New York. Living in the city is hard as it is, but the school system is tough and the kids tougher, even though I was lucky, teaching in Brooklyn."

No wonder Jerod can't get enough of this woman-child, an ingénue who looks like a Michelangelo carving with the poise of a sophisticate. Yet a serration behind her beauty, in her eyes and in the timbre of her voice, makes me think of something Tolstoy once said, something I can't remember just now, though I can always count on Leo's expertise in soldiers, aristocrats behaving badly, and beautiful women.

"You *do* know what a cad my brother is, right? Probably a world-class con man, undoubtedly a thief and—if I were a betting man—an undercover operative for anybody willing to pay him enough for whatever odd scheme he can dream up."

"I don't mind that y'all are talking about me as if I'm not here," Jerod says, busy filling his mouth with forkfuls of breakfast.

"We don't talk about work. Much," she says. "He doesn't listen to me talk about my classroom. And he's not about to discuss money, business issues, unless maybe we're in bed."

Jerod coughs into his fist, and I almost drop my fork. "So. What do *you* like to talk about?" I ask when my breathing resumes.

"Books. Sex. *Some* money, but not so much. Politics, although I would bet"—she looks around at the hand-painted wallpaper of roses, the silver tea service, the china cabinet packed with crystal, and again at PeeCee's commissioned portrait—"that you and I would see a lot of things a little differently. And music."

I don't hear too clearly after she says "sex," but I know she's lying about money. I can feel it. She could walk into a bank and rob it just by blinking those long, luscious lashes. Hell, if I were a teller, I'd give up *my* drawers for this woman. And politics? Discussing politics, especially local, with this young woman would be like discussing the nuances of Southern barbecue with a vegetarian. I clear my throat of something—a lump of sexually phlegmatic discomfort, I suppose. "I imagine you don't talk much about those subjects in class, not in high school."

"Most schools today are simply holding pens, in my opinion. As far as I'm concerned, parents have abdicated all their responsibility and are forcing teachers to become surrogate parents."

Jerod's fork has already returned to work on the Wedgwood plate. The trimness of the man's chassis says nothing about the volume of fuel he dumps into its engine.

"You, um, mentioned music."

She smiles and finishes her breakfast. My grandmother would be giddy about an appetite like hers. "I've read some of your pieces on the Internet, Mr. Duncan."

Her flattery is devastating, not to mention the "Mr. Duncan" thing. "Please, call me Randol."

"Of course." She blushes, and that's just as devastating. "You know one heck of a lot about music, especially the music my kids listen to."

"You have *kids?*" My cheeks ignite.

She laughs and puts her hand over her mouth. "No, no. Not *my* kids. I mean, the kids in school!" She laughs harder, this time a full, openmouthed laugh. "You seem to speak their language."

I look around my chair. "Guess it's easy when you're at their level."

Jerod flips open his cell phone, apparently to check the time. "Listen, I, uh, we, I guess, better get going."

"Are you planning on seeing Dad?"

Silence.

Annie shifts in her seat. After a pause broken only by another rubber-soled squeak from the pantry as Volusia comes to collect the breakfast plates, Annie says, "Jerod tells me that you may be able to help me find a job here."

For the first time since Grandfather died, I lose myself in helpless laughter. The inexplicable paroxysm won't stop.

I catch a mischievous spark in Volusia's eyes and see something in Annie's, too, that I can't figure out: Is it excitement about the possibilities of a new life here? A realization that she has signed on as Jerod's prisoner? Resignation that she has landed in a small town whose future is about as insecure as hers? Or is it delicious, hopeful optimism, a look that you can't help but love, a look that needs nurturing and constant attention?

Most of us would rather wallow in other people's histories than our own complexities, but it disturbs me that Annie is more questions than answers. If I could figure out how to look at her without reeling, I might be able to help her through whatever situation she's found herself in with my quixotic brother.

For no fathomable reason, Annie starts laughing, too, and my head spins. As sophomoric as it sounds, a man without a penis—a working one, anyway—is worse than a man with one. I feel as if I can only pine like a high school boy.

When the joviality finally fades and Jerod takes Annie away with him, a void takes its place. Grandfather is no longer in the next room, but I hear his final whispers to me, hear him tell me that trust has gone AWOL in our household. I feel something I haven't felt since the crash, since the nerves went dead below my waist:

Alone.

CHAPTER THREE

PEOPLE WITH spinal cord injuries, we call ourselves SCIs. We can recall every detail of the moment our lives changed. The pain. The shock. A lot of us still live with both, even though we can't feel anything in parts of us anymore.

For me, it was June 20, four months shy of three years ago, the day before the longest day of the year. That warm, late Saturday afternoon felt like pulled taffy, thick and sweet; you could pull and pull and pull, and it felt like it would never snap.

Doug Straithorn, Sonny Batson, Denise Merkins, and a couple others from the old Wrenton crowd had spent the day at Wren State Park. That meant passing the languid summer day laughing and swimming in the park's cold mountain-green pond, passing a jar of peach moonshine, as clear as crystal and as smooth as sugar-coated fire. We also passed around a roach or two. Whenever we got up from our spot on the lawn for a swim, we had to dodge park rangers, squealing kids, swarms of mosquitoes, bushels of

Baptists, and clots of families laden with picnics, yapping pets, and values, not to mention strategic piles of dog shit.

Doug sobered everybody up when he announced his enlistment in the Army Reserves; he said he wanted to work only one weekend a month. So right then we started calling him Duffel Bag. Denise was looking especially hot, and not just because it was ninety-one degrees. She kept asking me about Elsbeth, even though she knew we were already divorced; anyone who watched CNN could see she wore no ring on her finger. Sonny lounged around and laughed at everything, stoned out of his world and ours; he worked as a surveyor, so he was never in any big hurry to go anywhere.

"Are you ever going to get a *real* job?" Batson slurred to me, his eyes crimson slits.

I touched my chest in mock offense. "I work."

"At your father's gas 'n' git. That's hardly the role model of ambition—"

"Look at you, bong head. What're your kids doing at the trailer park right about now?"

He chuckled. Actually, Batson had a nice little ranch house for himself, his wife, and their two children.

"Listen," I said. "My son, Eddie, can visit his mom. Hell, he can watch her on TV and get all the inspiration he wants. It's nothing to get him from Wrenton to Atlanta whenever he feels like it. Besides, he's only eleven."

Denise leaned toward my shoulder. "Say, Randol, how did you ever get custody of Eddie in the first place?"

"Elsbeth and Eddie decided they didn't want him to live in Atlanta, that she would have to travel too much, and, besides, we all agreed I would be a suitable parent—"

Duffel Bag busted a gut. "If you learned your disciplinary techniques from your grandfather or your old man, Eddie's in for a treat." He winked at me and crushed another empty beer can. D Bag knew all my stories; he knew about the time my father had taken me to the Rhine River just so I could puke my guts out and the time my grandfather made my father parade around town with his rickshaw.

I packed up my towel, T-shirt, and sandals and began to say my good-byes. Elsbeth had Eddie that weekend, so I was planning to drive down to Atlanta the next day and pick him up after work. "The old man's convenience store opens at six A.M., boys and girls, so I'd better be off."

"Aw, I didn't hurt your feelings, did I, Duncan?" Straithorn asked.

Batson slapped him upside the head.

"Jupe can't open his own business tomorrow morning?" Denise said with the last come-hither look she ever offered me.

"That's why he hired me."

"I'll drop by tomorrow," D Bag said. "I got something I need to talk to you about."

I nodded, but moved toward the parking lot, Denise following me to the edge of the trees.

"You okay to drive?" she asked.

My red eyes said otherwise, but I told her I was fine. She hadn't taken a single toke all day, and if she had sipped any moonshine or beer, it had been hours before. She was as sober as one of the celebrated coeds from Wrenton International Bible College; I often had fantasies about those young ladies in their ankle-length skirts, wrapped in their homely virtuosity. But I never dreamed about Denise. Above her bikini, the look on her face bespoke innocence, too, but her hand happened to brush against my crotch.

"I'd be happy to take you home, Randol." In a tone that was

less an offer than a peremptory suggestion, she reached into my pocket and confiscated my car keys.

We climbed into her rust-red Mustang, which reeked of cigarette smoke. The backseat was littered with fast-food trash, her kids' toys, and the other detritus of a woman who lived with ends she would never make meet.

Winding through the park, she cranked up the classic-rock station and the air conditioner. You could almost taste her anxiety about going to work the next morning. She hated her bank-teller job, but she also worked twice a week at Weezle's, the most popular bar downtown, where she earned three times what she did at the bank, especially considering that her tips were tax-free. Still, she said, the situation sucked. She had two kids and a redneck husband to support. He would jig a Cherokee rain dance every day, she told me, to avoid going to his construction job. I had no such anxiety. All I had to do was show up at Jupiter's Fuel 'n' Go to open by six. Dad's stable of eight part-timers, whose cumulative IQ looked like the calorie count on a diet yogurt container, would roll in, usually late, to relieve me of such complicated duties as sweeping the floor and arranging the candy, snacks, and beef jerky, the cold-drink walk-ins and the cigarettes. Jupe never checked on me, only the previous day's receipts, which we never discussed. He never once asked me to handle inventory, not that I'd have obliged him if he had. I was too busy having fun back then.

Driving out of the park, Denise slid into the dusk. I remember the sky's muddy pastels and something Jupe told me: that the helicopter pilots in 'Nam used to hate this time of day. Nautical twilight, they called it. "Those warrant officers and army aviators who flew the Hueys and fixed-wings, they were crazy sons a bitches just by nature. But the light at that particular time seemed to scare 'em as much as the shooting did." Half of what Jupe said you could take to the bank; the other half either lacked principle, interest, currency, value, or authenticity.

He happened to tell me that *after* I got out of the hospital, I suppose to explain why Denise didn't see the Jaguar flying toward us that particular evening.

I remember thinking that I heard an engine singing up the state highway over my right shoulder; the park road yields onto SC 232 at a forty-five-degree angle. I turned just in time to see the silver glint of the sleek cat hood ornament.

The champagne-colored car was heading toward Denise's door.

Cops later said the eighteen-year-old frat boy behind the wheel of his daddy's Jag was doing eighty-two miles an hour. The speed limit on the state road is forty-five miles per hour.

Cops said it was a good thing that Denise wasn't wearing her seat belt. That it was a good thing my head had smashed the passenger-side window so that Denise met no resistance when she flew through it. That if the Jaguar had hit us head-on, instead of at an angle from behind, we both would have been killed. That our survival, especially Denise's, was a miracle.

All of which explains why she quit drinking and smoking and now sings at one of those huge God warehouses, where every Sunday some thirteen-hundred-odd people find in her a reason to never give up hope. She got a job there, too.

Denise sailed onto the shoulder, rolled a dozen yards, and landed in a thick bed of fescue. She ended up with a few bruises and a sprained wrist. Paramedics told me later that they couldn't believe she hadn't at least broken her hands, arms, or a few ribs.

She doesn't come around much to see me, mostly because I live in New Cumbria, almost an hour and a half away. She divorced her no-good husband and now devotes all of her time to working at the church, where she makes a lot more money.

As for the guys at the park that afternoon, Duffel Bag was killed in Iraq. I actually heard about that from Elsbeth, in a snippet on CNN. The report she read said Straithorn was looking behind a date palm tree on the outskirts of Baghdad while on patrol with a buddy. The two part-time GIs ran across an IED, one of those improvised explosive devices; the army sent D Bag home in one. Batson and the rest of the Wrenton crowd have actual lives or keep on with their old ones. I don't see them anymore, either.

When my head pounded against the door window, it felt as if a heavyweight boxer had landed an immense blow, then jerked his fist away. The paramedics and doctors later explained that my skull had lurched toward the Jaguar for a split second, then snapped back against the window, smashing the glass. They also said that because I was belted in, my body yanked into an S, then reversed itself, which explained the lesion I sustained on my T-12 vertebra, the lowest of the thoracic bones that envelop your spine. That was the good news. Any higher up the spinal column and the paralysis would have been worse.

My arms and chest are strong. I can breathe without a ventilator. I can't move my hips or legs. I *can* get it up, but that's a function of blood, not nerves. It doesn't do me much good anyway, because I can't feel pleasure when "that" happens, and when it does—during misty late-night dreams or, say, when a woman like Annie appears—I experience a certain deep internal pain . . .

I definitely remember my head shattering the window, or maybe it was the window shattering my head.

After that, I only remember being cold, as cold as if I were freezing to death, though it was eighty-nine degrees. (I checked that out on the Internet later.) And I remember my eyes flying open and staying open, as if I would never blink again. I don't remember *seeing* anything.

But I could hear. Crashing, crushing, shattering, tearing, twisting, rattling, skidding, and screeching. Then I heard Denise moan my name.

I couldn't answer. They say I was in shock.

Of all things, I do remember the car radio, and it was playing Lynyrd Skynyrd's "Freebird."

Other than the cold and the warm syrup of blood on my temple, I felt nothing. I felt no fear, only the need to survive. Shock handled that.

After surviving the operating room, the recovery room, and the ICU, I found myself lying in my own room, in a cast up to my abdomen. I could simply push the button on my handy patient-controlled analgesic machine to pump a few drops of superior narcotics into my IV for another trip into a pain-free haze.

I don't remember exactly how or when it happened, but I gradually emerged into my new reality. Once, as I surfaced from another drug-induced nap, my head vibrated with noises reminiscent of a car wreck. Then I began to make out distinct sounds that could belong only to rock bands: wailing guitars, thundering floor-tom drums, and now plaintive, now growling vocals.

Sometime while I was sleeping, Eddie had clipped a tiny digital music player onto my hospital gown and slipped its stereophonic buds into my ears. He had filled the quarter-sized device with songs reflecting the only life he could know at that age: his own. The songs brimmed with angst, rebellion, loathing, loneliness, fear, love, hate, anger, violence, misogyny, drugs, and, above all, passion. The songs included guns and sex, too, but I hoped those weren't a feature of Eddie's life.

A nursing assistant soon came in and found my head shaking,

my eyes closed. I felt a push on my shoulder. Another push. Then a pinch.

Having no idea how to turn the damn thing off, I pulled the smooth white buds from my ears.

"What the—?"

"Are you okay, Mr. Duncan?" Her smooth complexion re-minded me of chocolate ice cream, which sounded like another marvelous salve right then.

Her concern melted the second I smiled, the first time I had managed one of those in recent memory. "Don't kill me, God, I swear, I ain't gonna kill you, *bee-atch*," I tried to rap along with slang I'd never known, let alone used, before. She looked as if she might give me a well-deserved smack, but I grinned and held up the tiny machine from which a tiny hip-hop voice blared through the tiny speakers.

"Sorry, Ms. Gittens," I said, reading her name tag.

She swatted away my non-apology and laughed. "Oh, yeah, that crunk-head. He a'ight. I got his last CD."

That's when I realized how out of touch I'd always been, with the world, with my family, my son—even myself.

"You all right, too, Mr. Duncan," Ms. Gittens said. She put the earbuds and music player on the bedside table and turned me over, telling me, again, about the hazards of bedsores. "Let me just tell you a few things. They gonna put you in rehab. And don't let nobody there tell you that you can't do nothin'. Fact is, you can do anything you want; you just gonna do it sittin' down from now on. If somebody say somethin' negative round you, you stick them earphones in yo' head, turn up the music, and tune 'em out. Lord knows we ain't got time in this life for stinkin' thinkin' like that."

As she wiped mine, she continued, "Bottom line, make 'em treat you like the human bein' you is, rather than a patient on wheels. Make 'em look you straight in the eye, and make 'em bend the rules to you, not the other way round. 'Cause the fact is, the only difference 'tween now and three weeks ago is . . ." She rolled me back into my supine position and patted me on the chest; that felt sublime. "Your son, he's a honest kid, and I just know he's not gonna treat you any different. And your doctor, Dr. Lawson; he's the best brain surgeon there is, but I asked him about you, and he says you've always been slack-ass, anyway."

Her reverberating guttural laugh sounded like a hymn from an entire Gospel choir. Why couldn't Eddie have packed his little machine with some of *that* music?

"Now you got plenty of opportunity to be just as slack as you want, only now you got a good excuse for it. But life ain't no pity party, Mr. Duncan, and don't let 'em give you any reason to make you think things any different." She tapped my chest. "I bet that in here, where God's at, not much else has changed."

Over the course of the next several days came the parade of friends, well-wishers, and most of New Cumbria society. Meanwhile, when I was alone, I pushed the drug button less and less and the MP3 player's dial more and more, escaping into the world of music, my pain abating. In exercising my upper body on the silver triangle hanging over my bed, I decided that typing would exercise my arms, hands, fingers, and brain. So I also persuaded Toby Lawson, my brilliant neurosurgeon doctor friend, to ask his computer-geek son, Tyler, to research the best laptop computer available. I got Volusia to buy it and Eddie and Tyler to show me how to work the damn thing.

Next thing I knew, I was discovering the infinity of cyberspace. Though I was unnerved by the things those two boys knew, the portals they could find and enter, the worlds they could explore and manipulate, they also pointed me toward my own new universe. They showed me thousands of songs and hundreds of places I could go to discover my inner music critic. In my bed, I was finding a life inside myself—a life I never knew existed in a body I never knew I'd be forced to have.

The day before my discharge from the hospital, my grandfather's only brother, my great-uncle Lemuel, tottered in. A bear of a man whose hair had turned sea-foam white during his knob year at the Citadel, Lem had a cherry-tomato nose and bulbous purple-veined cheeks. The years had grown around Lem, mostly his gut, which entered the room a good six or so inches before he did, along with his megaphone voice. During World War II, Lem served for a year in the Pacific, a Navy signalman, then he returned to his wife, Eleanor June Hallonquist, who died before I was born.

"We were all heroes when we got back," Lem said. Despite his age, his Southern-operatic baritone had lost none of its timbre. "And even though I'd done nothing but sail around the deep blue on big boats, and my brother was the real war hero . . . well."

He fished around in his seersucker suit, dotted with various stains, and pulled out an old war medal. Leaning into my bedside, he stabbed the decoration into my thin hospital gown.

"This here belonged to one of your grandfather's GIs, Corporal Matthew Dahlgren. When your grandfather tried to pin it on him during the ceremony, why, Dahlgren refused, told Ed to keep it. So I'm giving it to you, since you got wounded."

"I haven't fought any wars."

"You haven't really done much of anything, Randol"—he winked—"but that doesn't mean you can't start trying to fight the good fight."

He settled back in the chair and lumped his kaiser-roll hands together. Expecting him to say something, I took off the medal.

The heart-shaped decoration featured a profile of George Washington on a purple shield with a gold border. On the other side was a raised bronzed heart, along with the embossed words "For Military Merit."

My throat and eyes stung. "I don't deserve this, Uncle Lem." I shifted my eyes away from him. "Where'd you find this, anyway?"

"The Plunder Room. Your grandfather told me to give it to you; he didn't want to make a fuss. He also told me he's going to pay for your rehab, at the best facility in the state, in Columbia. It'll be about a month, but they say the staff there makes you feel like a real person, somebody who never really ever lost anything."

I thought about what the nursing assistant had told me and fingered the Purple Heart.

"Want to hear the story behind it?" He reached over and held my hand with the medal in my fingers.

I pulled myself up by the triangle over my bed, fascinated that my grandfather would have told his brother much of anything.

And Uncle Lemuel began.

The medic from Cannon Company showed his regimental commander, Colonel Edward R. Duncan, the letter he had just written to his fiancée on a war loan poster:

> *The war is moving plenty fast and furious: my hands have been literally steeped in blood from the wounded. It is pitiful to hear four or five wounded men yelling, "Medic! Medic! I'm bleeding to death!" It is bad enough during the day, but at night a wounded soldier (whether he be German or American) is terri-*

fied by the utter separation in the pitch blackness lit only by the bursting shells. There may be hell in another world but this one is sure putting up some stiff competition. Compare "fire and brimstone" with twisted steel and bodies, splattered chunks of brain and intestine, shambled buildings, the screams of shells and the crack of bullets, the stench of death, the earnest soul-searching prayer of the dying. The longer this war lasts, the greater toll and hole this living hell will cut into humanity.

The Technician Fifth Grade had handed the poster to the colonel after they crossed the Ludendorff Bridge together at Remagen.

On March 10, 1945, German artillery blasted the bridge and its environs around the Rhine with rounds every thirty seconds. The regimental command post was moving so fast that field operators couldn't keep up with rear commanders. Officers had crossed the bridge with the dogfaces—bullets, body parts, shells, shrapnel, and screams flying—to make the first Allied toehold on the river's eastern bank.

"Are you sure you want to show this to your girlfriend, Jimmy?" Colonel Duncan asked the fresh-faced medic with the brushed-back hair. The young medic's hands were stained with India ink and blood.

"Why, yes, sir." His dark brown eyes were as intense and earnest as the men whose prayers he'd heard. "It's real. And I want the world to know. And she, my fiancée, she's my world."

The colonel knew; he knew all of it. These boys had started out in Mississippi three years before, a bunch of green volunteers, patriots, farm boys, orphans, misfits, and adventure seekers. In the previous five months, they had fought the Battle of the Bulge, tearing through the Ardennes and Belgium and now into Germany. Duncan had seen ruined towns, stayed awake in his command post less than three thousand yards from the front, listening to all-night barrages. He had watched arms and legs and guts soaring through the air, seen enough blood to fill a dairy truck or two back home. Along the way, he and his boys had picked up all manner of German handguns, Mausers, Walther P38s, a couple of Lugers, a few Nazi banners and flags, even a couple of leather pouches with ID cards. Now his doughs were exhausted, hungry, and angry. And they were men of the highest and hardest caliber. They were his. As for the young man's letter? He knew all about that, too. Colonel Duncan hadn't seen his wife, PeeCee, for going on two years now. And their letters to each other, combed by army censors, could be little more than brief how-do's about the weather and the comings and goings of folks back in New Cumbria.

"Your note here's awful graphic, son."

"Yes, I know, sir."

"And it's beautiful writing."

The poetry of war. Duncan remembered one snowy night the previous November in the Hürtgen Forest, near Aachen. He had ordered light armor thrown on the road through the forest to assault the Jerries in support of his infantry, but the tanks got bogged down in winter's slushy muck. He knew almost from the moment he uttered the order that it was a mistake, but even *being* in the godforsaken forest had been a mistake. The brass should have known it; everyone else did. For all anyone cared, the Boches could've rotted in that evil hell until Berlin fell. This same disastrous campaign would later cost him his command.

But while the armored cavalry was getting pounded and his men mutilated, one of his dogfaces heaved into the CP without a weapon. His right arm was maimed, and blood streamed down his temple.

"Why aren't you with the medics, son?" the colonel asked.

"Too many other guys need a lot more attention than me, sir."

The regimental commander nodded. "What can I do for you, Dahlgren?"

"Mind if I have a seat, sir?" The GI collapsed on a field cot without waiting for permission, then started to throw up and heave wailing sobs.

It was the first time the colonel had ever held a man.

Duncan's embrace calmed the soldier without a word.

"It's hell out there, Colonel, hell in a place that should never exist, hell that I never asked for, hell that people created, human beings just like me. Why the hell is that, sir? Pardon my French."

"Your French is good, Corporal. I guess war brings out the poetry in men."

The dogface laughed.

"Where are you from, Corporal?"

"North Carolina, sir."

"A Tar Heel. Good man. I'm from South Carolina myself, Matt. Thomas Wolfe, he's a writer from there—"

"Yes, sir, from Asheville, my hometown."

The colonel nodded. "You know, Matthew—Corporal Dahlgren—Mr. Wolfe was wrong. You *can* go home again, and"—Duncan swabbed at the GI's wounds with his fingers—"you've earned your ticket out of here." The regiment's commander had accomplished the mission God had put before him, saving this soldier.

"I've heard the stories about you, sir. Is it really true that a Kraut buzz bomb landed just a few yards away from you and a couple, three officers at a CP in France, and you were the only one who didn't move a muscle, you just stood there and looked at it like it was a football somebody'd dropped?"

Colonel Duncan chuckled.

The soldier stood and offered a weakened salute.

"Where are you off to, son?"

"Begging the colonel's pardon, but I think I'm gonna go shoot me a Natsy or two." Matthew Dahlgren turned to go, but before he left, he handed the colonel an Iron Cross he'd lifted from the corpse of a German officer. "Thought you could use a real souvenir, sir, even though I know you have plenty of your own."

"I think, when you get back home to your mountains, Dahlgren, you should write a book. Probably be better than that Wolfe fellow's." He winked at him "Besides, Mr. Wolfe died back in 'thirty-eight, and I guess he needs a reinforcement."

"I reckon I got a war to get back to, sir."

Nothing like Duncan's Doughs, the colonel thought, that's for goddamn sure.

Lem shook his head and laughed. "I don't know why I'm laughing. Not all that funny, but that's why your grandfather never talked about the war."

"I guess," I said, fingering Corporal Dahlgren's award and wondering whether the Iron Cross might also be hidden away in the Plunder Room.

"Your grandfather's still got faith in you, Randol." The old man pushed himself up from the faux-leather chair and squeezed my left big toe, which stuck out of my cast; he didn't realize I couldn't feel his pinch. "I'll give your regards to everybody back home. Get well soon, son."

Uncle Lem shuffled off, and I heard his drawling megaphone ask one nurse for a date and a doctor for cocktails all the way down the hall.

Later, back in New Cumbria, I never mentioned the medal to Grandfather. He never asked about it.

We never spoke about my rehab, either.

His war, my war.

I guess we both came out lucky.

CHAPTER FOUR

E D D I E   S L I N K S into the dining room for his breakfast just as Volusia is wiping off the table. Black denims hang to the crack of his ass and clink with chrome loops running down the outside seams. Under a navy blue hoodie, which won't keep him warm this morning, droops a black T-shirt emblazoned with the name of a metal band. The band's members, whose piles of hair could clog every drain in New Cumbria, dance under their logo of fanged-font letters spiked in blood.

His wardrobe notwithstanding, my son reminds me of my grandmother, only in reverse. Where my grandmother wasn't so much pretty as she was handsome, Eddie is beyond handsome—he's downright pretty. His face is just shy of round, with ruddy cheeks and a dimple in his chin, shaggy black hair that he wears in an untamed ponytail, and a perfect button nose. His smile would be disarming if he ever used it, and his bovine brown eyes betray the very innocence he yearns to deny.

"You plan on going to school?"

Eddie looks for a moment as if the question might be rhetorical. "Could be why I got dressed."

"Right. And I thought that was the volunteers' uniform for airport security or the daily satanic ritual. Curious, though, how you decided on the bomb-your-school ensemble, rather than the more charming rape-your-teacher outfit that you wore yesterday."

He picks at his clothes. "I wore the exact same things yesterday."

"For only a fraction of the day because you actually didn't even *go* to school, remember? You spent the better part of your afternoon at your grandfather's funeral, where you chose—sorry, *Volusia* chose for you—a blazer with a regimental-striped tie of blue and gold. For a shirt, you wore a pressed white Oxford button-down. And your hair was actually grease-free and in a controlled, discreet, and I'll even go so far as to say attractive style." I clap my hands in mock applause. "Today, I see, you've visited the Goth Outlet."

"Bite me, Dad."

"I forget, nonconformity is all the rage."

He slinks into the kitchen, where I hear him open a cabinet here and a drawer there. Volusia asks Eddie whether he wants some "real breakfast," if she could heat him up a good, hot plate right quick. Then he stops in the pantry before eventually returning to the dining room with a Corning Ware bowl, a casserole-serving spoon, a yellow plastic milk jug, and his favorite cereal, a revolting mix of chemicals and sugar that's neither agricultural nor pharmaceutical. He dumps milk into the bowl until the cereal floats to the rim and drops himself into the seat Annie has freshly vacated. The space seems profaned, violated now that incontinent spurts of bubble-gum milk dribble down my son's chin.

"You're a pig," I tell him.

"Bite me."

"Do you really expect to get chicks like that?" I ask, and his eyes meander up from his trough. "Your guyliner, Eddie. I mean, it's pretty, but I would call your mom about application techniques."

Across the polished-table distance, he gives me the finger.

"Y'know, I'm just saying, if you put that stuff on wrong, you could get it in your eyes and go blind. Now, *that* would, like, suck. On the other hand, by the age of fifteen, you could be a blind visionary. You're onto something. Being a 'blind visionary' could actually be cool enough to work to your advantage!"

"You really like the sound of your own voice, don't you?"

"As a matter of fact, I do, but in your case, just to be honest—which we could all use a lot more of around here—it's called a defense mechanism." I look straight into his eyes and remember what the nursing assistant, Ms. Gittens, told me. "I can't be at your level, so giving you shit distracts me from these useless legs."

I notice his guilty swallow. "Well, at least the girls who read your music blog think you're funny."

I scowl to hide my juvenile pride. "I'm more concerned about your plan for the day." I pull closer to put my elbows on the table, to look more paternal.

"Plan for what?"

"Oh, I dunno. Getting to school? After school? After graduating from high school three, four, five years from now? Homework after school today?"

"I can walk to school—"

"Did you have an estimated time of arrival?" I look at the time on my cell phone. He's already five minutes late for his first class. Ari Manios, the principal, would be calling any moment.

Eddie finds his cereal far more interesting than me; true, its molecular makeup would fascinate a chemistry class.

"Did you know your uncle Jerod was here this morning?"

Eddie jerks his eyes up. For the first time today, he looks alert. He has always worshipped his uncle, who, though only partially a blood relative and rarely in New Cumbria, gives Eddie the kind of masculine love every boy needs, and embodies a rough-hewn mystique earned from having gotten away with just about everything. Me, I've always been too honest, too forthright, and, frankly, too ignorant to deal with Eddie other than as his father. Jerod, on the other hand, floats in and out of Eddie's life, giving only hints of how glamorous, dangerous, sinful, mysterious, and fun it must be to be Jerod. What Eddie doesn't realize, because he is only fourteen years old, is that Jerod treats everybody like a fourteen-year-old, and most people older than fourteen know that Jerod is either full of himself, full of shit, or just plain patronizing.

"He didn't come down and wake me up?" Eddie's disappointment could hurt my feelings and stir me to jealousy, but I also realize that Eddie would have been more disappointed if Jerod had paid him less attention than usual, then rushed off.

"He had things to do, places to go."

"People to see." He sighs. "He's amazing—Jerod. Dude's got game, that's for sure."

I can't help but laugh.

Eddie stops mid–sloppy spoonful, picks up his bowl, and empties it. The very thought of the saccharine slurp rotates my stomach, but fortunately, Volusia's breakfast rests as hard in my gut as set concrete.

"What?" he asks, though I've stopped laughing.

"Whaddya mean, what?"

"What's so funny?"

"Nothing." I shake my head. "You would've been amused.

Impressed, even. It's just that he has . . . Jerod had a friend with him."

"F'real?" Eddie reaches out and grabs my shirt, a long-sleeve white Oxford. His touch, neither soft nor tender, isn't violent but playful. I appreciate the gesture.

"His, um, friend . . ." I begin.

"What about him?"

"See, Eddie, that's where you think you're all grown up and smart."

"Bite me."

By this time, I'm laughing harder, this time *at* my own son. Probably not the best thing to laugh *at*, rather than *with*, your children. But I have only one kid, and he has worked at being laughable.

I imagine my grandfather and me sitting here and talking. The fact is, we would be doing one hell of a lot better than my son and I are. First off, I wouldn't be wearing anything that makes me look like a cross between a medieval executioner and a hardware store. Granted, times have changed, and I once saw a bumper sticker that read "Change the way you see, not the way you look." I gave up on Eddie's sartorial issues a long time ago. Second, I would have been far more attentive to my grandfather than Eddie has ever been to me. I suppose that's because Grandfather had my respect long before I could even say the word, let alone know what it meant. I'm beginning to wonder, especially with Grandfather's funeral yesterday, how and when, even where, Eddie lost whatever respect he may have had for me.

"You *assume* everything, Eddie, because you think you *know* everything."

"A safe assumption's better than a bad bet." He picks at his T-shirt, as if he's picking the nose of a hirsute band member. "For instance, you or somebody else may assume I'm a bad kid just by looking. But that's not a good bet. I may be the guy who walks a little old lady across the street. Not a bad return on her don't-judge-a-book investment. Now, I admit I wear what I wear partly to piss you off, and it *might* look like something a kid would wear to Columbine his high school—"

"That's a *verb* now? *'To Columbine?'*"

"At New Cumbria High School it is." He leans back in his chair and pushes his bowl away. Sitting next to my grandfather, I would have done neither. "Fact is, Dad, I am way too smart for that."

"Way too *'smart'* to bomb your school, murder your friends, and commit suicide? Golly, how do you figure?"

"Well, I'm much too good-looking, much too charming—like Uncle Jerod, on both counts. And you'd have to be a complete moron to want to kill yourself that way."

"What's a, um, better way to kill yourself?"

"By getting into a car, stoned, drunk, with a chick who's not buckled in herself—"

I put my hand up for him to stop. At least he shows enough maturity to shut up.

Pushing back from the table, I suck in a deep breath and move toward the kitchen, hearing Eddie's sigh of . . . exasperation, I suppose. I stop, still turned away from him, but glance over my shoulder.

"Speaking of smart-asses, Eddie, you just *assumed* Jerod's friend was a guy." I turn to face him again and try to laugh, neither easily nor sincerely.

"Oh?"

"Jerod's friend. I'm just saying." Eddie now leans into the table. "'Hot' doesn't begin to describe this woman, my high-strung little offspring. If the sun is hot, if hell is hot, this woman makes them seem like our fridge by comparison." I love hearing Eddie laugh. It seems harder to get that kid, any kid, to laugh. "Let's just say . . ." He raises his eyebrows, and his big brown eyes grow to the size of muscadine grapes. "Let's just say you're so late for school, the day's almost over."

"You suck."

I raise my hand as he slaps me a too-aggressive high five.

"Bite me, Eddie."

His laughter and clanking jeans harmonize on their way out the front door. He is missing his first-period class, maybe second period, too.

Ari Manios should be calling . . . right . . . about . . .

A tap on the front door rattles the beveled glass. Like the people inside the house, the leaded panes have been losing their hold through all these years, getting looser in the frames. The doors, with their overhead fantail windows, have outlasted most of us here.

Another church lady is coming to call, I suppose, to drop off another squash casserole, as if the refrigerator and freezer aren't packed enough after the funeral. Eddie loves fried chicken as much as the next Southern boy, but if I let on just how much fried chicken is going to fill his backpack for the next week, he may start trading drumsticks for condoms and selling them at school. I caught him doing *that* last year when Uncle Lemuel died, just a year after he'd given me that Purple Heart. You'd have thought Lemuel Alastair Duncan was a poultry-processing magnet, judging by all the chicken that wound up at his visitation.

Actually, my great-uncle Lem had owned the Buncombe Mill, a 320-loom textile plant that collapsed in 1936. He left his shareholders, including Grandfather, with a return of twenty cents on the dollar. Lem retained ownership of the four-story brick factory. He expanded his real-estate holdings and bought into retail, where he *sold* textiles, primarily men's dress suits. Lem made a fortune after losing his first one and everyone else's, too.

In 1939, just before the war started, Grandfather couldn't afford a loss like the one Lem had handed him. My grandfather wasn't broke, per se. He was making a half-decent living, considering the job he was doing: He was a captain in the United States Army.

I know all about such things because every now and then I would take a break from watching Grandfather die and riffle through his intimate possessions and personal papers. Grandfather left some of them in his rolltop desk, a magnificent oak antique wedged between his bureau and the door to the guest quarters. It was hard enough to wheel my chair in there, and once I did, it was harder still to push away from the documents he had slipped into every nook, drawer, cranny, slot, and secret compartment.

While I watched him live out his last few months, among the first papers I found was Grandfather's tax return for 1939, the year Germany invaded Poland. The U.S. government form doesn't look much different than it does today, except that Grandfather's has far fewer entries; the sheet probably took him a minute or two to fill out. The paper is green, not even tinged brown around the edges with age. The heading reads "For Net Incomes of Not More Than $5,000."

In those sixteen boxes, he claimed his wife, a dependent with a $400 exemption, and a $25 personal exemption; listed his army post at the time; provided his signature; and specified his earnings: $2,880. Which would amount to about $38,000 today. Pretty good money, I suppose, in a country hungover from the Depression. Barely five years later, Grandfather was earning a few hundred dollars more, fighting at the Battle of the Bulge and getting promoted to colonel, the chief executive officer of a fifteen-hundred-man corporation designed to destroy the German war machine.

Today's colonel takes home nearly $110,000 a year, while his counterpart CEOs earn well into the millions, some even billions. And in Grandfather's line of work, he and his boys were on the job 24/7, on yearslong business trips, working in mud, stench, and snow with no office suites, stock options, or golden parachutes. Most chief executives don't watch their people get slaughtered at work, although that seems to happen with some regularity these days.

The Duncans, at least in the last four or five generations, weren't poor. The family has been in South Carolina since 1670, a rebellious bunch seeking more freedom and more real estate, which are usually the same things. The original American Duncans made their living off the land, as farmers and property owners, evolving then, like Uncle Lem, into manufacturers, retailers, and businessmen. A lot of soldiers. A solid living there, and a solid dying, too.

The family cemetery in Little Brook, South Carolina, about six miles outside of New Cumbria, has markers that look like ink-stained elephant tusks. Three are etched with such sentiments as "Priv. Thaddeus O. Duncan, 1759–1840, *Fought* Battle of Cowpens 1781, with *Valour*." At Uncle Lem's burial, I heard Grandfather tell Jupe that in 1832 Private Thad had been awarded a $30 annual pension, which amounts to about $650 today, and Thad didn't even start getting *that* until fifty-one years after he'd done the job.

I've never understood money. I guess that accounts for why I'm so emotional about it and why I'd rather be detached from it. Grandfather never talked about money. Jupe talked about it even less, and only in the context of never having enough, figuring out more efficient and usually underhanded ways to get it and despairing over the impracticability and unfairness of ever having to work for it.

I guess money is just one of the many things I'll have to start getting a handle on now that Grandfather's gone.

Rolling toward the rap on the door, afraid of yet more food and little old ladies, I see a man through the lacy sheers. I pirouette in my wheelchair to open the door.

On the porch stands one of the most elegant people I've ever seen, a black—or should I say, African-American—man. He's of indeterminate age. It may not be politically correct to say, but it's also hard to put an age on men of color. Perhaps he's seventy, eighty; eighty-five, tops. He carries himself without a stoop, his bearing strong, despite the sadness he seems to carry. His complexion is like an old baseball mitt. A small pinkish scar curves around his left eye, which I begin to think could be prosthetic glass. He wears a blue pinstripe suit, a crisp white shirt, and a dark blue tie dotted with American flags. On his lapel there's an American flag the size of a dime.

"Sir?"

"I came to pay my respects to your father."

"My grandfather?"

He chuckles in a sweet melody, like the bugler's "Taps" at grandfather's funeral yesterday. "My apologies."

"No worries." I wave him in. "Please, come in, it's chilly out." I wonder why he's not wearing a hat; I thought most men of his generation did. My grandfather rarely went out without one.

We move into the China Room. He looks around, his head rolling this way and that as if it were a toy top finding its way around.

"Place hasn't changed much at all." He sighs.

"You've been here before?"

He nods toward the door to the guest quarters.

"Used to stay in there when the Old Bird and the missus would have me over. We would be the talk of the town, a Negro bivouacked in the colonel's quarters. That was back in the fifties and sixties, back when they'd started to desegregate the army but hadn't gotten around to the rest of the country yet."

"No disrespect intended, sir, but you are . . . ?"

"Sorry," he says, his chuckle even warmer now. He seems diffident, deferential as he extends his hand, as rough as beef jerky. "Oliver Duncan Barrows."

An electric spark shoots through me, even through my legs, as if Grandfather himself is ordering me to stand and salute the general from Charleston.

I roll back from him and bid him to sit down. "Excuse me for a second, if you don't mind."

He eases into the Chinese couch, where, so far today, Jupe has slouched and Jerod has crossed his Cole Haans. The way things have been going today, it wouldn't surprise me if Bill Westmoreland rose from the dead just so he could sit here and swap a few war stories with ol' Blast-'Em-Up Barrows.

Rolling into the kitchen, I see Volusia is already settled into her morning soap operas on the seven-inch TV set she installed under the cabinet that holds the glasses.

"You know, Veronica, that once Sam gets her claws in him . . ."

"Mind?" I nod toward the television, then toward Volusia.

"They got lots more interesting things to talk about than you."

"We've got a visitor here who's lots more interesting than these little white people." I love the way she raises her eyebrows at me. "Come see for yourself."

"You sound like a kid 'bout to wet his pants."

"Who says I haven't?"

She smacks me upside the head and starts toward the swinging kitchen door.

"Hang on, V. Stop!" I throw up my hands. "Coffee. The gentleman would appreciate some coffee, I'm sure, cold as it is outside. He didn't just come from a nice warm snooze in the guest quarters, y'know, though he seems to be familiar with them."

A current of curiosity flies off her like static electricity.

Volusia sets up the coffee service, pouring her perfect brew from the percolator into Grandmother's engraved silver pot, and takes down three cups and saucers; evidently, she plans to join us. She even turns off the TV. She fills a silver creamer and sugar bowl, grabs a monogrammed spoon, and puts everything on a silver tray, and off we roll.

"Ollie!" she cries when she lays eyes on him.

I'm just as surprised as he is.

He stands, and his gallantry fills the room like a furnace kicking on high.

"Miss Volusia." He doesn't move. She doesn't, either. I wonder why they won't touch each other. "You look . . ."

. . . like the teenager she was when she met him? I begin to wonder.

"You're still the strapping young soldier you always were, Ollie." She puts the silver service down on the mahogany coffee table inlaid with jade and mother-of-pearl dragons. Fluttering, she flaps around the coffee table and throws her arms around the old man. "Sit, sit. Have some coffee." She pours him a cup. "With a little sugar, if I remember."

He laughs this time, full-on.

"I remember the time you snuck into the guest quarters to warn me that old Bill . . ."

I must have looked bewildered because General Barrows stops and explains that he's talking about General Westmoreland.

"She came to warn me that Westy was going to be here in this house the next day. Well, seeing as how I had no real fondness for the man"—I see restraint, as if God Himself slapped a hand over the old soldier's mouth—"I appreciated the warning, and I knew I had to cut my stay short."

They share a laugh that I can't, a history I've only read about and could never fathom.

"That was in 'eighty-two, just before the CBS lawsuit," the general says, shaking his head, "and even then, in this town, two black people, unmarried, in the same bedroom under a white man's roof! Mmm."

"But, you know, Colonel and Mrs. Duncan, they wouldn't have said a single word to a single soul. Just—"

"Well, see, that's why I'm here, Volusia, Mr. Duncan."

"Please, General, my name is Randol."

He begins as if he doesn't hear me, "Granted, Westmoreland did go to Fort Carson in Colorado during the racial uprising there . . ." He stops and waves his hands, aware that Volusia and I aren't likely to care about such details, especially if they don't concern my grandfather. "Point is, Colonel Duncan did more for us, for me, than a whole division of Westmorelands."

I lean toward him. Volusia still stands. She beams with pride as she sips from the coffee she has poured into her saucer to cool.

"Oh, yes, sir," he says, leaning back. "Colonel Duncan . . ."

My mind slips away. I hear my grandfather's name, my own name, and then I remember how he introduced himself. Oliver . . . Duncan . . . Barrows. I think of our family name, Duncan, my brother's middle name, Barrows. I realize that in the Old South names routinely exchanged between the races, as did, well . . .

"Excuse me, sir," I ask, "where were you born?"

"Charleston, son, the Holy City, born and raised. Same place ol' Westy passed. My house isn't too far from where his was. Poor Kitsy, his wife. Bless her soul, brave woman." He waves his hands again. Age allows tangents because time can only go backward, with so little left forward. "Most of my people started there, migrated to Cumbria County." His smile dissipates.

Volusia settles into Grandfather's recliner.

I get where he's going, but to understand his meaning would be to try to grasp, in a few seconds, the psychological history of the American black man.

"I joined the army when I was seventeen years old because I thought a black boy in those days could pretty much stay an ignorant farm nigger in South Carolina or go to work in a textile mill, where seven people were killed in the strike of 1934—" He shakes his head again. "I'm sorry. What I meant to say was—"

"No need to apologize for anything in this house, General." I paraphrase a Faulkner quote to fit the moment: "In the South, the past is not dead; it's not even past."

"Well, I joined the army to get out of the fields and the mills and see the world. Your grandfather was in the cavalry then, and we, the troops of color, were horse soldiers. That was shorthand for grooming the officers' mounts and mucking out the stalls." His chuckle returns. "Funny thing about the colonel, who was still a captain then, he treated us like men, even though, like I said, in civilian white society we weren't people."

Listening to the general is like watching PBS tape a documentary. I can't move. I can't move half of me anyway, but now the top half is transfixed.

"I owe my confidence, in those early years, to him. That's why I'm here."

Volusia stands up to leave, her coffee cup rattling on the fine china saucer. "Ollie," she says in her big, gregarious voice, "you shouldn't stay away till we all dead."

He apologizes and puts his hand on her forearm, then rises to peck her on the cheek. "You're still as beautiful—" He stops and a blush tinges his leathery face.

"I remember when he bought this house, he was so proud." General Barrows looks around. "Bought the place for twenty-six five, if memory serves. I imagine he paid that off years ago."

Not too long after the Korean War, according to the papers in Grandfather's desk. By then, he was earning a bit more than $51,000 in today's currency. He retired in 1954, as a colonel, denied the single star he would have loved, the only thing he had ever yearned for in his life. Barrows earned not one, but two stars: major general.

"He was making pretty good money in those days," the general says, "and he had a good life, too." He looks around the house before making himself comfortable again on the couch. "He was a damned fine horseman; I guess you knew that. Played polo as if he was riding on air. He could smack that ball like Tiger Woods, but on a pony galloping at full speed and swinging a wooden mallet with a sweet spot no bigger around than the bottom of this cup!" He stops, sips his coffee. "That Volusia. Beautiful creature. Brews the finest cup in the Palmetto State. She'll keep you straight, keep your heart clean—your mouth, too. I never will forget the time your grandfather and I were trading war stories . . ." His voice trails off again.

"We fought two different wars, your grandfather and I. He was gone for two long years. I was gone for one. In his day, see, when I first enlisted, more than a million African-Americans served, but only seven hundred of us died in that war. Different story in Vietnam.

"I was in the Fifteenth Artillery in 'Nam. We had guns that could shoot darn near twenty miles. I was in 'A' Battery, a young lieutenant, under the command of a black lieutenant colonel, good-lookin' young fella, sharp as they come." He shakes his head. "Poor SOB died in a Huey crash that killed all four aboard, including the pilot, a warrant officer. Damn shame, too, because the army needed brilliant young black officers like him. He would've made general officer, guaranteed."

He pours himself another cup, puts the saucer on his knee, and sips again, enjoying the coffee far more than the memories.

"We held a firebase not too far from the Laos border, like a bald spot on a big green monster's head. Thankfully, we had Montagnard gunners at our perimeter, tough little sumbitches."

He stops, his eyes ahead but somewhere past. Like most men I've known who've seen combat, that's as close as he comes to talking about it.

"Seems like, for what? I don't know." He sighs and empties his cup. "Looks like you've been wounded in action, son."

"Yes, sir. Car accident. Drunk driver."

"Shame. Sorry to hear that." He reaches for the silver service, but the coffeepot is already empty. "I'll just help myself." With the ingrained courtesy of an officer and a genuine-article Southern gentleman, he stands and moves toward the kitchen, rebuffing my offer to serve him.

His absence leaves a deep silence—what it must be like after a 155 mm howitzer unleashes its walloping 181 decibels.

He's gone a long time. He and Volusia must have a lot of catching up to do.

Pulling the cell phone from my pocket, I punch a couple of buttons.

"Yeah."

"That's some nice phone etiquette, Jupe."

"At least I answered. Caller ID is great."

"Guess who's here?" I tease the old man.

"Jerod."

"Come and gone. He says he's on his way to buy you a new house. I gotta say, he looks pretty spiffy in his Cole Haans." Silence. I might as well be talking about coleslaw. "Are you busy today?"

"No more'n usual. Why?"

"Buy me lunch."

"Is that a question, Randol, or a request for an audience?"

"Little bit of both. I guess I miss you."

"That's funny. Either that or you've suddenly become a senti-mental son of a gun," he says. I think I can actually see a smile through the satellite that connects us.

I laugh to ease whatever tension might be between us. "Seri-ously, though, y'know who *is* here? Oliver Barrows."

"Blast-'Em-Up Barrows? The man who put the 'art' in 'artil-lery?' You know he left the army under a cloud?"

My father might as well have punched me square in the nose. My head begins throbbing with incredulity. Then, again, my fa-ther *is* incredulity. If ever I needed a grain of salt, my father would be the shaker.

"For real," he says into my silent disbelief.

"You sound just like Eddie, old man, like, really."

"The poop on Barrows is that he was a skirt-chasin' fool, fraternized with a female Marine gunnery sergeant at Quantico while he was stationed at the Pentagon. No investigation. Just kind of . . . left the service."

"Sounds like bullshit to me."

"A lot of it usually is, especially when you get into all that thin, rarefied air around the Beltway. He was never much of a water-walker, Barrows, he just did his job, pounded the hell out of gooks, got paid for it, kept his profile low. What I heard was, he took it really hard when his CO went down in a 'copter crash in 'sixty-seven while he was still in-country. They said he never forgave the army for that."

After hanging up with Jupe, I swallow, trying to digest what my father just told me, trying not to believe him, trying to keep down the lump of disillusionment, as if *I* have any right to *that*. Amazing that we can put a man in uniform, pay him a fraction of what we pay our movie stars and athletes, ask him to die for the country that enslaved his kin, then make him a standard-bearer for valor, for duty, honor, country, and personal integrity.

Then I realize why Barrows came today. He wanted to say good-bye to Grandfather and the life the old colonel had led. I think he also wanted to give me deeper insight into my grandfather's principles, perhaps with the notion that I might provide the same example to those around me. I suppress a chuckle at the lost cause that Jupe and, I'm afraid, Eddie have become.

General Barrows strides back into the room. It's amazing to see an eighty-some-year-old man walk with such purpose, with such upright dignity. He's laughing now, Volusia having brought back all the happy times.

"Did Volusia ever tell you about the time your grandfather was approached by three men in China the day he got off the boat in 1935?"

I'd never heard this story, so I shake my head and smile.

"Well." The old general sits down, his coffee cup clattering like the tail of a glass rattlesnake. I see he has already finished half the cup. "Three little Oriental—I guess the proper term now is 'Asian'—men greet him near the Chin-wang-tao wharf, where he's about to start his two-year tour in China. One's a tailor, one wants to sell him a car . . ."

I start laughing so hard the lower part of my body hurts; those muscles don't get used enough. "This sounds like one of those 'A rabbi, a priest, and an imam walk into a bar' jokes."

"Well, with your grandfather, it sort of was." General Barrows drains his third coffee and slides his cup and saucer onto the table. "And they all have business cards, one side in Chinese—"

"Who's the third guy?"

"The third guy? Well . . ." The general laughs harder than I've seen him laugh yet, so I start laughing harder, too. "The third guy's card has an address on it, 'Branchatmucgooloo, Tientsin. Chin Wang Tao.' But the other side is in pidgin English, and *it* says, 'Chu Poon Tang, Number One Whore House.'"

"'*Chu Poon Tang*'?" I can't hold back anymore. Tears roll down my cheeks; the general's, too. "'Number One Whorehouse'? So what does he do, my grandfather?"

"Well, he takes all three cards, he bows to each of the men. Then says to them, all three of them, 'If I ever need to hitch a ride or get a hitch in my britches or hitch my britches for a ride, I'll give each of you gentlemen a call.'" General Barrows leans against the sofa, falling deep into the Chinese silk, and wipes tears from his eyes, finally resting his hands on his gut.

After a moment, his breathing returns to normal. He leans back toward me. "Let me tell you a little secret about your grandfather." He looks into my eyes with sincerity, wonder, and seriousness. "I'm sorry, with all my heart, that I missed your grandfather's services yesterday. I just . . . well, it doesn't matter now. The day, the opportunity, is missed. But not this one. What I mean to tell you, Mr. Duncan, is this: Your grandfather was one of the bravest, toughest soldiers, one of the finest, most honorable men I've ever known. He didn't give the ultimate sacrifice, as some men on the battlefield must, but he didn't live and die so that his legacy could be forgotten, neglected, or tarnished."

I gaze into my lap, where tingles of phantom pain begin. Like the pain that creeps in on me and takes over from time to time, General Burrows has gotten inside me, become a gnawing addition to my existence.

"Your grandfather gave everything he had for this country," he continues through my silence. "And everything he had left went to his family. Y'all may not understand that."

Like the silence following the cannonade boom, a deadly silence fills the room.

"Well," the general says finally. "Wish I could take a few gallons of Volusia's coffee home with me."

I look at him with fondness that fills me with hope.

"Thank you for your time, Mr. Duncan, and, again, my condolences."

Nodding and smiling with something akin to renewed pride, I say good-bye as the screen door bangs its farewell. And rather than feeling melancholy, I am aware of something strange, a swelling resolve that's strong and bright, a new obligation. Something akin, I suppose, to a call to arms.

CHAPTER FIVE

THE PRISON-ALARM phone bell rings—jangles my nerves clear to next week. I guess I can dismantle the thing now; that is, arrange for somebody to take it down. Until the day he died, Grandfather had most of his faculties, except for about forty percent of his hearing, which explains why he had the monster telephone bell installed over his recliner. Loud enough to make even a politician pay attention and certainly loud enough to roust me from the melancholy that General Barrows forgot to take with him when he left a few minutes before.

Volusia finally picks up the phone in the kitchen before I reach the one in the China Room. She's not long in fetching me and handing over the cordless receiver.

"It's for you. Mister Mangyus."

Ari *Manios*. She never did like the man and bends over backward to mangle the Greek pronunciation.

The Manioses have been in New Cumbria four generations,

immigrants from the Peloponnese. Ari's grandfather Pete, originally Petros, started Hero's Diner, a spin on gyros, which are lip-smacking delicious. The diner also serves the best onion rings, souvlaki, and baklava in the state. Pete was a U.S. Marine, killed in Okinawa during World War II. His wife, Sophie, remarried, to his brother, Darius, who kept the diner's name and opened another place, also called Hero's, in nearby Coker Mills, and Hero's, Too, in Wrenton. My father eats there all the time; he loves their Pete's a'Plenty Platters, an avalanche of fries, onion rings, and grease. Jupe even has a Hero's Heart Card; if you eat five meals, you get one lunch free. It bothers me that I know trivia like that about my father's life and so little about the man—how he makes a living or manages to keep breathing.

"Aristotle." He always bristles at his full name, so after he pauses, I ask him how his grandmother's getting along.

"Sophie's flagging a bit in her old age, but still a firecracker."

"What can I do for you today? I take it you're not calling about the weather or the New Cumbria Bridge Club or inviting me to speak again at the Rotary."

He finally lightens up. Ari once asked me to speak to the upstanding gentlemen and women of the Friday Breakfast Rotary. Why the estimable high school principal would ask me, a sometime freelance music critic and full-time wheelchair operator, to address these civic leaders still mystifies me. But for fifteen interminable minutes, I talked about contemporary music, mostly how politicians try to force artists into dialing down the often-vile lyrics that accompany today's frenetic rock melodies. I might as well have suggested that we give Communism another go, only on a smaller scale, say, in New Cumbria, just to see if it might catch on better this time.

He admits, "We'd run out of available speakers."

"No doubt."

"I'm calling about Eddie."

"Of course you are."

"Two issues."

"Straight to the point, Ari; I like that about you." Even over the phone, I can see his square jaw moving, his black kalamata-olive eyes narrowing under thick black brows, the small tube of middle age fighting against his belt, the gray hair wisping at his sideburns.

"Eddie was late to school again this morning."

"Duly noted, and for that he got a serious upbraiding."

"Third time this month. One more time, and it's—"

"It's what, Ari? Dismissal, expulsion, suspension, detention?" I feel as if I'm about to break into a rap song. "You graduate roughly half the kids in this school district. Mine, if you happen to run across his latest report card, has grades that will send him to one of the top colleges in the country, if—"

"That's precisely my point, Randol, if. It's the biggest word in the English language with the fewest letters."

I sigh. I also happen to agree with him, but—the next biggest word. "What's your second point?"

"The T-shirt. Gotta go."

"Heinous, isn't it?"

"It's advertising."

" 'Scuse me?" I can't suppress a laugh because his comment is simply too absurd. "*Ad*-vertising?"

"We had to come up with guidelines for our Zero Tolerance Dress Code; we couldn't just make stuff up. Remember how Mark Twain said, 'When I was a boy of fourteen, my father was so ignorant I could hardly stand to have the old man around. But when I got to be twenty-one, I was astonished at how much the old man had learned in seven years.' They all think it's stupid, sure, but rules have to start somewhere."

"Right. Mark Twain never said that. It's just been attributed to him so many times—"

"Whatever, Randol. You've always been smarter than everyone else, and that's the point. Kids are smarter than us in a lot of ways, and they figure out the loopholes faster than most lawyers."

"Maybe that's why lawyers are such—"

"Randol, please. I've got a school to run, not a rhetorical race with you."

"Right. Got it."

"School district guidelines say that T-shirts are allowed on school property as long as they don't 'advertise' a product, band, concert, service, et cetera, et cetera. T-shirts may also contain no foul language, no innuendo, no symbols, signals, gang-related colors, or signs. We have, oh, I'd have to guess, fifteen hundred, maybe two thousand words in our Zero Tolerance Dress Code. The Gettysburg Address has two hundred and seventy-two words; *those* words changed the country. With nearly two *thousand*, we can barely get our freakin' kids to change clothes!"

I burst out laughing. "I'm sorry, Ari, I really am, but what do you want me to do, run right over with a new outfit?"

"Well, yeah. I mean, work with me here. Your kid is one of the brightest in my school. I could use him as an example, but I'd prefer that he is a positive one."

"Sounds like a threat, Ari."

"Take it any way you want. He's not wearing those clothes—that T-shirt—on my campus."

"All right. I'll see what I can do."

"See to it soon. I don't have all day, and I don't want a Duncan kid running around school grounds naked."

The man's got brains a'plenty, if not the zest of Zorba. But he has the same charm as his father, who still runs the cash register at

Hero's, the same robust character that Darius used to attract enough customers over the years to send Ari and his brother and sister to college and one of them to law school—all on spanakopita and chili dog platters.

I'd needed a plan for the day, anyway, because I can't simply sit around and wait to levitate up the stairs to the Plunder Room.

I'll shower and change and take Eddie a different shirt, then drive on to Wrenton and call Jupe. We could eat lunch at Hero's, Too, and I'll tell him about General Barrows's visit.

Jupe hasn't told me much about his time in Vietnam. Apparently, he had this love-hate thing for the place—at least, he *says* he did. He only talks about it if I get him going or someone else does, but what's weird is that whenever the subject does come up, he's at his most lucid. My grandfather didn't talk about *his* war, either. I guess that's the combat experience, though I know for certain that Jupe never saw any combat. Not in Saigon. Regardless, after listening to General Barrows this morning, I think it's time to get to the bottom of a few things, find some peace in this family that has been so much about war.

Perhaps Volusia will run down to the SQ to grab a clean and legal shirt for Eddie. That would be asking a lot. She doesn't much care for our backyard bungalow. She once called it the "bachelor bivouac from hell."

So I roll down to the SQ, which sits at the edge of the tree line and Grandfather's property, where the old house backs up to the ten-foot-high fence that separates us from Duncan Park. We never lock the door back here.

The eight-hundred-square-foot bungalow, with the original wood siding, was built before the turn of the last century. The front door opens to the living room, the largest of four rooms, not including the single bathroom. The living room, such as it is, serves as a breakfast room, recreation room, den, study, library, parlor, and make-out room, if Eddie would ever bring a girl home. To the left, wedged into the southwest corner, is our one-butt kitchen with a counter, a sink, and a dorm-sized refrigerator, which contains little more than soft drinks and Eddie's perishable junk food. There's no room for a table or chairs. The back door leads to a jungle of trees and kudzu. Through the kitchen wall is my bedroom, then the lavatory, then Eddie's bedroom. The bathroom has rails I use to vault from my wheelchair to the toilet to the fold-down seat in the shower.

When I roll inside our house, the chill hangs like paintings nobody wants. No point in turning on any heat; nobody's home. I reconsider moving up to the house. Grandfather's bathroom is a lot easier to use; everything is closer to the kitchen and to Volusia; we have a lot more space to navigate. While I do love Eddie's company and maybe he enjoys mine in our little bachelor pad, he's probably getting to where he could use more privacy. Besides, as the general had intimated, maybe some responsibility— the upkeep of a small *house*—might do a fourteen-, almost fifteen-year-old kid some good.

I roll past the footlocker that Eddie used once for summer camp and that now serves as a coffee table. Past the red fold-out futon couch. Past the thousand-dollar plasma TV, a gift from his mother so that Eddie could watch her read the news. Past a book-case with glass-paneled doors that open to shelves packed with books, mostly mine. And past a hundred-odd-year-old oak armoire that Grandmother brought from France while Grandfather served as a judge in the Nuremberg war trials. (They both returned briefly to Europe after the war so Grandfather could help try a few Nazis.)

Eddie's room is tidy.

Apropos of every other mismatched piece of furniture in here, Eddie's Contemporary Americana chest of drawers took a half hour to assemble; a hard rain would melt the pressboard in half the time. Rather than go into his closet for his "good" clothes—no point in giving the kid sartorial whiplash; he'll be upset enough to see me—I dig around in the second drawer and find all manner of T-shirts.

A simple black one with no pictures has small white sans serif letters proclaiming READ THIS, I DARE YOU. Though it may violate one of the fifteen hundred words in Ari's dress code, I'm okay with it. In the next drawer, I find an actual pair of *blue* jeans, pants that wouldn't set off an airport metal detector and would stay on by dint of their perfect fit, as opposed to what he's wearing now, which, if gravity really were the law, should have long since fallen off him.

For no particular reason, I reach into the top left-hand drawer. I feel a crinkling plastic bag and a box about half the size of a deck of cards.

Yanking the drawer onto my lap, I find single socks, old marbles, a near-empty pack of cinnamon-flavored gum, and a twenty-five-cent box of Nag Champa incense. The stuff smells like earthworm guano rubbed around the armpits of a dreadlocked hippie from the North Carolina mountains, one of those trustafarians who showered the last time he had a job. Next to that and wrapped in one of *my* black dress socks, which has been lost for years, is a pipe with a gold screen and the smallest bit of resin. The Baggie, of course, is full of weed.

The Trojan Supras box hasn't been opened. *Supras?* "For extra body heat stimulation," the box advertises.

Like every other parent who finds contraband in his child's room, I feel the predictable stew of emotions: anger, confusion, despair, denial, anxiety, disappointment, worry, the feelings of failure and hypocrisy, hatred of whatever kid led mine down this path of self-destruction.

Worse than the collision of conflicting emotions is the indecision about what to do next.

I want to laugh aloud. I have just discovered drugs and contraceptives in my son's bedroom. I want to shoot the kid, but I also, hypocritically, want to add a pinch of weed to the pipe's bowl and light up. Not that I plan to shoot my kid or steal his pot.

And who can I talk to? Certainly not Volusia. I know exactly what *she* would do. I can't talk to Jupe, because I have an inkling of what he's doing, though he should have learned his lesson the last time. I could try talking to Jerod, if I could find him and he's not too busy with whatever mysterious errand he's up to at the moment. Even *that* would be taking my chances. Of all the people I want to talk to now, I can't. I buried my wisest sounding board yesterday.

Gathering up the articles that in my opinion should be legal and the clothing that isn't, I roll out of the house and back up the driveway to my car.

The midmorning sun is gaining strength now, burning off the early chill; it's going to be a pretty day after all. A few high clouds hang in the sky, giving no thought to where they might go.

I wish I could follow them, but since the crash I've learned that wishes are for beggars, beggars can't be choosers, and my chair is the only horse left to ride.

Ari Manios pulls open the glass-paneled door to the principal's office.

"Great to see you again, Ari."

He seems relieved that I didn't call him Aristotle this time. "Likewise, Randol. You look good."

"I'd get up to greet you, but I'm afraid you might kick my ass over this whole T-shirt thing."

He smiles. Heavens, yes, he's a handsome man, and he knows it, despite his paunch. Heck, if I had a lifetime pass to Hero's onion rings and the only chili-cheese dogs I have ever seen make a grown man cry, then I'd be wearing a few extra pounds above my belt, too.

He asks, "Shall I call Eddie so that you can hand him the change of clothes, or would you prefer to leave them here so that he can come and get them?"

"Do you have a clothes-changing goon squad?"

"Complete with fifty-thousand-volt Tasers, duct tape, handcuffs, and all the other tools necessary to ensure the smooth insertion of the prisoner into the appropriate school wear, yes."

"Greeks. Yes. A funny lot." At the rate this day is going, a year couldn't last much longer.

He signals for a student to come into his office. I recognize her, a pretty girl, but I can't remember her name.

"Marnie," Ari says.

"Hi! Mr. M, you wanted something, sir?" If she gets any windier, it seems to me, she might simply blow away.

"You know Mr. Duncan, don't you?"

"Oh, gosh, yes!" she verboses, and, yes, Marnie is doing just that, verbosing windily, neither of which is a word, but, like, whatever! "Everybody knows Mr. D."

"They do?" I ask. "And how would they know Mr. D, Miss M?"

"You write those columns for the online music zine, don't you?"

I beam for the first time in years. I know from e-mails that I have readers, who taunt me with cyber names like "rockphu-quer" and "stareEOgrrl and "hairbandage" and say things like "u rok!" and "think u'r so smart, dikferbrainz" and "such-and-such band kicks thus-and-so's band's ass, dumshit!" But I've never re-ally thought about them as people, not as pretty girls who inspire thoughts that could get me thrown in jail, though the age of con-sent in this state *is* only sixteen.

"You actually read my stuff?" I try not to sound too dumb-founded.

"C'mon, Mr. D, *everybody* here reads seriousmusic-dot-com. Are you kidding? It's, like, y'know, the most *serious* music Webzine on the entire Web!"

I hear Mr. M clear his throat.

"Miss Jennings, Mr. Duncan, shall we get on with the busi-ness at hand? Marnie, would you mind locating Eddie Duncan for me?" He glances at his watch. "Early fourth period. He should be in Ms. Everude's math class."

I detect a grimace on the delectable Miss Jennings's face, in-spired, I suppose, by Ms. Everude or the class she teaches.

Ari clears his throat again. Marnie flits out of the office.

"How are things going, Randol? I mean, other than . . . I am terribly sorry about your grandfather. Colonel Duncan was a true gentleman in every sense of the word, one of the last in the Old South, a real hero, a genuine soldier, and a fine . . . a fine man." He clenches his jaw in emotion. I can almost feel the burn in *his* throat. "I should have been at the funeral, but . . ." He gazes through the office window into the vastness of his respon-sibilities.

I imagine he's earning about the same salary as a high school principal that my grandfather did as an army colonel. It occurs to me that my grandfather's chances of getting killed in World War II, given the millions of people who served in that incalculably tragic conflict, were about two percent. With the insanity and violence in today's schools, I wonder whether Ari Manios's chances might be about the same.

When Marnie escorts my son into Ari's office, the principal has the presence of mind to pull down the wooden shutters before he leaves the room.

"She's hot," I begin.

"Huh?" Eddie looks at me as if I'd emptied his sock drawer and finished all his stash.

"Marnie Jennings."

He doesn't say a word. He just looks at me with the angry look of a kid who doesn't get it, doesn't want to get it, and doesn't care.

I pretend not to notice. "If we ever had girls that hot when I was in school . . ." I shake my head. "No, I swear, it's evolution. Really. Think about it. A zillion years ago, people were plug-damn ugly, with jagged teeth and arms that hung down to here. Short, too. Look at the old houses in those preserved colonial villages: little beds, little rooms—little people. You think them little turkeys could play basketball against the telephone poles we have slammin' dunks today?"

He sits down.

"I'm not saying that the women in, oh, say, a John Singer Sargent portrait weren't hot, but that was in the late 1800s, early 1900s, right? And you can always airbrush a woman—"

"You don't airbrush an oil portrait."

I feign a chuckle. "My point is, they were aris-*tocracy*, those women. They were born and bred and raised and groomed to be beautiful; they were *trained* to be. Sargent was working with quality material."

"What the fuck are you talking about?" He knows he's far enough away from Volusia's little soaps.

"Change your clothes." I hand over the "Read This, I Dare You" T-shirt. He unfurls it and smiles. Without comment or complaint, he whips off his heavy-metal T. So tough. And thin, pale, and vulnerable. I want to hold him. "We get taller so we can slam-dunk baskets, get hotter so we can get better guys and babes, make better-looking and maybe even smarter babies. We e-*volve*. That's the design, Eddie, the grand plan."

He jumps out of one pair of pants and into the other.

I manage to fasten my eyes into his. "I'd hate to think that my grandfather was the end of the evolutionary chain for this family."

Eddie looks at me blankly. I may have finally gotten through to him. While he collapses into a chair older than he is, I say a silent prayer to General Barrows, who may have finally gotten through to me.

"Y'know, Dad, you are such a freakin' windbag."

"By the way, mister, watch your fuckin' language, before Mean-Ass Manios walks in here and watches it for you." Eddie so rarely hears me cuss that he's caught off guard. "What I mean, Eddie, is that we are all supposed to grow, not just as people, as boys grow to men, but from one generation to the next. It's how civilization is supposed to survive. We're not doing such a hot job of it these days, and I'm not going to get into all that now, because I've got some places I need to go—"

"People to see." His smile is wry. He thinks he's going to get out of our chat with a philosophical slap on the wrist.

"Marnie Jennings, I can guarantee you, is a hundred percent prettier and healthier than her great-grandmother. That alone should be an object lesson."

He shakes his head.

"My point is"—I stop and fire another glare straight into his eyes—"my grandfather gave everything he had for this country and would have given his life for it—everything this country meant and stood for, believed in, and asked of its people. Your grandfather, my father, well, I have to admit we have some issues . . . but the man I'm here to talk about is you." I point a finger at him as if I were Uncle Sam. The gesture startles him, and he leans against the chair, his arms crossed. "You're incredibly smart."

"How do you figure?"

"Because I am."

"Now *that's* humble."

"No, that's simple evolution, Eddie. I got it from my grandfather and from *your* grandfather." I nod toward the pile of black denim and chrome loops at his feet. "But I'm not about to let a pair of crappy jeans and a ridiculous T-shirt stand in the way of your evolution."

"Change how you see, not how I look." He stares at me with defiance.

"Bumper-sticker philosophy. Get your own."

"Are you going somewhere with this, Dad?"

"See how smart you are, Eddie? You don't put up with a bunch of bullshit, even mine." I tap my temple hard enough to give myself a little headache. "Caught you, ya little shit. I actually got you thinking!"

He smiles. "Okay, so?"

"So." I pull out the bag of pot and the pipe, knowing full well that if Ari Manios walked in right now, Eddie and I would be thrown in prison for having drugs on school property.

Eddie's retinal Ping-Pong balls look as if they might explode out of his head. He grips the arms of the wooden chair so hard that his knuckles turn from red to white and back to red again. The chair starts shaking.

In a whispering rage, Eddie hisses, "And . . . what . . . the . . . *fuck* . . . DAD . . . were . . . you . . . doing . . . in . . . my . . . stuff?" His face flushes. I can't tell if he is near tears, near homicide, or near both.

I pull the condoms out of my other pocket. "I was looking for these. If I can get a date tonight with that nice young lady your uncle Jerod brought over this morning . . ."

He flies out of his chair. "You smart-ass son of a bitch asshole!"

If he were older and stronger, his flailing fists would have connected, and I would have deserved it. But I had evolved into a pretty strong guy. I grab his wrists and hold him still.

He backs away and slumps into his chair.

"C'mon, Eddie. Turn on your brain. That's what I mean by smart, by evolution, by growth." I stuff the condoms and the drugs and the pipe back into my pocket. I hear Ari and one of New Cumbria's numerous Lolitae chattering in the hall.

"What's going to happen to me?"

"Think about that for a minute, will you?" I stare into him that much harder.

He stares back.

"You *are* smarter than this, Eddie"—I pat my pockets—"not because of what a great father I am or what a great role model I've been, but because of the gift of evolution. You're smarter because you've got some great genes, and it's your job to exploit those and the resources you have."

"Resources? Give me a fucking—"

"Mouth, champ."

"Give me a break, Dad. The only horse this one-horse town has is the granite statue of the loser Confederate near the county courthouse!"

We both start laughing. The tension explodes, the relief blasting out like a giant fart.

"Okay." I wave my hand. "I get that, okay? But I *know* you get what I'm saying."

"So. All right. Indictment. Verdict. Conviction. Sentence."

"Sentence?" I think for a second. "Yeah. You're going to do two things." I pause. "No, three."

Defiance creeps back into his eyes. "I could run away."

"You could. But, see, that would work to my advantage. Lack of courage in the other guy always does."

He looks away again. Eddie hates when I call his bluff. "Okay, then try."

"First, as soon as I get the chance, and I hope that's sooner rather than later, I want you to get me upstairs to the Plunder Room."

His eyes widen. He's getting a serious ocular workout this morning.

"You will help me with whatever may be in there. Ghosts, dead bodies, historical research, car engines, whatever."

His body visibly tightens, as if he's trying to figure out whether his thin muscles could lift me up the stairs all on their own.

"Second, we will destroy the contents of my pockets at a time mutually convenient to both of us."

He relaxes.

"And third, you will ask Marnie Jennings on a date."

"You are out of your freaking mind!" he yells.

"I will be looking for proof; receipts. Photos would be . . ."

The door swings open. Ari Manios slides in. "Everything okay in here?"

"You bet." I wave my arm toward my son in his fresh change of clothes. "Fashion plate, no?"

Ari Manios sizes up the T-shirt and smiles. "Better get your ass to class, kiddo."

I smile at Eddie, too.

To my astonishment and relief, he smiles back.

CHAPTER SIX

SHOW ME a man with no skeleton in his closet and I'll show you a man with no closet. Driving out of the parking lot of New Cumbria High School toward U.S. 36 Bypass to get to Wrenton, I wonder whether that's why Grandfather had footlockers. Of course, he had closets, too. In fact, the room opposite the Plunder Room has a walk-in closet big enough to qualify as another bedroom. Once, when I was a kid, I even found a trapdoor from that closet with a ladder leading up to . . . I wasn't about to find out. Talk about creepy. Talk about skeletons. I wonder now how much space I would need to accommodate all of mine.

I glance at my watch. It's almost noon. Leaving now would put me in Wrenton sometime between one-fifteen and one-thirty. Traffic shouldn't be too bad on the interstate.

Driving north on Buncombe Boulevard takes me past my grandparents' house. I look around the neighborhood. Nothing has changed. Nothing ever does. Except people dying. Most of the homes are painted white on this two-and-a-half-mile stretch of Buncombe, from downtown until it fizzles into auto-body shops and remnants of the Buncombe Mill villages. I pass the Maris house. Like Doug Straithorn, Putt Maris came home in a body bag; his was shipped home from Tan Son Nhut, Vietnam. His mother, Alva, almost as old as my grandfather, still lives there. His father, Ned, a vice president at New Cumbria First Federal Bank, died years ago. A few houses down is the Greek Revival plantation-style mansion belonging to Whitman Carlisle, far and away the wealthiest man in the county. Carlisle owned three cotton mills, but not the Buncombe Mill, which he'd help put out of business; my great-uncle, Lem, always thought the world of Whitman Carlisle, even though Carlisle got the better of him. "Friends is friends and bidness is bidness," Lem told me once. Carlisle and his wife, Issa, short for Issabelle, still live there; she's a cross between fireworks and an enema, colorful to watch but a pain in the ass. I love these people. These are my people, my people's people. History, blood, and money have created a bond that time, even death, can't break.

As I approach my grandparents' house, I look at 519 South Buncombe Boulevard. The house somehow doesn't look the same now that Grandfather and his wife, who died twenty-two years before him, are gone. A half-acre lawn spreads before the house. A driveway curves from one side of the property to the other, arching toward the six stairs ascending to the wraparound veranda. Smack in the middle of the lawn is a massive magnolia tree, whose enormous white blossoms look like the very palms of God. Two-hundred-year-old oak trees line the left side, between the house and Duncan Park, a three-and-a-half-acre gift Grandfather gave to the city of New Cumbria. Spanish moss hangs like tattered uniforms spattered into the trees after a tragic Civil War set piece. Whenever I take the time to notice, the romantic effect leaves me near tears.

On either side of the veranda, two tapered Corinthian columns hold up the slanted copper roof, with smaller matching columns and a railing forming a balustrade along the rest of the veranda. The roofs are oxidized to green, the only part of the house that isn't white, except, too, for the dark window screens. The house has no air-conditioning; upstairs, an enormous attic fan that has to be the size of a Sopwith Camel propeller blows hot air out of the house through four vents dotting the roof. I've slept through more steaming Carolina afternoons than I can count under the narcotic white noise of that fan. Two chimneys, one coal- and one wood-burning, face each other like eternal Beefeaters, sentinels overlooking the house and providing warmth. The fireplaces are two-sided: One drops into the China Room and into the guest quarters, the other into the formal dining room and formal living room. Grandfather had the flue bricked up in that one because they never used it, and it was the coal-burning one, anyway.

I slow down near the driveway when I notice movement on the porch . . . and stop breathing. Standing next to one of the columns, her arm wrapped around her perfect waist, her head buried in her ivory left hand, is none other than Annie, Jerod's companion.

She's heaving sobs.

Would that I could race up the stairs and hold her.

I grab my chair from the backseat, hop in, and roll up the ramp. "What in the world?"

"She kicked me out." Annie raises her head. Her face is red, mottled. She looks like Persephone, beautiful, grief-stricken, in hell.

Still, I can't help but cover my mouth to keep from laughing. I can picture the scene I missed between Volusia and this young woman—"girl," as folks call even middle-aged women in the South. "Get the hell out my house," I can hear Volusia say. "This isn't your house," Annie must have said. "And who the hell are you to say it isn't?" Et cetera, et cetera, until Volusia picks up either the telephone, a knife, or a cast-iron skillet or simply moves in her direction until Annie has no choice but to flee.

I'm in an awkward situation: go back into the house and overrule Volusia for the second time today or sit in the cold.

It's still just a bit too cool out here.

All my plans for this morning, the day after Grandfather's funeral, keep going to pot.

"Would you like to go for some coffee?" Of course, I can't help but imagine that Randol Duncan accompanying such a beautiful creature on Main Street would create a buzz louder than if the pastor got caught with his needle in the quilting bee.

She brightens up in an instant, the way gray weather often does here.

"Y'know," I say as I roll back down the ramp to the driveway, "I don't even know your last name." Fact is, I don't really know the first thing about her.

"Harkin. Annie Harkin."

"Irish name, isn't it?"

She slides into the car with the same liquid grace as mercury. "My predecessors came over during the potato famine, moved to upstate New York in the 1840s, been there ever since. Merry bunch of alcoholics, cops, firefighters, the lot of 'em," she says with a put-on brogue.

"Y'know," I say, "it's been theorized that the War of Northern Aggression had a little to do with the fact that the Scots-Irish held a mighty grudge against the British and still wanted to do some redcoat ass-kickin'."

"I'm a history teacher by vocation," she says, heavy on the hint.

It takes two minutes to arrive in downtown New Cumbria, a glum place with unemployment topping twelve percent and at least a third of the storefronts shuttered. When the textile mills started closing during the latter half of the last century, no replacement manufacturing moved in.

I'm impressed that Annie Harkin doesn't offer to help me out of the car or into Winchell's Café. Annie understands that we SCIs can be strong, resourceful people who usually handle life better on our own, that "helpers" often get in the way. She does open the café door for me.

Winchell's has been here since coffee was invented, and only Volusia brews a better cup, but Marty Winchell has a better mug, the thick ceramic diner model.

"How the heck are you, Marty?" He's big and garrulous and wears a flour-dusted apron and baggy chef's trousers, though he's no more a chef than I am. Marty's walrus mustache reminds me of my grandfather's; in fact, I wouldn't put it past Marty to have grown the mustache to imitate my grandfather, perhaps his most beloved customer. Grandfather would come in at least once a week to buy a New Cumbria *Record*, even though he got the paper delivered at home. He and Marty would talk news and politics over a cup of Marty's coffee, even though Grandfather had already had his fill of Volusia's.

"Two of your best, big guy, and a table, if you don't mind."

Marty looks at me, then eyes Annie. I glare at him. He looks as if he's about to explode into a paroxysm of laughter. Which may or may not have anything to do with me—or with Annie. Marty's the type who if I cut myself shaving, would hear about it in less time than it took to put a tissue on the spot. And somebody here at the diner would hear him chuckle about it.

"Say, Randol, I hear your brother's in town."

"In fact, this is Annie Harkin, Jerod's girlfriend."

She shifts in her seat, her first noticeable reaction to anything I've said in her presence. Maybe she doesn't appreciate the word *girlfriend*. Maybe she doesn't appreciate that I'm telling people her business. I find her impossible to read because I can't see through her beauty, but for the first time, I'm sensing something beneath her stunning mask.

"Great to have you in town, miss." He reaches over me and wraps his Kodiak paw around her small hand. With the delicacy of a professional wrestler, he shakes her arm up and down. She's strong. He's impressed. I see it in his eyes. "What's your plan? For New Cumbria, I mean?"

"For the moment, to enjoy your café, sir." The girl just swung the verbal sledgehammer on that conversation. I've never seen that happen before.

"Best of luck, young lady," he says, sliding two mugs in front of us. "Cream and sugar?" Sledgehammer or no, he wants to be near her. A man's a man, after all.

She nods, then reaches for my arm, out of instinct, I suspect.

I notice an eye here, a glance there, mostly from the wizened patrons who would give what's left of their eyeteeth to be sitting where I am now.

"Wow." She sips her scalding coffee and smiles. "This is really good."

"'Winchell's Works Wonders.' Been his motto since the day he opened, before I was born." I point to a sign posted on the stainless-steel hood that reads "The Carolinas' Finest Coffee, a Curative from Cradle to Coffin." She laughs. I can't stand myself. "Want a doughnut or something? Those are good here, too."

She shakes her head, smiles, and pats the erotic plain of her flat tummy. She needn't have done that. "I'm not sure my physique can accommodate all this Southern hospitality, this epicurean largesse."

Epicurean largesse. Nice. She's killing me.

"So"—I try maneuvering a little conversational plane onto the flight deck of her heavily fortified battleship—"what brought you to my house this fine morning?"

"I thought Jerod was going to meet me there."

Something sounds wrong, but her azure eyes look straight into me. I know from TV crime shows that when she shifts her eyes away from mine, she's lying.

"You settling in okay?" I try again.

"It's a small town."

I nod. "Sure, but you're a beautiful woman"—I've never said that to anyone, and I feel an embarrassing blush rise in my cheeks—"and Jerod did say you wanted to get away from big-city—"

"Jerod wants to be back home, stay around here."

"I guess that begs the question, then: Do you care enough for the cad, I mean, the man? I mean, care enough to want to stay with him. Stay *here* with him?"

She nods and offers a coy half smile. "I guess. He's a great guy. I mean, I'm twenty-six years old."

Jerod, you cradle robber, you—but a damned elegant one! "Okay . . ."

"And I'm anxious to settle down, but not in upstate New York."

"I totally understand that." I get the feeling she's never been interviewed like this before, so I wonder whether I should back off. She already has aroused more than just my curiosity, but I'm feeling the need to satisfy the curiosity, at least.

Her smile hasn't faded. "But *here*? In new Cumbria?"

"Hey!" She knows my protest is tongue-in-cheek.

For a time that stretches from awkward to uneasy, loaded silence separates us, filled only with spoons clanking against porcelain coffee mugs and the tidal ebb and flow of conversations nearby.

"You mentioned back in the car that you're a history teacher by vocation."

"That's right." She nods with startling alacrity, her eyes dancing again. "I really do want to teach. High school would be best. That's where I'm most qualified. My specialty is history, yes, but I could teach math, some geometry, English, not much science. I'm certified in New York and Connecticut, but could get certified here, I'm sure. I've taught for four years, including two in the New York City system—now, that was something. P.S. Two Eighty-Two in Park Slope, probably one of the finest schools you can ask for, in Brooklyn. I went to school at Lesley University, used to be Lesley College, right next to Harvard, in Boston—"

I raise my hand to stop her. She has a gold-plated résumé; the New Cumbria School District can't afford her but would roll over and die to recruit her if it could. I can almost see the look on Ari Manios's face were I to introduce the two of them. Not because of Annie's outrageous beauty—Ari is accustomed to beautiful women; he's Greek—but because of her gorgeous credentials.

Trouble is, I just had a little trouble of my own with Ari this morning. Still, I could make one call to Mabry Hollander, the district superintendent and past president of the New Cumbria Chamber of Commerce and retired CEO of Sykes Foods, the largest wholesale food distributor in this part of the state, and she'd be hired. On second thought, it would be better to call Ari first so he doesn't think I've gone over his head. Trouble with *that* is, I'm not sure going to Ari Manios first is protocol, either.

"Morning, Chief!" Marty says, as if Terry Magnus's arrival needs an announcement.

The former ACC linebacker packs just the right mix of charisma, authority, and constraint in his 246-pound frame that people feel compelled to behave.

Oh, crap! I suddenly remember Eddie's contraband in my pocket.

Marty buries a coffee mug in one hand and shakes the other as the door swings shut with a little bell tinkle.

If I weren't wearing a catheter, I'd wet my pants.

Terry slides onto one of the empty chairs between Annie and me.

"I'll be damned, pardon my French, but it's rare to see Mr. Randol Duncan out and about, especially on a chilly winter day." He winks at Annie, obviously unimpressed with her seraphic beauty. "Now, I know you can get coffee every bit as good as this at home, Randol."

"You're leading the witness, Chief Magnus."

He laughs, a big laugh. If he were white, he'd be in charge in this town. He's in charge in a lot of ways, but not in the ways he should be. I'm sad about that. My respect and admiration for Terry Magnus run deeper than he could know.

We stir our coffee together in silence, until I say, "How 'bout them Tigers?"

"It's February, Randol. Football season ended in December, and our season wasn't what you'd call the best we ever had." He shifts in his seat. The pause feels like a furnace about to kick on. "So. I hear your brother's in town."

"Yes, and this is his girlfriend."

He looks at Annie with a friendly gaze; she's innocent until proven guilty. But I can see him thinking: You *are* known by the company you keep.

"Annie Harkin, Chief Terry Magnus, New Cumbria's finest. He was in Desert Storm. Our local war hero."

He laughs. "Some war. We killed a bunch of rag heads, got out, came home." He shakes his head. "Sorry, no politics, not today." He gulps his coffee. The man's composition is an alloy of indestructible metals.

"How's Jennie, the kids?" I ask, looking for something, anything to keep the subject away from us.

"Good, all good." He looks around, always on the job. "So." I can feel it coming, like one of the Patriot missiles Terry saw flying toward him. Those always missed; Terry's don't. "Your pop been busted yet?"

I laugh as hard as I can, just to defuse the question. "Only once, and that was years ago, fifteen hundred miles and a whole different country away." I'm afraid that if my smile gets any more wry, Magnus might feel the urge to slap me.

"Just a word to the wise is all." He sips his coffee again, his big brown eyes never leaving mine. "You know everybody's watching him."

"Dad's not a bad guy, Chief. He's just . . . unique."

Annie clears her throat and stands, excusing herself and looking toward the ladies' room in the back.

The chief moves to stand, but she waves him back to his seat, clearly impressed by his courtesy.

"What's her story?" Magnus asks, even before he's certain she's out of earshot.

"Don't know, really." I shake my head. "She and Jerod are a package deal."

I watch his eyes follow Annie, but not for the reasons any other guy's would. Terry Magnus was nominated for the Heisman

Trophy because he could read a quarterback better than any defensive player in the Atlantic Coast Conference, nearing the record with eighteen sacks in his senior year.

He shakes his head and chuckles. "Now Jerod, there's another one."

"C'mon, Chief, cut my people some slack."

"I just don't . . . I don't know," he continues, shaking his head. "I can't put my finger on it. Mama used to say that a woman so pretty she doesn't have much to say must be a Boo Hag waiting to do her mischief."

He's referring to the supernatural woman of Gullah folktales, similar to evil old women from all over the world, like the witch in "Hansel and Gretel." But in Gullah lore, the Boo Hag can also appear as a comely seductress who targets wealthy and handsome men. The Boo Hag flies through a crack or a keyhole in her victim's house and "rides" him while he sleeps, rendering him helpless. Sort of like the first time I met Annie.

"Don't let de hag ride ya," he concludes in fluid Gullah.

"I suppose I could always put one of Grandfather's shotguns across my threshold." According to the folklore, Hags don't like the smell of gunpowder, so it's one way to ward them off. Another is to leave a broom beside your bed, because the Hag will be distracted counting the straws and won't be able to ride you before the sun comes up.

Folktales impart truths, and I shiver with the heebie-jeebies. He's right: I know nothing about Annie, and I wonder whether Jerod does, either. I would bet that the moment my brother laid eyes on Annie Harkin, he decided ignorance really is bliss.

Annie returns to our table, and this time Chief Magnus rises. He drains his coffee and moves toward the door.

"Randol, Miss Harkin, my pleasure." He winks at me, but not at her. "Hold 'em in the road, Duncan, and tell your father to clean up his act before one of my colleagues has the pleasure of doing it for him."

My face drains. My entire body, what I can feel of it, begins to ache, and I fear a bout of oncoming pain. Lunch with my father is now out of the question.

Annie Harkin has become the question. With no immediate answer.

CHAPTER SEVEN

BACKING INTO the nonexistent traffic on Main Street, I glance at Annie in the passenger seat, sitting like a schoolgirl, her lovely hands folded in her lap.

Finally, she breaks the silence. "So, back there, the police chief, what *was* all that he was saying about your father, if you don't mind my prying."

Annie sounds as innocent as an octogenarian lost in a gift shop. I realize how much Chief Magnus has unnerved me because I'm wondering whether Annie might be looking to do a little shoplifting.

As much as I would like to confide in her, I can't tell her anything about Jupe—certainly not about his arrest and imprisonment in Honduras. Nobody in New Cumbria knows about that, not even Volusia. For all Volusia knows, Jupe was conscripted by the U.S. government for some ultrasecret mission in some exotic foreign country: one of those if-he-told-us-he'd-have-to-kill-us junkets. Volusia dutifully zipped her lips and swallowed the key and promised not to tell anyone. Which means I heard from a half dozen folks around town who said *they* had heard that Jupe was on some super-dangerous covert mission that could get us all kilt.

Now that Chief Magnus just aired our family's sullied laundry, I feel no small amount of vulnerability, as if sitting in a wheelchair doesn't beget that all on its own. But I'm not about to make myself more so by divulging family secrets to Annie Harkin.

"I'm sorry," she says, responding to my silence.

"Back to the problem of you."

She nods and chews on her fingernails. Aha! Maybe I have found a flaw in the perfection that is Annie Harkin! Maybe the young siren has perfect hands and elegant fingers ending in gnawed and pruney stubs. As if that would make any difference.

"The New Cumbria Motor Lodge isn't such a bad place," she offers.

"Nicest place in town."

"Jerod says—"

"It's more or less the only . . ." I think for a moment, then snap my fingers. "Hold on a sec. I remember an article in the paper about a retired Fortune Five Hundred exec and his wife who bought a hundred-year-old house and converted it into a bed-and-breakfast, about ten, fifteen minutes outside of town."

The Jessamine Plantation Inn opened for business back in November, probably the worst time of year. New Cumbria and its environs certainly are not what you'd call a tourist mecca. But Hampton and Margaret Owens—he worked with one of those massive computer-chip outfits—wanted a gorgeous place to live, found one, and opened their retirement hobby.

I tell Annie that if Jerod were to drop by with all his charm, his Duncan name, and his New Cumbria pedigree, I'm certain he could secure a deep, long-term discount.

I pull out my cell phone and call directory assistance and ask for the Jessamine Plantation number. The computer connects me. "Would you mind giving me directions, please, from downtown New Cumbria, South Buncombe Boulevard, right off Duncan Park?"

A woman on the other end of the line, likely Margaret Owens, confirms that the antebellum mansion is located on the way to the Duncan family cemetery. I need to tell Annie that, as a historian, she should peruse the resting place of my kinfolk. Then it occurs to me that she could get into the Plunder Room and help me go through Grandfather's things, catalog them and . . . my head begins to spin again. I picture us wading through Grandfather's keepsakes, splayed all over, through endless cups of coffee and enthralling conversation, preparing a historical narrative that would set the world on fire. Together.

My heart beats so fast it almost stops. Or maybe it just stops. The air in the car is close, and I'm relieved to pull into my driveway, where Annie has left her white rental car.

"I don't know what I'm going to do, Randol," she says, touching my arm. "I really don't."

"I don't understand." Here I am thinking *I'm* the one who's vulnerable. Or is she playing me? "What are you asking? What do you need?"

"I just don't know if I can last in this town or whether this town can accept me, but I know Jerod's counting on me to try." She chews a bit more on her fingers. "I guess I'll figure out a plan soon enough."

"Well, you held your own against Chief Magnus back there." I want to wink at her and make her laugh. "In fact, I really think he liked you, big ebony teddy bear that he is." I think I hear a faint giggle.

"And Jerod . . ." Her words evaporate as she lifts her hand from my arm.

"What about him?" I ask.

"He's busy, and he told me he probably isn't going to be around much."

I'm beginning to feel like the clown in the circus who picks up a few poles and plates and starts spinning the plates on the poles and then starts adding plates and poles and tries to keep them all spinning. Since General Barrows's visit, it's more than dawned on me that I have to start minding each plate more carefully. Apparently, though, the clowns in the Duncan circus are going to keep piling more plates on my poles. I know this for certain: I'm not capable of handling the Jerod plate.

All I can do is nod as exhaustion and pain slam into me.

The pain doesn't seep in, it gushes, the locks on the Pain Canal opening in full flood. The day started too early, with too much of a jolt, and nothing has been smooth.

The pain assaults in stabs and aches, sears and jabs, sometimes here, sometimes there, then all over, all at once, then it's gone, but only for a seeming instant, and then not really. Pain doesn't want to be described, which is why we have the capacity to forget it so easily, to rub it out of or let it slip from our memory. They talk a lot about managing pain, but pain manages you. Pain doesn't knock your body for a loop so much as it rearranges the intricate wiring of your emotions, your psyche. Pain messes with your head, does things to the person you're otherwise supposed to be.

I need to get inside, out of the bone-stabbing bitterness.

Her voice blows in a cold front that adds to the terrible chill.

"Jerod says you know everyone in town. If you could just talk to someone at the high school or . . . maybe . . . please . . . maybe talk to them about a job for me. It would just be so much faster than if I—"

"Seriously? Here? In New Cumbria? Y'all really do plan on *staying* here?"

"Could you? Please?" She returns her hand to my arm. Electricity shoots through me as if I'd just been Tasered.

"You don't want to teach here, Annie, you really don't. You don't even want to *live* here."

"Why not?"

The sound of my own laughter not only makes me laugh harder but creates a distraction from my pain, which already has compounded threefold.

"Listen. Annie. I need to have this discussion another day. Another time." Finally, I manage to look at her. Her beauty unravels me, but this time only for an instant. The pain resumes in a hammer blow. I look at my watch and feign urgency about another matter. "Listen, I really hate to do this, but I promised my dad that I'd be in Wrenton an hour ago, and it's more than an hour's drive away. So . . ."

She reaches across the seat and pecks me on the cheek. Strike me dead now, Lord. Call me home. Everything I have ever needed in my life I have gotten—thank you, Jesus.

"Thank you, Randol. I know you'll take care of me. Jerod says you're like that."

My cheeks, now both of them, feel napalmed. I don't have pain pills strong enough for what I'm experiencing right now.

She climbs out of her seat, and I flop out of mine after pulling down my chair.

Annie glides into her car, then out of the driveway. Her blond hair looks like a halo in the winter sun.

I roll up the ramp and call to the kitchen for Volusia.

"You look like the Devil's breath has blowed right over you, Mister Randol."

"Rough day, and it's barely started."

"I'd say. That girlfriend of Jerod's, the little hussy—"

I put my hand up. I don't want to hear another human being say another word. "I just need to go to bed. Take me to Grandfather's room; it's closer than mine."

"Want something to eat or drink? Some Goody's Powders?"

I shake my head. "Just . . . please." I look up at her.

She knows.

She rolls me into the bedroom without a word or resistance. I let her yank me out of my chair and dump me into the king-sized bed where my grandfather died four days before.

"One more thing," I say, trying not to moan through the agony.

"You don't *sound* too good neither."

"Could you reach into the medicine cabinet and pull out my painkillers? They should be on the bottom shelf."

Volusia goes into the bathroom, which still smells more than a dozen years later of Grandmother's lavender powder, and returns with pills and a glass of water.

In a few minutes, these 160 milligrams of OxyContin will send me to my cranial Plunder Room and whatever's stored there.

It's been a day.

While the opioid tablets begin dissolving into my system and the pain into the universe, my mind wanders to Tegucigalpa, Honduras, and the man I was six years ago when I went there to fetch my father from prison.

At the time of Jupe's incarceration, I was living in Atlanta's Buckhead neighborhood, whose motto is "Where old money lives and new money parties." One spring afternoon around four o'clock, the telephone rang.

"Mr. Randol Duncan?"

"We're not interested. Thanks."

"This isn't a sales call, sir. I'm calling from the U.S. Department of State."

My pulse doubled. "Well. That *is* the ultimate long-distance service."

"Not quite," the crisp male voice said. "It's about your father."

I exhaled, mostly in exasperation. Jupe was supposed to be in South Carolina, doing whatever he was doing in his "retirement." He had been honorably discharged from the United States Army thirty-three years before as a sergeant with a ribbon or two and twelve years' service, just enough to qualify for a minor pension and veterans' benefits.

"And you would be . . . ?"

"Excuse me, sir, yes. I am Chance Tolliver, Central America desk, Washington."

You could hear the Ivy League in his voice, that of an erudite young white man with manners matching his IQ. I used to think I would be one of them. Unlike my father, I couldn't wait to go to college, especially since my grandmother whispered into my ear that Grandfather would pay my full tuition—a gift, she said, to ensure that I would have a carefree education. So I attended Columbia University in New York. When I walked through the big iron gates at 116th and Broadway for the first time, I harbored fantasies of being a dashing State Department officer, dining on fine china with the American-eagle seal in exotic embassies— Quito, Ecuador; Jakarta, Indonesia; Paris, London, Madrid. I would meet elegant women in ball gowns and glittering jewels, with delicate accents that lingered like perfume. I would bed them all, of course, after late-night cocktails in smoke-filled rooms choked with people chattering in the many languages I understood. Or we would drink scotch in burgundy leather wingback chairs discussing why the United States had just given al-Wheresis billions of dollars in munitions. But after my first glance at the State Department test, I instead partied my way through Manhattan, tanked my grades, and destroyed any chance I might have had to join the U.S. Foreign Service.

"Okay, so you're calling about my father. What could my father possibly have done to involve you?"

"We got word from our people in Tegucigalpa that he was arrested a few days ago and charged with drug possession. They have him in custody, in the Central Prison there."

Prison, no huge surprise. The locale couldn't have been more startling.

"Any chance, Chance, that you could shed some light on how dear ol' Dad wound up in Teguc?"

"I, we, haven't demobbed—sorry, debriefed—your father yet; we're still negotiating with the authorities in Honduras." I could almost hear the jingle-jangle of money in his voice, as in the jingle-jangle it was going to take to unlock my pop. "The Honduran government supposedly has a zero-tolerance policy regarding drug smugglers, especially yanquis. But from what I gather, our Teguc station indicates that your father is very much a small-time operator."

I snorted. "Small-time doesn't *begin* to define Jupiter Duncan."

"Right now, they're saying they won't let him go for at least six months regardless of what we do."

"Six months? Why?"

"That's just what they're saying."

"What else are they saying?"

"They're saying nineteen thousand, six hundred and seventy-seven lemps a month until they can get this thing cleared up. But, of course, they would prefer American currency."

"*What?*"

The Honduran lempira had been stabilized at around nineteen lempira to one U.S. dollar, so the authorities in Tegucigalpa were trying to shake us—me—down for a thousand dollars a month, six thousand dollars, to "get this thing cleared up."

"Well, they have expenses—prison fees, court costs, what have you."

"What about those pictures, the ones you see in the magazines, with poor Third-World kids, flies buzzing around their adorable little faces, huge eyes, bulging tummies, 'Your donation of thirty cents will feed Juanita for a year'? So what the hell—sorry—are they talking about? A thousand dollars a month? I bet a thousand bucks would provide Thanksgiving dinner with all the trimmings to the entire Honduran population."

"That's what they're quoting us."

By now, I was talking so loud that little Eddie, who was eight at the time, came bursting out of his room to join the fun.

"I'm not sure he's worth their quote."

"Excuse me, Mr. Duncan?"

"Well, let's figure this out, Chance. I can *buy* the old guy for six grand. Or I could leave him there for free, except the cost of a guilty conscience, which I may not even have to pay. Or I could . . ." I scratched the three-day beard that my wife hated—and realized how much she would hate this breaking news.

"Well, it appears the Honduran government is willing to wait until you're ready to discuss your father's situation. They would be more than happy to get acquainted with you and, of course, your wallet. The longer your father sits in Central Prison, though, I fear . . ."

I'd seen the movies about Americans in foreign prisons. My imagination didn't need much stretching to see what lengths the Honduran government might go to get what they wanted out of me in exchange for a prisoner they probably didn't want.

"I'm sorry, I really must go," he said. "So, please, think about what you would like to do and get back to me at your earliest convenience."

I hung up and looked down at my son, my gorgeous little boy with his big cow eyes and his mop of black hair and his sly little smile.

"Everything okay, Daddy?"

"Oh, yeah, big fella." I sighed and swung him onto my lap. "Something has come up that I need to talk to Mommy about, so we'll just have to wait for her to come home from work."

Elsbeth and I had planned to attend a concert that night at Chastain Park. We lived within walking distance of the Atlanta amphitheater, where I could get free tickets to almost any show by scamming press laminates from area newspapers.

As soon as the deadbolt turned on the door of the town house Elsbeth had purchased for our new family, I thought about possible escape routes.

"Hey, guys, I'm home. Accomplish anything today, Randol?" She sounded exhausted.

"Other than feeding, clothing, and acting as a marvelous role model for our child; writing a few thousand words here and there to contribute to the welfare of the Duncan tribe; and getting a six-thousand-dollar government quote to release my old man from a Honduran prison—no."

She unpacked three plastic bags of groceries that she knew she didn't have to buy. Eddie and I always went to the grocery store. Her seventeen-minute commute was long enough after a stressful day, and I had told her I could handle the shopping as part of *my* job description.

"We were out of half-and-half, and I needed some tampons."

"I'm not shy about buying feminine hygiene products, honey."

Eddie started easing out of the living room, like an animal sensing the tsunami before it smashed ashore.

She put her hands on her hips and looked up from the grocery bags. "What was that you just said?"

"You look cute as all get out when you do that." I sensed the tsunami, too, and would do anything I could to water it down.

"Something about your father? Honduras? Prison?"

"Uh, yeah." I stood up from the couch and moved toward the kitchen. "I, uh, yeah, got a call just before you got home. From the State Department."

"Right. The U.S. Department of State." She put her hands on the counter, as if to balance herself. Against a tsunami. "As if people get calls from the State Department every day. I don't guess they were calling to sell us long-distance service."

"Hi, honey! I'm glad you're home! How was work?" I wrapped my arms around her and tried to kiss her. She was so beautiful. She still is, at least on TV.

She pushed me away. "Randol. Really. Enough of the bullshit. I mean, can't you *ever* be serious or, at least, *pretend* to show even a *little* panic? For pity's sake, we're talking about your father, who apparently is in some damned dangerous situation." She moved from the kitchen, sat on the couch, kicked off her heels, and rubbed her sore, panty-hose-encrusted feet.

"Dad's in a bind, is all, according to the State Department guy. Drugs or something."

"Sounds like more than a bind to me. Sounds like he's in deep shit. Drugs? A Honduran prison? I'd say it doesn't get much deeper than that. You don't get charged with 'drugs or something.' Knowing your father, it's a drug-smuggling felony, and he's there for what they call in Central America, 'the long haul.' *Comprende?*"

She slumped into the couch. Whatever energy she may have had after a long day doling out the world's news to the world, Jupe and I had stolen it away. And he was about to steal more.

"So, I was wondering, do you see a problem with asking your father to intercede on Jupe's behalf?"

She was finished looking at me and continued massaging her feet. "It's embarrassing, it's dicey, and it could cost him a lot of political capital."

I knew the ramifications. Her father, Collins Pearson, could do a lot as a United States Senator, especially as a member of the all-powerful Senate Ways and Means Committee. But I understood how sticky things could get.

"I haven't talked to anyone about this, Elsbeth, I promise." I touched her arm as softly as I could. "And we don't have to ask him." She looked at me sideways. "Seriously! From the moment this guy at State, this Chance Tolliver guy, called, I really just figured I would handle this on my own."

She flashed those jade-green eyes at me. "'Zat right? And how would you propose to do that? You and what division of your grandfather's Grand Old Army are going to march into Honduras and spring Jupiter Duncan from jail?"

"That's funny, sweetheart."

"Listen, I'll do what I can. I mean, I've always known you have an allergy to full-time work, and when I met your father, I realized the allergy is genetic. But you've always told me I would never have to worry about *your* family causing *my* family a problem." She closed her eyes and pinched her nose, the way Jerod always did. I swear, at times, I wonder whether those two would have been happier together. "You're incorrigible, you know that? Never mind that you're also lazy, diffident, and self-absorbed."

"Thank you, honey." That pissed me off, never mind that most of it was true.

I stomped into the bedroom and started stuffing T-shirts, jeans, and underwear into an overnight bag, along with the wad of cash I had stashed in my sock drawer.

Then I walked out.

"Where are you going?" she asked, stunned.

"Honduras. I'll call you when I get back home with my father."

CHAPTER EIGHT

I WAKE up back in the real world feeling as if I've just had marathon sex, hardly remembering the dream-memories of my ex-wife and my father's Honduran odyssey. Every millimeter of my body feels better than it ever has—even the regions I can't feel. Sweat soaks the bed, leaving the sheets a cool, delicious shroud that tells me I bled out all my agony.

Grandfather's ancient round-faced alarm clock, with two bells and a clanger and a real second hand, orients me to the fact that I'm disoriented: It's almost eight o'clock. At night, I presume. A halogen lamp from Duncan Park throws frozen bars of light through the leafless oaks outside my grandparents' bedroom window. I've slept in this room before, but never when they were both gone.

I stretch and shake myself to fuller consciousness.

My thoughts soon pick up where they'd left off, with Jupe stuck in Tegucigalpa's Central Prison.

I wonder where my son is.

The house is dead quiet. I don't want to stay in this big, cold, empty house by myself, not tonight. Besides, I need to check in with Eddie, see what he's doing, tell him goodnight, that I love him. After this morning, I can't abandon him.

I get out of bed and into the chair, then wrap myself in a bathrobe and a blanket and roll out of the house and down the driveway. Every light is on in the SQ. Not one but two heads appear inside.

You don't enter our bungalow quietly, and you don't enter anyplace quietly when you're in a wheelchair. I might as well have been a marching band crashing Eddie and Tyler's party.

"Tyler, what brings you to this fine establishment so late?"

"Whaddup, Mr. Duncan?"

"The Lawsons said it was okay," Eddie says, his eyes big and pleading to head me off at the disciplinary pass.

You have to admire the kid. He may commit the occasional felony, getting off with a punishment lighter than helium. But he's not short on compassion. He takes a kid under his wing who's a little shy. A little shy on brains, on looks, and on—what's the best way to put this?—cultural advantages in the Deep South. Tyler Lawson's father, Toby, is the finest neurosurgeon in the state, *my* neurosurgeon, and the only reason he moved to New Cumbria is that his wife, Rachel, begged him to leave New York and return to her hometown when her parents got sick. That was a spectacular blessing for this town, where Toby Lawson is a rarity by profession and by faith, considering that only eleven thousand of the state's four million souls are Jewish. And here sits the kid who climbed out of the shallow end of the Lawson gene pool.

Tyler's not ugly, it's not that. In fact, he has a winsome dopiness about him that's akin to that of a show dog in the toy category: You just want to scratch him behind his ears and rub under his chin and hug him around the neck until he starts panting. His nose is a tad on the bulbous side. He wears his bushy black hair spiked. He could stand to lose a few pounds. He's pale as self-rising flour, though he's not given to self-rising. His small, dark eyes skate around the room the same way the boys do on their skateboards. He's a bit older than Eddie, at fifteen, sprouting a ludicrous little mustache and willowy hairs on his chin. His father could stand to take a few minutes from his practice and show the boy how to shave. While Tyler's unlikely to ace the SATs, I've watched those kids on the computer, and I fear the boy could hack his way into the Pentagon and wind up in *my* bank account.

They look up from Eddie's desktop monitor, where they're huddled around flashing images I can't see; height does have its advantages.

"Any decent porn?" I ask. "I like to visit the big-tits-dot-com site myself."

Tyler shakes his head in disbelief. "He's kidding, right, Eddie?"

"He only *thinks* he's kidding. Because he *thinks* he's funny."

"No, actually, Eddie, my son, former friend, and soon-to-be evil nemesis"—I swivel and say to Tyler, "Turn away if you don't want to see embarrassment or raw humiliation," then level my gaze back in Eddie's direction—"you were grounded, as of this morning, and under Code Sixteen, Section Twelve, Point Three, Subsection One of the Grounding Until Dead Manual, 'it is not permissible to have a friend over at one's house and in one's company while one is grounded.'"

"I didn't read that section."

"Don't be a smart-ass, Eddie."

"Fruit don't fall too far from the tree, Dad."

"Tyler, I have tried to be lighthearted here, have I not? I have tried to make this easy. Now he wants to take advantage of my easygoing nature and piss me off." I sigh. "Listen, Tyler, you're a good kid, a decent kid. You do need fashion help, in my opinion. Your hair sucks, but that's just me, and you shouldn't take advice from a forty-three-year-old cripple, even though I am revered in certain circles, and by many of your peers, as being one hip and badass Internet music critic."

"Dad, really—"

I point my finger at Eddie. He looks as if lightning just shot out of it. "You, mister. One more word out of you, and I'll—"

"You and what legs, pal?"

Even Tyler knows that Eddie has stepped *way* over the line.

The pause is so awkward I feel fear peeling like cheap paint from these boys—mostly, unfortunately, from Tyler.

"Tyler, do you have any idea what the word *disenfranchised* means?" Of course he doesn't. He wouldn't have learned a concept like that in school, though New Cumbria High School might have tried to teach it to him.

"Oh, no." Eddie sighs.

"I swear to God, Eddie. One more word, and I will call Chief Magnus right now, and I will discuss with him the contents of your sock drawer. Then I will ask him to charge you as an adult. After that, I will tell him the entire story of your grandfather Jupe, and maybe he will figure out a way to make all *that* a part of your rap sheet, too, because you are definitely trying to prove that, as you say, 'fruit don't fall too far from the tree.'"

"What are you talking about?" His eyes widen.

Obviously, I couldn't legally use Jupe's sordid history against my son, but I could use it as a potent parental threat.

"Here's what I'm talking about, Eddie, and I swear to you, one more interruption, even the mere *thought* of one, and it's straight to Terry Magnus. Word?"

He knows I am fatally serious now. My heart begins to crack like a piece of glass. Then I have an idea. I roll into the bedroom and return with an old postcard, a panoramic view of Teguci-galpa that I had mailed to Eddie when he was eight. My hands tremble when I reread it after so many years.

I return to the living room, where the boys sit in rapt attention, wondering what I might do next.

"Fellas," I say, "move away from the computer. Now. Faces forward and not a sound. Let me tell you a story."

Not long after Chance Tolliver's telephone call, I was on a direct flight from Atlanta to Honduras.

With a short layover in Miami, the flight to Toncontín International Airport took a little more than five hours. That was just long enough to compose the fumigating harangue I planned to spray on my father in the hope of killing off the bugs of self-destruction that were infesting him—along with the lice he had probably picked up in Central Prison.

The 757, the largest aircraft allowed to land on the world's shortest and most dangerous runway, tipped to what seemed like a ninety-degree angle and slid between broccoli-green mountains for its final bounce onto the tarmac. Dense gray clouds squatted over the city of nearly a million people. Lower on the hillsides, wispy sleeves of fog laced over thousands of shacks that crawled like struggling vines up rutted hillsides.

Toncontín itself looks like a penitentiary you might see driving past Cornfield, USA, its drab ivory terminals sporting thin windows and a squat control tower overlooking the grim expanse of concrete. During the 1969 Soccer War, the Salvadoran air force bombed the airfield, which is still used as a military staging area. Crowds were thin when I deplaned, and with nothing but carry-on luggage, I swung by the *bureau de change* to convert a few dollars to lempira and off I went into the cool Central American air.

A baby-shit yellow Pinto taxi picked me up outside the airport to whisk me the seven miles to the Hotel Maya. The *taxista*, a young man with gold-plated teeth, a cigarette bouncing from his chapped lips, and the same kind of goofy fuzz on his chin as Tyler's, asked me if I wanted the scenic route, women, or "record time."

"Well, seeing as how this ain't no vacation, Pedro—"

"I'm no Pedro," he said. He smiled so broadly it looked as if his investment in gold futures had doubled. "*Mucho gusto; me llamo Ricardo.*"

"Great. *Mi nombre es* Sam Zemurray," I said in my best Humphrey Bogart, slit eyes and all. I had no idea whether Sam Zemurray or Bogey looked anything alike.

Ricardo almost fell out of the cab laughing. "Sam Zemurray! Ha! He died the year my mother was born, so you look pretty good for a dead guy." He took a final lingering drag on his cigarette and flicked the butt out the window. "Besides, I don't think you made any fortune in bananas like Sam Zemurray, *señor.* Otherwise, you wouldn't be riding in my taxi, no?"

You have to be impressed by a guy who knows enough about his country's history to remember an immigrant American Jew named Sam Zemurray. Zemurray was born in Russia in 1877. By the time he was twenty-one, Zemurray was living in New Orleans and making a fortune in the banana business, buying the fruit in Honduras and selling it in the United States. After purchasing five thousand acres along the Cuyamel River in Honduras, he wound up deeply in debt, and Sam the Banana Man returned home. At the time, around 1912, deposed Honduran president Manuel Bonilla happened to be living in New Orleans, so Zemurray smuggled Bonilla back into Tegucigalpa. Bonilla overthrew the government and put Zemurray back on top of his fruit empire, giving him land concessions and tax breaks. In America, people Ricardo's age couldn't name their *current* president.

"Just drop me off at the Maya, *por favor*. There's good, hard U.S. currency in it for you."

"*Sí, señor*." His smile vanished.

Ricardo took spaghetti-thin side streets leading to the hotel, which was perched atop a prominent hill in the city's ritzy Colonia Palmira section. Children played while heavily armed men, some in civilian clothes, some in paramilitary outfits, patrolled outside walled-in homes.

During my layover in Miami, I had picked up a guidebook to Tegucigalpa: "Despite the crumbling decay of the old-town homes and the crime at night—which has led to problems with robberies and issues with prostitution and street children who've either vanished, been killed, or wander in the streets in a glue-snorting haze—the capital city retains a magnificent charm filled with modern wonders. The downtown shopping mall rivals some of America's best, the cathedrals are breathtaking in their architectural splendor, the people are warm (and handsome!), and the hotels are world-class." In short, a pugilist of a town still hanging onto the ropes and trying to beat its way through history's split decision.

Somewhere in the middle of this bedlam sat my father.

Ricardo dropped me at the Hotel Maya, where I tipped him enough to satisfy his wages for the next year. After checking in, I flew up to my room—in those days, I could still run—on the twelfth floor and dropped my overnight bag. The view displayed a sprawl of beige and brown skyscrapers and low-slung buildings, a few with red-tile roofs; billboards; streets crisscrossed with wires and cables; and miles of traffic. The lovely pool and patio below were unused; the seventy-two-degree September weather was too cool. The hotel wasn't full.

The beauty of Honduras is that a telephone call to the United States is all but a local call; Tegucigalpa has an area code just as Los Angeles does. I called Chance Tolliver.

"Where are you, Mr. Duncan?"

"Tegucigalpa."

"I'll withhold my judgment on that for the moment." I couldn't tell if he had choked on a snort of derision or an outright laugh.

"Hang on a sec here, my advocate friend. I flew all the way down to the Third World to pick up my second-rate father, so I'm counting on some first-class American resourcefulness here to get this thing done."

"Believe me, Mr. Duncan, I understand your frustration, but we—I—*never* advised that you simply hop on an airplane."

"I never suggested that you people simply sit on your ass and let my father sit on his in Hotel Prisono down here until the jefes in Honduras feel they're goddamn ready to spring him loose!"

"No need to swear at me, Mr. Duncan."

"I'm sorry, I just . . ." I tried to compose myself. I wasn't angry at *him*, of course, I was angry at Jupe and angry at my ridiculous situation.

Perhaps I had acted on impulse, but I figured that the best

way to get the job done was to do it myself, just like in the movies. Maybe I could mosey down the street, flip a few bills to the guys wearing camo, buy an M249 Squad Automatic Weapon, and at 725 rounds a minute Rambo my way through Central Prison and yank dear ol' Dad out of his cell and out of this damnable country.

"Okay, Mr. Duncan. I would advise that you contact Major Felix Gonzalez at the American Embassy at the Avenida La Paz. He's one of our military attachés."

"Military?"

"The Honduran military runs the prison; they charged your father."

"Okay."

Now I was picturing Jupe surrounded by men in olive-green uniforms with ribbons stacked from their breastbones to their shoulders, men with faces as big as Virginia hams and huge evil smiles. *"Tell me, Señor Gringo, were you selling cocaine for your CIA? Where are the weapons caches? For whom were you working? Give us names!"* They would be hovering toward his bared testicles, their cigar-shaped fingers anxious to apply black and red wires attached to a twelve-volt car battery.

"In the meantime," Tolliver said, "I hear the El Arriero, right around the corner from you, is a good steak house. Check it out."

"Thanks for the dining tip. I'll return the favor and take you to the Old Ebbitt Grill if I'm ever in D.C." I hung up, in no mood for some bureaucrat at the American consulate to make me an appointment to see some low-level military attaché who could keep me waiting for days while he jumped through the obligatory hoops.

Hungry, tired, and disgusted, I decided to take Tolliver up on his recommendation and headed back downstairs.

I passed the duty-free shop and noticed the exotic rums, panoramic postcards, and genuine hand-rolled, honest-to-God Cuban cigars, which you could *never* get in the United States. Not that I'm much of a smoker, but a regal cigar, especially the Grand Dames of Cigars, is too good to pass up, especially when it can be legally obtained. As Rudyard Kipling said, "A woman is only a woman, but a good cigar is a smoke." I also bought a disposable lighter, all for a princely sum. My father was already costing me a fortune, and I had barely arrived.

At almost four thousand feet, the Tegucigalpan air felt thin and cool. Above the cacophony and pollution of the city stretching beyond the Colonia Palmira neighborhood, the world smelled smoky, rain-wet, and earthy. A few people in light jackets, black linen trousers, and swirling jersey skirts walked arm in arm, free-floating toward dinners, discos, dirty dancing, and dreams.

At the El Arriero, a maitre d' wearing a white dinner jacket welcomed me to a wooden table dressed with a white cloth and a chair that appeared to be made of rain-forest logs.

I didn't bother looking at the menu but took the waiter's suggestion and let him order the *riñon*. After I downed a dirty martini and two near-frozen Salva Vida beers, a charred black moon rock the size of a baseball arrived on an ivory china plate. The entrée was served with plantains and carrots and sweet peppers julienne. In the dim ambient light, I stabbed at the *riñon*, which began leaking clear hot ooze.

Marvelous, I said to myself, the most pleasant dinner companion. Here we have a strange but obviously juicy Latino steak of some rare variety. I carved my first morsel; a bit rubbery, I had to admit. With delightful anticipation, I took my first bite.

Grease sprayed all over my mouth, a taste of burned hide and fatty rubber bouncing from cheek to cheek across my tongue. Even the last of my cold Salva Vida, which I learned later means "lifesaver," couldn't wash away the foulness.

After calling the waiter, I asked him what I had ordered. He snapped open the menu. In English and Spanish, the words over his perfect fingernail read Riñon *(or kidney)—a typico house delicacy, grilled to absolute perfection!*

"Listen, Pedro, I just realized I have a dinner meeting at the Multiplaza Mall downtown, where, I think, there's a Pizza Hut, and an old Italian buddy named Pepperoni . . ."

I was talking so fast that I really hoped he couldn't understand a word I said. The restaurant was nearly empty; the *real* dinner hour wouldn't start here until well after nine-thirty or even ten-thirty. It was only six-thirty.

I threw a couple of bills on the table. "On second thought, ace, could you bring a doggy bag?" A little sign language and hard currency went a long way. In less than a minute, my grilled urine-filtration organ was boxed, and I was out the door.

Around a corner or two, I came to the prison's mottled gray walls, topped with concertina and barbed wire. A couple of dozen people crowded outside the arched gates, mostly wailing women in colorful white and pink and purple peasant skirts with garish flowered blouses. The women banged tin plates and pots against the bars. Most of them were crones, many with long silver hair tied back in thick ropes, and faces the texture of dried apples. A few shoeless boys and girls milled about, trying to be good while their mothers and grandmothers tried to do whatever it was they were doing.

I edged my way into the mayhem. "Ladies. Evening."

The crowd parted some.

I must have arrived at Tegucatraz for feeding time. If the military wanted me to pay my old man's room and board at a thousand dollars a month, they certainly wouldn't be shy about taking tortillas and frijoles from these poor *familias*. Well, how about some fresh-off-the-grill *riñon* for dear old Dad?

Guards languished around the mouth of the prison, cigarettes hanging from lips. With the agonizing tedium of a high school graduation, one inmate after another approached the guard in charge to collect the mess kit his family had delivered.

"Excuse me, ladies, everyone. Anybody here *habla engleis?*"

A middle-aged woman stepped out of the crowd. She was big-boned, with sparkling brown eyes, perfect rouge on puffy brown cheeks, and thick black hair that fell to her shoulders. She wore the same peasant fashions as everyone else.

"*Si, señor.* I am a missionary from Texas, working on prison reform."

I shook my head, incredulous that someone would *choose* to be here, someone who spoke English and might actually know the system, someone who, apparently, wasn't a bureaucrat or a *militarista*.

I introduced myself and told her my father's name. If I'd hoped for a spark of recognition or sympathy, I found none. "So, um, okay, we're out here, he's in there, and I'm told he'll be stuck there quite some time unless I figure out a way to spring him." I patted my left pants pocket.

She shook her head. "That can get you only so far, but it works . . . sometimes." She extended her hand to shake mine. "Mirabelle." She stopped short of offering her last name. "How can I help you, Mr. Duncan?"

I'd never before had to size up anybody in a life-or-death situation, and I'd never known what it felt like to put my entire trust in a complete stranger—in a place so alien, so dangerous as this.

I looked into her dark brown eyes and saw a glimmer of concern. Was it concern for her own safety? For my father's? For mine?

"Excuse me, but what is your father accused of?"

"Drug trafficking." The words scraped off my tongue like filthy sandpaper. "Cocaine." I realized I didn't have to reveal any more information than that—and probably shouldn't have revealed even that much.

"Honduras is like any other country, Mr. Duncan," she said in a matter-of-fact tone that bordered on patronizing. "It has its laws and its punishments."

I looked around the towering walls and the grim throng of bawling women banging against the bars. "How is this just punishment?"

"Tragic, I know, but . . ."

I could tell she was trying to withhold judgment of a man she didn't know, a man who just might deserve whatever justice awaited him.

"I get it," I said. "Okay, well, I was told by a State Department guy that a Major Felix Gonzalez . . ."

The only response she could manage was silence. Then she shook her head and smiled. "I hate to laugh, Mr. Duncan, but Major Gonzalez is an American military officer, and he will have to go through a maze even more complicated than the Pentagon to get you what you need. And he is fully aware of that. I'm certain he has already been halfway through that maze on your father's behalf."

If her information had been a glass of water, I wasn't sure whether it would have been half full or half empty.

"Isn't there anything I can do," I asked, "right here, right now?"

"In Honduras," she said, smiling, "it never hurts to ask for what you want." She glanced at my left pants pocket. "And, yes, it looks like you did come prepared to ask."

I stepped through the crowd, got clocked with somebody's dinner tin, and beckoned a guard.

Opening my bag of savory *riñon,* I offered him a whiff, then reached into my pocket with my other hand and surreptitiously rolled a hundred-dollar bill. "Now, Pedro, get a whiff of this." I pulled the tight straw from my pocket and waved it through the bars.

The guard, with teeth courtesy of the same metallurgic dentist as Ricardo the *taxista,* took a drag on his cigarette and blew a billowing cloud toward the archway.

"And you are?" he said in slow English.

I introduced myself and told him my father's name.

"I will see to it that your—father, is it? *¿Su padre?*"—we nodded at each other—"gets his delicious meal from El Arriero. Excellent choice, *señor.*" He winked at me and turned away.

"Hang on a sec, Pedro, don't you want your Ben Franklin?" I twirled the bill between my fingers as he glared at me.

"Ah, yes," he said, snatching the hundred dollars, "one of only two American notes that do not have an American president on them." He winked again.

(I stop my story long enough to study the spellbound faces of Eddie and Tyler, both of whom wallow in material possessions, while they remain naive and ignorant about so much, including volumes of American history; I search their eyes to see whether my tale is making any headway.)

"Ah, yes," I said, "but my old friend Ben did say, 'Money has never made man happy, nor will it.' "

"Franklin was a wealthy man." He winked at me a third time and took another draw on his cigarette, shifting his automatic rifle and blowing the smoke through the bars toward the women. "Señor Ben also said, 'He who waits upon fortune is never sure of dinner.' Tonight, you bring dinner *and* fortune. I like you, but you could be a *grano* in my *culo* tonight, so . . ." He rubbed his thumb and forefinger together. "Señor Ben never liked loneliness." He patted his pocket.

I knew this would be an expensive trip. I was glad I had packed for "contingencies." Now, I was hoping my amigo would finish greasing the skids.

The guard pushed his way through the others, who, chattering at him rapid-fire, opened the iron gate while managing to keep the crushing mass of crones out.

The cobbled passageway led to an open-air courtyard, two stories of cell block after cell block surrounded by balconies ridged with rusting railings. The place stank of sweat, urine, shit, and occasional wafts of vomit. Hay and sand were strewn around in lazy attempts to soak up the man-spews.

Low-wattage bulbs burned from their own cages along the walls. Men in olive-drab fatigues and scuffed black combat boots patrolled the darkening corridors. I couldn't see well enough to tell how many inmates were locked up, but I could make out a passageway from the upper level to even more cell blocks. The Central Prison was probably holding two thousand men—surely a notorious violation of its capacity.

The guard led me to the nearest corner of the old colonial building.

"You are most fortunate, Señor Duncan. The warden, Lieutenant Colonel Eduardo del Hoya Bonilla, was just about to leave for the evening." The guard opened the door, whose window was covered with yellowed venetian blinds.

I wasn't prepared for what I saw next. Stepping into the cold air from a humming window unit, I could have been standing in a drill sergeant's office in any U.S. Marine barracks, replete with stacks of papers and files, a laptop computer on the massive mahogany desk, and another computer and monitor in an armoire. Filing cabinets stood at attention, also overwhelmed with paperwork. Even the requisite coffee machine and its helter-skelter accoutrements of Styrofoam cups, mugs, and sugar and cream packets filled the top shelf of a bookcase crammed with bulging binders. Photos and other memorabilia covered the walls: military units in review, military men receiving military honors, military parades, and framed newspaper stories about the military and military heroes.

Lieutenant Colonel Bonilla stood about my height—in those days about six feet tall. He rose as I walked in and offered a thin smile; Grandfather always used to say, "The thinner the man's lips, the stronger the man's leadership qualities." He looked like a man of steel, a solid cylinder of strength, but above the neck he was all pomaded black bouffant hair and Carmen Miranda makeup. In his uniform, the color of an olive, with his red rouge and red lips, he looked as if he should be floating in an enormous martini glass, waiting to be stabbed by a plastic sword. On his left breast was a cascade of ribbons.

"Lieutenant Colonel Bonilla," I said as fast as I could to stifle a snicker. "Hmm. Name rings a bell . . ." I snapped my fingers to jog my memory. "That's it! You wouldn't be related to *the* Manuel Bonilla, would you? The *presidente* who returned to power here with Sam the Banana Man?"

He chuckled and eased into his chair. Slick as a Vegas poker player, he sized me up without looking at me and determined his next move. He snapped his head toward the guard, who slipped out of the office with a click of the door.

I slid some bills onto my knee and, with one eye, counted out five hundred, then slid those over the mountain of papers to the warden.

"Surely you jest, Mr. Duncan."

"Oh, that's just a little pocket change for a cup of coffee, Lieutenant Colonel Bonilla."

He smiled with a smugness I've never seen, except on New Cumbria's own police chief Magnus when he knows he's got you by the cojones. But even Magnus couldn't be *that* smug.

"I'm not your *camarero*—your waiter—Mr. Duncan, but please, help yourself to the best Honduras has to offer. Over there." He pointed to the coffee machine by the window, whose iron bars looked down a corridor into faint light and ambling guards.

I poured myself a cup, returned to my seat, and reached into my jacket pocket. Pulling out one of Fidel's finest, which smelled as if it had been grown in the Garden of Eden, I said, "Would you accept this token, then, sir?"

He reached for the brown-leaf tube and studied it like a diamond merchant does a stone. "Flor de Cano."

I whipped out my Bic before he could pick up his gold Zippo.

Then he reached into his bottom left-hand drawer and withdrew a clear glass bottle shaped like one of those shiny silver bells you see in a Christmas handbell choir. The dark juice inside would have me caroling in no time.

"El Dorado rum, from Guyana. Aged fifteen years."

I thought about my father, rotting somewhere in here for a crime he probably *did* commit but for which he probably hadn't been arraigned, let alone judged guilty *or* innocent. Jupe *absolutely* could wait for me to enjoy a cocktail and a cigar.

"A toast," I said.

The colonel looked at me in wonder and amusement, or perhaps the other way around. He puffed his cigar in haughty contentment. "To what?"

"To you, Señor Bonilla." I raised my glass, then sipped the most sublime rum I'd ever tasted. No wonder pirates loved this stuff! I imagined myself with a wooden peg leg, a parrot on my shoulder, and then I began to wonder who the pirate really was here between us. "After all, I am sitting in the presence of presidential material!"

"Pardon?"

"*Si, señor.* You are a Bonilla, are you not?" I took another sip of the ambrosial liquor.

"You are a madman or a drunk or just plain *norteamericano*, Mr. Duncan." His eyes twinkled nevertheless. "Yes, my family is distantly related to the former president, Manuel Bonilla, but I'm afraid I am stuck in this post"—he waved his hand foppishly around the office—"for the time being."

"With a man of your talents, good nature, and immense intelligence, *señor*, not to mention your pedigree"—I swear I batted my eyelashes as I slapped five more Benjamins on the table—"and your wealth, why, I can see you moving up the ranks faster than ol' Ike became president."

"I preferred your General MacArthur." He slid the bills into his tunic and went back to making some serious love to his cigar.

Cocktail hour was clearly winding down here. "Fidel may not run the best government, but he's got some fine cigar, cane, and rum factories."

Del Hoya Bonilla slid his smoke into an ashtray with the gentleness of a woman putting a baby in a crib and took another sip of rum. Licking his lips, he tightened them, then said, "Señor Duncan, don't misunderstand, but your father—"

"Is a world-class moron. I believe he's listed in the *Guinness Book of Records* for being the world's biggest idiot. Believe me, sir, if I had the weapons, the bullets, the men, and the rank, I would organize the firing squad and say, 'Fire!'"

He looked as if he was trying to suppress a laugh. He picked up his cigar to plug the hole.

Clouds of pungent smoke filled the room, and I began feeling light-headed and disheartened. He hadn't even broached the subject of how much my father's freedom would cost. The government had quoted Chance Tolliver six grand. Bonilla must have known that, as did every gun-toter and paper-shuffler between here and Plaza Morazán, the central plaza and the location of city hall. And each of them had already calculated his slice of the pie.

"Three thousand," I blurted out. I had a little more than four thousand dollars in my pocket.

Yes, carrying around that much hard currency was incalculably stupid. I might as well have worn a T-shirt that read I DESERVE TO BE ROBBED AND MURDERED.

"I'll have to think about your offer, Mr. Duncan, and get back to you tomorrow."

I was dumbfounded. No way Bonilla could turn down all that cash, especially if all of it would be his. I wanted to grab that cigar and shove it so far up his ass he could have used it for a flagpole and run his BVDs up it for surrender. I tried to calm myself, gulping the last finger of rum.

Then I saw his dilemma: Take the money and let the prisoner go, or wake up the next day with no money and a valuable prisoner. One way, you're broke and stuck with *un grano en el culo*, but nothing to explain to your superiors. The other way, you've just bought your wife and your mistress each a diamond necklace, but you're going to have to do some fast talking to explain the missing gringo *criminale*. Of course, you could always do the smart thing and save a few hundred for the guy up the food chain.

Watching him think, I nodded toward the guards at the gate.

"With all due respect, *señor,* I'd prefer to leave here with my father tonight." I patted my pocket and moved to stand, but I was careful not to stand up too quickly. I wanted him to stand up, too, so we would be on the same level.

His pause was brief enough to let me know where we stood. "I think that could be arranged." His fingers twitched.

"Gracias, señor." Another five hundred emerged. "I think a fifty-percent deposit is fair. I'll pay the rest COD."

He moved to the door to call a guard, and when he returned to his seat, I tried to make small talk. No telling how long the prisoner's retrieval would take.

"Say, y'know, my son's name is Edward, too. Eduardo. We call him Eddie."

"Fast Eddie, just like Paul Newman in that movie." Del Hoya Bonilla shook his head and laughed, the clear winner in this deal.

God, I prayed, I hope not. He's only eight. Give me strength.

The lieutenant colonel picked up his cigar and his Zippo. The flame seemed to shoot clear to the ceiling, but he sucked most of it through the stogie.

In time that seemed to defy orders, we sat in silence, our transaction finalized.

I could have used another glass of rum, a celebratory drink, but I knew none would be forthcoming.

In what could have been ten minutes or an hour amid the thickening smoke and the dying haze of rum, the office door banged open.

The guard thrust my father inside.

Jupe, still in handcuffs, nearly fell over me and onto the warden's desk.

"Hello, Dad." I picked him up and turned him around. His

skin, clinging to thin bones, looked jaundiced, dry, and scaly. His hair hung thin, and his fingernails were brittle and spooned—all signs of malnutrition. "Room service must be awesome here."

"It's good to see you, Randol." He didn't touch me. For once, he had the sense to keep his piehole shut. "Do you have my ticket outta here?"

"Sure, Dad. Our friend Ben bought it for you. You can thank him later, but, meantime, be effusive to your hosts, thank them for their hospitality and generosity, and wish them well."

He offered his shackled hands to the lieutenant colonel, who motioned for the guard to remove the cuffs. Raw, red circles remained.

I gave a slight bow to the warden, nodded at the guard, then turned back to del Hoya Bonilla and slid the balance due across the desk before the guard could notice what I was doing.

"Sir, it has been my utmost privilege and pleasure to share this evening with you, and if I can ever do anything for you or your generous nation, please don't hesitate to call me."

He didn't offer his hand, but palmed the money. I suppose he couldn't wait to feel his cash. Either that or he didn't want to sully his hand with that of a filthy yanqui who had just bribed him for the freedom of this drug-smuggling gringo.

I pulled Jupe out onto the street and barely gave him time to suck in the almost-stench-free air of his costly freedom.

"Listen up, Dipshit"—the first time I ever called him that—"you and me, we're going straight home, and I swear to you and to God and to my wife and son that if you ever pull anything even remotely like this again, I will do *exactly* what I told the warden back there that I would do."

"What's that?" He wobbled toward the hotel.

"You don't want to know, but it ends with the phrase 'Ready . . . aim . . . fire!' "

I looked at him and wondered where the doggie bag from El Arriero had gone. "What'd you do with the food?"

"What do you think I did with it? I ate it."

The thought made me want to throw up.

Back at the hotel, I ordered a cot while he took a long, hot shower. I let him sleep in the bed, where he seemed to die in its comfort. I didn't leave him for a moment.

Our plane left Toncontín the next morning after an enormous *norteamericano* breakfast in the hotel restaurant—though nothing that could come close to Volusia's, except maybe the coffee.

At the airport I dropped into a mail slot the postcard I had purchased the night before from the hotel's duty-free shop. The postcard, with a view of Tegucigalpa, including the old Central Prison, arrived in Atlanta long after my father and I did.

Eddie's hands shake when I hand him the postcard. He studies the panoramic picture, then flips it over. Tyler crowds closer to read it, too, the way they huddle at the computer.

> *Dear Eddie:*
>
> *I have just picked up your grandfather from hell. He was arrested for being a bad man. He did something no thinking man should do—he got involved with drugs. Drugs will kill you. If they don't, they will send you to a place like hell, a prison in a country where nobody cares if you eat or if you sleep or if you die. It's a shameful thing. That's what drugs are and that's what they do. They cause shame. And they kill people, Eddie.*
>
> *I love you.*
>
> *Daddy*

Eddie passes the postcard to Tyler.

The boys look as if they've heard a ghost story, a real one, the kind that scares you so stupid that you can't sleep.

"That's a *true* story, fellas, and the ghosts are still alive. They haunt you, they haunt me."

Their eyes look like small lightbulbs, bulging and bright.

"So, what happened to him?" Tyler asks.

"To who?"

"To your dad?"

"Well, Tyler, you know my father. You see him from time to time. But none of us knows what haunts him." I tap my temple with my forefinger. "And let me just say one more thing, guys." They both lean into me with anticipation. "Nobody—and I do mean nobody—in this town knows anything about what I just told you. Not Volusia. Not Chief Magnus. Not Mr. Manios. No-body."

I detect a slight grin on Tyler's face.

"Okay. Well." I sigh. "Tyler, look, you may think you have something on me, on my family, and maybe you do, now. Maybe now you've got something that might be useful to you one day. A little information that could help you, should you decide some day to turn against me or Eddie—"

"Against Eddie? No way. That would *never* happen! Never, Mr. D! We're best friends for life!"

"Just remember what Ben Franklin said: 'Glass, china, and reputation are easily cracked, and never well mended.' Once busted, a friendship, too, is hard to fix, and words are usually the easiest and fastest way to break one."

He looks as if his stomach just flipped a cartwheel. I suspect he never considered that his friendship might not be "for life."

"Don't get me wrong, Tyler. All I'm saying is, discretion is the better part of valor. What does that mean in your world? That it's better to be a good friend than to bury one for the sake of popularity."

The boys look as dazed as I'm beginning to feel, and I fear I may have crammed too much into the small part of their brains that was open to me.

Clapping my hands, I release them from their trance.

"Alrighty, then. Tyler, have you checked in with your mom lately?"

"Yes, sir."

"If that's a lie, I'll find out about it tomorrow . . ."

Tyler reaches into his knapsack and pulls out his cell phone. Though he's no more than six feet away, I can't hear what he says. He flips the phone shut and offers it to me. "You're welcome to confirm."

I wave the phone away. "Dude." I roll toward my room. "If you testify, I don't need to verify."

"Night, Mr. D." He folds down the futon and arranges the blankets and pillows that Eddie has already pulled out for him.

I'd never seen Eddie more anxious to pull his grandmother's quilt over his head.

"Hey, Mr. D, one last question. When you told your father, 'I swear to you I will do what I told the warden that I would do,' what did you mean, exactly?"

"You didn't pick up on that?" I glance at Eddie. "You caught that, didn't you?"

Eddie nods and says to Tyler, "He told the warden he would gather the firing squad himself and order them to pull the trigger on his own dad, if he did anything like that again."

"Whoa," Tyler says. "That's cold, dude."

Through the thin white-plank walls of our little cottage, I hear the boys say good night to each other, then Tyler, the older of the two and a sophomore next fall, whispers, "Hey, Eddie, you still awake?"

"Yeah, Ty."

"Do you really think your old man would shoot his own father?"

"Yeah."

"Hey, Eddie?"

"Uh-huh."

"Who's Ben Franklin?"

Part Two

SPRING'S

HOPE

ETERNAL

CHAPTER NINE

A BLACK SUV PULLS into the driveway and rounds the glistening magnolia tree. Cool spring mornings are a memory, like the dogwoods that have shed their delicate pink and white Easter clothes. Green leaves have returned to the oaks. Clouds in the deep-blue sky sleep like fat Persian cats with no place to go. It's already easing just above seventy degrees with a warm breeze. The air is clean and honeyed with jasmine and fresh-cut grass, compliments of the Gervaises' yardman, who mowed the next-door neighbors' yard yesterday.

Out on the porch, Volusia has served my breakfast of fried eggs, bacon, and fruit ambrosia made with citrus and hand-shredded coconut, and, of course, her perfect coffee. Today's *New York Times* adds up the number of casualties in the country's latest war. How many wars has my country started since I was born? Vietnam, Grenada, Panama—Somalia? Bosnia?—Afghanistan, Iraq. In the latest Middle East war, the tally is about a fifth of what it was in the Vietnam War, and so is the length of time we've spent there. At this rate . . . I never got the chance to ask Grandfather what he thought about America's wars, any of them, not even the ones he fought.

Almost four months have passed since Grandfather's funeral—it's early June now, a Tuesday, four days from the start of Eddie's summer vacation—and I have *yet* to get upstairs to the Plunder Room. Nobody has been available to heft me up the stairs and back down. I'm hoping that Eddie and I can make the Plunder Room and its treasures a summer project.

Jerod slides out of the SUV looking like a cross between a Secret Service agent and a movie star. He wears dark brown Italian linen trousers, a striped Oxford shirt with the sleeves rolled halfway up his hirsute forearms, and dark green aviator glasses, his black hair moussed. He might as well plug himself in and flash like a neon sign.

He springs up the concrete stairs as if to remind me of the spry athleticism I never had and certainly never will.

I whistle at him. "Hey, good-lookin', what brings you to the HQ?"

"Just wanted to check in." He takes a seat in one of the enormous green rocking chairs, Grandfather's favorite place in all the world to sit. "How're you holding up?"

"Good, as a matter of fact. How's it going with you?" I'm guessing that this is as far as it's going to get.

"Good. Better."

"Best." Reaching into the folds of the quilt draped over my legs, I retrieve my cell phone to summon Volusia from one of her soap operas. We've taken down the fire-alarm telephone bell and removed Grandfather's old recliner so that my wheelchair can fill the same space. I can hear the phone ring in the hall near my grandparents' room, which I use from time to time when the pain gets as bad as it did that night in February. "You look good, Jerod. You look as if life is agreeing with you."

"We've figured out a few things. Got a few things going right."

"Cool." I have no idea what he's talking about. And don't want to know. I wonder if it involves Jupe; if it does, it's probably at my own peril, whether I know it or not.

Volusia finally answers my call.

"Volusia, you'll never believe what captain of industry just showed up on our doorstep. Would you mind bringing some coffee, please?" I ask Jerod if he wants breakfast. He rubs his six-pack abdomen and shakes his head, though he probably hasn't eaten anything this morning. "And, Volusia, why don't you bring the man something to eat?"

"Capitalism, Randol," Jerod begins, apropos of precisely nothing. "Just the way the world turns."

"Hope you get rich."

"Hope I do, too."

"Since you're not selling faux *eau du Lord* anymore, what have you come up with instead?" I catch his trademark sad but hopeful smile. "You're amazing, Jerod. I wish I had your talent. Were you the guy who invented the Pet Rock? The guy who's been telling everyone that human urine can fuel automobiles? That kudzu contains the cure for AIDS *and* cancer?"

"Nobody's been doing that." He looks at me with authentic curiosity. "Have they?"

I glance down at the *Times*, as if to make sure, then look back up at him. "No. But you could be that guy." He jabs me in the shoulder. "Seriously, Jerod, what have you been up to all this time?"

Volusia steps out with a tray of breakfast, wisps of steam swirling from a china coffee cup. Jerod takes it and dives in.

"Not bad for a guy who ain't hungry, Mister Jerod." She stands over him.

"Morning, Volusia."

"Looks like you could add ten, fifteen pounds to that skeleton, son."

"Thanks for breakfast."

"Don't wave me off like some servant." She smiles at me. He's so busy with his eggs that he doesn't notice. "He's up to no good again, isn't he, Mister Randol?"

"It's useless trying to find out, Volusia. Talking to him is like talking to a screen door. Words go right through him, and if he ever does open up, all's you get is a rusty little squeak."

She laughs, hands on her hips, and doesn't move. "It kills me, you two." Her eyes dart between us. "You the one with all the brains, Mister Randol, and you don't do squat. He the one with all the looks and energy, and who knows what he does? But he looks good, though, in all them nice clothes."

"Y'all don't have to talk about me like I'm not here," Jerod says, wiping his mouth with the linen napkin Volusia brought with his tray. He sips his coffee. "God, that's good."

"You don't have to call me God, Mister Jerod, and it's a fatal sin to be taking our good Lord's name in vain—not fatal enough for me to stuff one of my soaps in your face, but . . ."

He jams the rest of his eggs into his mouth just to be certain nothing else gets there first.

She laughs again. There's nothing like Volusia's laughter to make the day feel better.

Jerod, happy to be in her good graces—for the time being, anyway—wipes his mouth again and takes another sip of coffee.

Volusia seizes the moment, too. "Just what is it you do to afford such fine fashions, nice ride"—she glances toward the car—"and, say, whatever happened to that red-hot ho—" She stops.

Jerod turns to me as if Volusia's voice belonged to a mocking-bird perched in the crape myrtle against the porch banister. "Yes, Randol, I came over to thank you for getting Annie a job."

"I heard about that!" Volusia says.

"Thanks again for breakfast, Volusia." Jerod holds up the tray but keeps his cup and saucer. "If you've got any more coffee—"

"You can get up and get it yourself. You know where it is."

Jerod takes the tray, cup, and saucer into the kitchen.

"I swear, that boy's got just enough evil in him, like his daddy, but you ain't never gonna find out what it is, and he ain't never gonna get caught, bless his soul." She shakes her head. "Umm-unh. I just don't want his stain to run on this household, is all, Mister Randol. I know it's not my place, but I'm just trying to look after you. And young Mister Eddie. I know how much that boy loves his uncle Jerod, like the big brother he never had."

"I haven't seen the guy in almost four months, since the day after Grandfather's funeral." I try not to sound defensive.

"So what's this about you getting that little bi—"

"Would you stop with that already?"

"I just wouldn't trust her to melt butter on grits, Mister Randol. She rubs me so wrong. I can't put my finger on it; looks all innocent and too pretty, kind of pretty she can use for somethin'. Like one of them sirens you read about, get all smashed up onto the rocks if you get too close."

Trust Volusia to know just a hint of Homer, while Tyler Lawson has no clue who Ben Franklin is.

"Word to the wise, Volusia. I'll certainly keep that in mind." Siren she may be, but Annie Harkin and I are never going to crash up on anyone's rocks.

Jerod returns with Volusia's ancient percolator, the secret font whence the magic black elixir of the voodoo java queen flows.

He pours me another cup. Volusia grabs the pot from him and squeaks her way back to the kitchen.

"Man, what got into her? Last time I saw her this talkative was when Jesse Jackson came to town to rip Mabry Hollander apart for that beating incident."

Nobody in New Cumbria would ever forget that. It was like something out of *To Kill a Mockingbird*. One warm May night about ten years ago, before I had sprung Jupe from Honduras, two white boys beat a fifteen-year-old black boy senseless under the bleachers of the high school football stadium. The suspects were of no social standing at New Cumbria High School, not athletes or scholars, just rednecks on a rampage. Mabry Hollander was the district superintendent then, as he is now. But Terry Magnus wasn't the police chief yet. Darryl Bishop was. And Darryl thought a little teenage roughhousing was part of growing up. "Boys will be boys," he'd actually said at a press conference. Never mind that the NAACP and the Urban League didn't see it that way, which was what brought civil-rights activist and South Carolina native Reverend Jesse Louis Jackson Sr. to New Cumbria.

"Reminds me of the Scottsboro Boys trial, Alabama, early nineteen thirties," my grandfather said at the time. Then he told me the story of the nine young black men from Paint Rock, Alabama, who were arrested and accused of raping two white girls. Nelle Harper Lee, one of my grandmother's dearest friends, based her story of Scout, Jem, and Atticus Finch and Atticus's gallant defense of Tom Robinson on that case. Miss Lee was among the many guests who used the room next to my grandparents' quarters. I never did meet her, though. The year I lived with them while Jupe was in Vietnam, Miss Lee was busy in New York, basking in the glory of her Pulitzer Prize and Truman Capote's *In Cold Blood*.

Back here in New Cumbria, Mabry Hollander handled the incident as best he could. Without so much as a trial, he ordered the two suspects to a summer detention camp, which pleased the civil-rights people no end. He agreed to pay all the medical bills for the victim. And he threw his support to Terry Magnus when Darryl Bishop, not too long afterward, announced his "retirement."

A few days after Grandfather's funeral, I visited Mabry in his office west of town. The new, low-slung brick campus housed the district administration's offices, built with money nobody had. But Mabry was that way; he just made things happen. He'd done it as a food-delivery wholesaler, which made him rich, and he did it with the school system. He once told me that graduating a kid from a Cumbria County high school was harder than making money.

Mabry was a big man, with big bones and a gut that hung like a twenty-five-pound frozen turkey over his belt. His jowls drooped in marbled slabs, making him look akin to a basset hound. His rheumy blue eyes had seen too much of this small world that had too much real world crammed into it—children doing adult things and parents behaving like children and expecting their kids to enjoy childhoods they didn't really have anymore. He looked a decade too old and a day away from a heart attack.

"Isn't it about time for you to pass the baton, Mabry?" I asked, wheeling close to his desk and surveying his office.

"Good to see you, Randol. Coffee? Course, I know it's nowhere near as good as Volusia's."

"No, I'm good, thanks."

"I was sorry to hear about your grandfather. One of New Cumbria's greatest sons."

"At least he got in a full retirement." I smiled at him. "And when are you planning on getting out of *here*?"

"Oh, I'm close. I'm just not done yet."

"It'll always be something, y'know."

He intertwined his bratwurst fingers and heaved his bulk onto his desk. "Colonel Duncan was one of the finest men I ever knew. He was an inspiration in this town."

"I've always said, Mabry, if I could be half the man my grandfather is, I'd be twice the man I am today. So let me cut straight to it and ask you for a favor."

He smiled. "I have no trouble listening to a petition from a Duncan."

"My brother."

"Except for *that* Duncan." He waved away a fat, wheezy chortle. "Just kidding. Go on."

"Actually, his girlfriend. It appears Jerod's probably going to stay in the area for a while and he's brought, well, a nice young lady—"

"You mean, she's beautiful."

My face turned a shade of red; I could feel it. "You're not supposed to judge a book, Mabry."

"Never have, but go on. Your grandmother, of course, is responsible for half the 'dirty' books we still have on the shelves in our school libraries."

"Anyway, she needs a job. She's a history teacher—"

"Need teachers in the worst sorta way, though we're not in a world of hurt for history teachers."

"Understood, but she's certified in New York and Connecticut, and she's done her homework. She says South Carolina has a reciprocity agreement with Connecticut, that y'all accept their teacher certifications here, that all she needs is the application and fee, her college transcripts, professional-test scores, a few verifications, some recommendations—"

"And that's where you come in . . ."

"Pretty much." I rubbed my chin. You can't help but like the man, which means you can't be dishonest with him. If anything, Mabry Hollander is a straight shooter, and he requires straight shooting from everyone else.

"Did she mention FBI fingerprints? We require those, too."

"Well, no, but she doesn't exactly strike me as a Rikers Island alumna."

"Tell you what, Randol. I'm in desperate need of a math teacher, a part-time biology teacher, and a Spanish teacher. If she could pinch-hit on any one or two of those . . ."

"I can ask. She's sharp."

"Among her other assets." He winked. "You're a pushover, Randol."

"This ol' chair doesn't have the best center of gravity, I'm afraid."

"Send her my way. I'll see what I can do."

That was Mabry Hollander's way of telling me she had the job. The next day it was official. And since mid-February, Annie Harkin has learned enough high school math, biology, and Spanish to get certified in South Carolina to teach all three and is edging her way into teaching some history classes, too.

Until yesterday, I was certain that she was doing me proud at New Cumbria High School. I haven't had a chance yet to tell Jerod about the phone call I got from the superintendent's office.

"Listen," Jerod says, clearly relieved that Volusia has taken herself and her opinion of his girlfriend back to the kitchen. "I really appreciate you going to bat for Annie, talking Mabry into offering her the job."

He eases into the sofa and savors his coffee.

"Are you kidding? It was nothing. I didn't talk Mabry into anything. This district needs quality schoolteachers worse than the federal government needs money; the deficit here is about as alarming."

"He's crazy about her, I'm sure. How could he *not* be?"

"Well, the superintendent is crazy about her," I say, trying to ease my way into another difficult topic. "But he called yesterday, and . . . he also has a few . . . I don't know. Concerns. He says he's a little worried about her."

Jerod shifts in his seat. His face betrays nothing. "How so?"

"I gather you're not around much." His lips twitch. I hold my hand up to keep him from saying anything. "From what Mabry says, Annie's been seen out a lot, at Herbie's, Cowboys"—one of New Cumbria's famed dive bars and the huge country-western line-dance joint on U.S. 36 Bypass—"mostly by herself, but she's also been hanging with some of the kids, a few of the parents. It's a small town; people talk."

"Any of that illegal?"

"Oh, no, nothing like that."

"So, what's the problem?"

"She's been working hard, really hard. Ten, twelve, fourteen hours a day. Spending a lot of her own money on materials."

"And *that's* a problem?"

"Mabry's a little concerned about burnout and, well, a bit worried about fraternization," I say, borrowing one of Grandfather's military euphemisms.

Jerod laughs, though his laugh sounds a little thin. "Get real, Randol. She's the star on his roster. Are you kidding? He's just freaking out because he's pinching himself, he's telling himself she's not real."

"Think about it, though." I finish my coffee and feel a bit shaky. Three cups is more than plenty. Good thing I don't have to worry about peeing. "She's working *all* the time. This is a hard town to get adjusted to, especially for a fine Yankee girl like her, and without you around, she's probably getting lonely."

"What's *that* supposed to mean?" He's rocking his chair harder now.

"You leave the rose alone in the garden long enough, big guy, someone's going to come along and pluck it."

"She's a big girl, she can handle herself. And besides, if she's been to places like Herbie's and Cowboys alone and gotten out alive—well, I guess that just goes to show she's got plenty of thorns, right?"

"Touché."

He gets up and paces the porch; he has plenty of real estate. "Besides, aren't you saying, basically, that she's already the most popular teacher in school?"

"I guess, but that's not my point. My point is that I don't think you should be gallivanting around so—"

"Hold on a second, Randol. Is this about me or is this about her?" The color on his face is rising to red. "Or is this about the two of us? Because if it is—"

"Okay, okay." I wave at him to stop. I already know that most of my brother's life is none of my business, and he's not going to let me anywhere near anything so intimate as his relationship with Annie Harkin.

"So," he says, calming down, "what's Eddie say?"

"About Annie?" I smile at Jerod's charm, his deft ability to defuse. "He thinks she's hot."

He smiles back. "About her *teaching* ability? About how she's *fitting in* there? About the *job* she's doing?"

"Eddie? Well, as a fourteen-year-old freshman, I guess he's qualified to offer high praise in her professional evaluation."

I've touched another nerve. It's a good thing Grandfather put fifty-some years' worth of gray paint on this porch; Jerod couldn't possibly scuff it off.

"You know, Randol, you think you're so damned smart and

better than everybody else. You're smug, you're judgmental, you think you're the funniest goddamned guy since . . . since . . . since I don't know who . . . and all you really are is a slack-ass dilettante—"

"Hey, wait just one minute." If I could stand up right now, I'd kick him so hard in the ass, his balls would tingle. "Who got her the job in the first place? Who's been here for her? And where the fuck *have* you been? I mean that. Where have you been? I've been asking you that since freaking *February*." Jerod slumps down into his rocking chair. I reach for his arm, with the same ginger touch my grandmother used on me. "Listen, Jerod, I know you're under a lot of stress, but I don't have any earthly idea why, and it appears you're not about to tell me.

"The fact is, Mabry Hollander called here yesterday to say that Annie may be getting a little frizzy around the edges, that she may need to 'collect herself,' in his words. That's all. He didn't say anything else. As far as I could tell, he just doesn't want his hot young hire to blow up in his face."

"How *could* she?"

"I don't know, Jerod. I have no idea. You're the only one who can tell me that. I'm just the messenger."

He leans back into the chair. The wooden rails saw against the planks of the porch. The sound reminds me of all the time I spent out here with my grandfather, saying so little but meaning so much.

"I'll try to spend more time with her." He sighs, as if being around Annie Harkin is a sacrifice.

I could press him, but I don't want to. He's not telling me anything about his life, for reasons that apparently make sense to him but not to me. He may not be doing anything illegal, but he's certainly not proud of the way he earns his fortune. And what- ever he does, he's not in any hurry to do it; after all, it's nearly ten-thirty on a Tuesday morning, and the man's sitting on my porch talking about his girlfriend.

"I guess I'd better go." He stands and puts on his aviator glasses, looking stunning again.

"It's good to see you, Jerod." I reach out to shake his hand. He takes it. That feels good. "I reckon there's really no point in telling Annie about all this. Just try to keep an eye out for her, okay?"

"Tell Eddie I said hey."

Not going to happen. Eddie wants to be just like Jerod. And I don't even know who Jerod is.

After school today, Eddie bounds, actually bounds, rather than slinks, into the main house, looking for me. He hasn't bounded anywhere in at least five months. He usually slinks straight to the servants' quarters, where he pretends to do homework while goofing off on his computer.

I'm where I've been since February, when Volusia suggested I convert the guest room of the main house into my study. She cleans the SQ once a month, only under duress, and only when I supplement her income. But when she noticed that all I had for an "office" in the SQ was a cheap pressboard desk crammed into my tiny bedroom, she said it was time to clean out the big house and take some ownership of the place.

Eddie was still grounded, thanks to the contents of his dresser drawer, so he and Tyler gathered up all of Grandfather's clothes and shoes, including old and mostly ugly ties and fedoras from the 1940s and '50s that hadn't been worn since. Eddie kept a few of the hats, but hasn't donned any yet. Volusia took some of the clothes, but most went to various Christian charities around town. Grandfather had never done anything with Grandmother's belongings, either—a vast closet of tulle and taffeta, skirts and dresses from the last thirty-five years; at least, she hadn't kept anything older than that. Volusia took none of those things, but boxed everything up and called her church to come and get it.

We decided to leave the canopy bed in the guest quarters, but we paid a couple of neighborhood kids to move Grandfather's old recliner from the China Room. To make room, an antiques dealer from Charleston came and bought Grandmother's busty armoire and chest of drawers for a few thousand dollars, which went straight to Eddie's college fund. We also decided to have the kids bring into my new study Grandmother's Victorian writing desk from the living room. I remember watching her write letters on the elegant walnut Eastlake piece. She was known for her voluminous correspondence, especially to her husband while he was away at his wars. The desk, with its slanted leather inlay surface, works just right for me.

In no time, my fingers started spelunking through the nooks and crannies of Grandmother's desk, where I discovered breathtaking treasures.

One of my favorite letters, folded to the size of a credit card and tied with a thin purple ribbon, is written in a perfect hand. On stationery bordered with delicate roses, Pearl Clementine's museum-quality penmanship slants to the right in India ink.

Dear Edward:

It's raining here today to beat the band, so I am indoors. Sutet Willkins and Eudora Matthews are coming over this afternoon for coffee. We thought to have Bridge Club, but decided against that. Wilbur Calvert went to see Dr. Albritton about that awful goiter on his neck last week, but apparently the cure could be worse, so he'll have to live with it. I was thinking of going to visit the Martindales in Asheville next week. You did hear that Frank was lead counsel on that case? What a strange situation, that! I would enclose a newspaper clipping, but I'm afraid your boys over there would simply discard it as part of their normal censorship of the mail. I'll keep you apprised of the verdict, and I know Frank will do the best he can to keep young Kip out of jail for accidentally shooting that poor fellow. Of course, Frank is not allowed to discuss the case, but I am certain Maisey could use company, other than that of a barrister. Besides, when it's not raining, it's become so beastly hot here. A few days' retirement to the mountains always does a soul good. And I think our young Edward Jupiter Duncan would love to come along. He adores the water so and, as you well know, the Martindales' cabin is so close to the lake he can almost swim in his sleep! The boy is doing quite well, though he often seems to find his way to mischief. His imagination is rich and active. He always seems to be lost somewhere in his thoughts; I just hope they are godly ones. I miss you, dear man, and pray for you and love you as much as always.

    Yours truly,

    Pearl Clementine "PeeCee" Duncan

Grandfather must have squirreled the letter away in her desk when he returned from the war, as a reminder of their unbroken conversation with each other, no matter how trivial. PeeCee herself pointed out that the military censors let precious little pass in private correspondence. In another letter folded next to PeeCee's, Grandfather, in his rough and rushed hand, didn't offer much information or intimacy, either:

My darling:

    Please be sure to ask after Harriet's health for me and offer her my very best. And if you would do me the favor of asking Winston to put extra fencing around the tomatoes. I remember two years ago, Petunia, the rabbit, had some fine dining at our expense from my garden! I would prefer that the fruit of our labors go to our table rather than Petunia's. I know that Frank will acquit himself well, but Kip's fate remains in the hands of God and a jury of his peers. I hope to hear in your next letter that you found the mountains a delight, as I myself always find them a fine respite. Please send my regards to Sutet et al, and tell them they are in my prayers.

     Your devoted husband,

     Edward Duncan, Colonel, United States Army

The formality of the letters moved me. It was as if they needed to remind each other of who they were, with full signatures at the end of their letters.

The dozen or so letters I found, dated 1942 to 1944, the entire time Grandfather spent in the European theater, are all short, concise, filled with news of people other than themselves.

I had wanted to share these with Eddie, but I don't see much point. They're not very telling, these missives. Besides, he's not going to care. Kids today don't understand censorship and the beauty of reading between the lines. I've seen their digital communication. Nothing is subtle or sacred; nothing is held back, nothing restrained. Nothing is spelled right.

I do plan to share with him the most valuable prize I reclaimed from the deepest cubby in Grandmother's desk. The name stenciled in delicate Roman script in blue ink across the top of the stationery says it all: Nelle Harper Lee.

Then in the sure handwriting of a woman practiced in stenography:

Dearest PeeCee and Edward:

    Your generous hospitality and warmth during the weekend's visit were nothing short of delightful, true Southern gentility that I hope doesn't see its death in my lifetime. Your love for each other is a marvel to behold. PeeCee, your grace is unmatched, and Colonel, I only wish I could tell a story the way you tell yours, with easy humor and devastating pathos.

Your son is a beautiful child, blessed to have been born in the bounty of such a household. Magnificent, too, that you should call him "Jupiter," after the pater of all Roman gods! (Perhaps it might be best to teach him that he is no god. But I am no mother!) I very much enjoyed playing catch with him in your big and beautiful yard; as, you know, I am quite the tomboy. Colonel, one day, the army will enlist women, and we will fight as well as any man, I assure you of that.

In any event, my wishes are to thank you for a fine weekend of splendid conversation, the best food in the world, and stories that will keep me inspired.

Warmest regards,

NHL

The letter is dated 1959, before her novel was published; I have to wonder if she scribbled some of *Mockingbird* during her stay in this very room. One day, I'll show this to Eddie and hope he appreciates it for the treasure it is.

"Hey, Dad," he says, poking his head into my new office space, which I am becoming loath to leave.

I have written a month's worth of seriousmusic.com articles about bands and musicians I never knew existed. My editor, whom I've never met and who could actually be a microchip somewhere, thinks I have been reborn into someone who cares.

I'm still not certain I'm wild about his Webzine, but I need something to do—a man can read only so much and give his kid only so much unsolicited attention. After all, some employment's not bad, and the paychecks bolster Eddie's college fund, boosted that much more now, thanks to some fine antiques.

Ever since hearing last winter about his grandfather's imprisonment in Honduras, Eddie, too, could be mistaken for someone who cares. As for Tyler, we don't see as much of him as we used to.

The day after our talk, Eddie and I had a ritual burning of his drug paraphernalia near Grandfather's erstwhile garden. I chanted a few faux-Buddhist moans and hoped for a contact high while Eddie torched his stash, the finest-smelling pot I'd inhaled in years—a rare father-son moment when Eddie promised never to smoke marijuana again.

Under a cold, full moon, I intoned: "By the Great Vow of the Four Main Moons of Jupiter—Io, Callisto, Ganymede, and Europa, each representing your great-grandfather, your grandfather, me, and you—do you, Edward Pearson Duncan, solemnly swear beside this cleansing fire that you will never take another toke, as long as you live, so help you God?"

"Sure."

That was the first of the three penitential trials I had set for him. He had two left.

This morning, I motion Eddie into the room as he walks past. He plops into an old chair and I turn my chair to face him. "What's the word?"

"A killer concert's coming to Wrenton."

"And did you read that in my seriousmusic preview? Tremendous writing and your ticket to college, thank you very much."

"I was thinking about going."

"Who are you thinking about taking?" He glares at me, but the anger dissipates just as quickly. He has begun to learn about the balance of power, that rebellion can go only so far and that so far his rebellion has failed.

"Tyler."

I shake my head.

"What's up with that?" he says, his defiance rising again with my resistance.

"Have you asked Toby—I mean, Dr. Lawson?"

"Not yet."

"Bet he says, 'No way, no how,' only not in so many words. Try again."

He knows he's walking into an ambush. "What gives, Dad? I mean, for real?"

"C'mon, Eddie. You've completed just *one* of three tasks I gave you. Hercules had twelve. In one single day, he diverted two rivers and mucked out the Augean stall. By himself. You accomplished your first task in February. And I *helped* you!"

"I swear, you think you're so freaking smart."

"Better watch your mouth, mister, or Miss Soap Lozenge will come in here and give you a faceful." I smile at him. "Listen, Eddie, I wasn't kidding. After all, you could have faced a felony charge. So I simply grounded you with two other conditions: You help me with the Plunder Room"—I look around the comfort of my office—"okay, so we haven't had time for that. But we—"

"No way."

I tap my temple. "*Yo no comprende* 'no way,' Pedro."

"You can't pimp me out to Marnie Jennings and call it a condition of my . . . of my parole. You can't!"

"'Zat so? This is *my* country club, pal, and if you want to learn to play with the pros, you don't noodle around at the putt-putt." He pauses to consider his next shot, which gives me the advantage. "So. Just how bad do you want to see this concert in Wrenton on Friday?"

"Right." His eyes light up. "Steely Black Steeple. Everyone says it's going to rock balls."

"Rock balls. Well, in that case. Nobody in this household would ever miss a show that is going to rock balls."

From working on my seriousmusic preview, I knew the poetic genius of Steely Black Steeple's front man T. J. Wrex, who had come up with this particular lyric:

You light me up, I melt you like a candle.
You wear me down, I wear you out, you lose.
You wax your ebb and flow, I'm more than you can handle.
Get back home before you light my fuse.

I try not to shake my head. If Eddie really did read my piece on the World Wide Web, the fact that I've trashed these guys makes them all the more heroic. Here's what I posted about the kids' new faves:

> *Talent in a musician is the ability to coax lasting and hopefully life-changing melodies from inanimate objects, their instruments. And talent in a songwriter is the ability to make sense. In the case of Philadelphia's four-piece Steely Black Steeple: Somebody please blog us and tell us what young Mr. Wrex is trying to say in SBS's 'No Easy Way,' the fourth track on their overproduced CD of the same name.*

My editor—not a microchip as it turns out, but Keith Chen, who fancies himself a second-generation Chinese Keith Richards—told me the site's server nearly crashed from the avalanche of e-mail responses.

"Hey, fuk-wad," reads the best of only three dozen that Keith forwarded to me, "u r either old as dirt, dumb as dirt, or have ears of dirt, s.b.s. phucking rawks & if u don't get the words, u r an idiot. lol." The return e-mail address was "retchidrokker."

"The writer makes his (or her) point so eloquently," I e-mailed back to Keith, who wisely forbid me from replying to any of our readers.

I tell Eddie, "I really didn't think Steely Black Steeple would be your speed."

"The Wrenton show's almost sold out already, and everyone's going." He sits up in anticipation, as if I'm about to give in.

"We still have one little problem here." I lace my fingers together in spurious condescension.

"But you just said—"

"I never said anything. That's not true, I've said a lot of things, most of which you've ignored, thanks to that Rebellion Thing." He shifts in his seat. "We've been busy in the last few months, but the fact is I *am* going to need your help this summer going through the Plunder Room. I never said you were done, that your penance was set aside, that you could just trot off and rock balls." He squirms even more, seeing that the battle and possibly the war aren't going in the right direction. "And I really think you should consider the Marnie Jennings part of the deal. If I were you, I wouldn't outright say 'No way' without considering the benefits." I hold up my hand to stop his obligatory insolence.

"And those benefits would be?"

"She's great-looking, she's smart—"

"She's a freak, Dad. She *so* kisses Manios's ass—"

"Is that any way to talk?" Of course it is, when you're fourteen years old in this century. "Look, Eddie. I know you think I'm being a jerk. And maybe I am. Maybe you think I'm having fun at your expense." I grin at him, then wipe the grin off my face. "But I'm not. I'm trying to teach you something—no, don't look at me like that. Try being normal just this once. A normal kid doing a normal thing. Like going on a date. With a 'normal' girl.

"There is a life out there beyond rebellion, a good life within the realm of responsibility and dignity. And, oh, yeah, you are good enough to ask a popular girl out on a date. You *are* good enough to have fun with a pretty girl, even one who happens to so kiss authority ass."

He sighs.

"It's one night, Eddie, *one night!* One night of being a responsible adult. Show me that much, and maybe, just maybe, I'll loosen up."

"A *responsible adult?*" He gets up and swings his arms like a wild man. "But, Dad, look at my role model! And me? I'm a *teenager!*"

I wish with all my might that I could stand, my face in his face, but since I can't, I fight dirty. I push him back into his chair, down to my level.

"Let me remind you of something, buster. You committed an *adult* felony. You are beyond lucky, do you realize that? I could just as easily have handed you over to the judicial system to be tried as an adult. You want to do adult things, try adult things, commit adult crimes? Fine. Then you will suffer adult consequences.

"Under *my* judicial sentence, you will, for one night, try to behave like an adult, with the mores and manners and confidence of an adult, in the company of a young lady who appears to be trying her damnedest to *work* toward being an adult and trying harder than most to *grow* into one!"

He collapses in what I hope is defeat.

"Will you at least buy the tickets?"

"For Steely Black Steeple? You have lost the last of your marbles. I wouldn't buy tickets to see that band if they were given to me. I wouldn't even pay the ninety-nine cents to download *one* of their songs."

His smile begs me to shut up. "So you'll let me go to the concert?"

"With. Marnie. Jennings."

"Okay, already." He sighs and looks away, a fine pout working to full throttle.

"Being a sore loser isn't part of adulthood, unless you're talking about coaching Little League."

He smiles. This one looks genuine.

"Eddie, you may use my credit card to order the tickets. Then you can pay me back later."

I pull the plastic out of my wallet and he reaches for it. We play a little tug-of-war with the card, knowing that his repayment plan will be a battle for another day.

CHAPTER TEN

BACK IN the SQ for the night, I'm in bed and flying through a twelve-hundred-page brick of a novel called *Once An Eagle*. I feel my grandfather in the pages of Anton Myrer's epic of Sam Damon, a World War I Medal of Honor recipient who rises from army enlisted man to major general. Myrer shows what life was like for the officers and their wives during peacetime, living in desolate and often substandard quarters. He unleashes horrific battle scenes from the Pacific to the European theater, where Grandfather fought. He paints a perfect picture of the German countryside, where as a teenager, I witnessed firsthand a column of tanks and heard their hellish rumble. That was *after* puking my guts up into the Rhine.

I'm lost in my grandfather's war when the phone's ring explodes beside my bed.

"This Rannel Duncan?" The voice is rough, weary, and, while slow, forgoes further formality. "They tol' me to call you ASAP."

"They who? Who is this? Jupe?"

The bedside clock, whose numbers are as red as my eyes must be, says it's a little after ten, much too late for anyone to be calling with anything other than bad news.

"This's Gunny. They told me to call you 'cause I live closest, here in Wrenton, and I'm the name on the sheet—"

"The hell?"

The voice, charred from cigarettes, belongs to Jupe's oldest friend and confidante and the longtime manager at the Jupe Box, my father's venerable dive bar in Wrenton. The crusty Marine gunnery sergeant and Vietnam veteran is too old, too jaded, and too mean to get worked up about anything. Tonight, he sounds worked up.

"Gunny, what's going on? Is something wrong with Jupe?"

"Yuh, I'll say. Hospital called, said it was an emergency. Your old man's there. Wrenton Memorial. He had a stroke."

Everything goes spinny. "Is he dead?"

"No, he ain't dead, but he ain't too good, neither. Gotta run, pal. Sorry 'bout Sarge."

Click.

Regrets are already gathering like elements of a powerful storm, ready to lash itself against the wall of my emotional core—regrets about fathers, regrets about sons, about fathers and sons, regrets about not knowing enough to care and not caring enough to know. But storms make you panic, and while the storm rises, I move as quickly as I can into my wheelchair and into some clothes, gather my cell phone, wallet, and keys. Nothing happens fast when you're in a wheelchair, but I tell myself I still have time, that my father will be fine. My heart beats a faster rhythm to move me toward the door, while I pray with all my might that in the hour and a half it takes to drive to Wrenton, my father doesn't die.

Thanks to the phone's blast and my clanking around, Eddie's awake now. He slinks out of his bedroom into mine, rubbing the sleep from his eyes.

I tell him what's happened. "Jupe's a tough old bastard," I say, and I remind him of Vietnam and the prison in Honduras, not to mention all the abuse my father has heaped on himself.

"Anything I can do for you?" he asks.

"Yeah, call Tyler and sneak him in for a sleepover."

"No, I'll be okay."

I wink at him, then notice the square of treasured stationery on my chest of drawers. I fold the note from Harper Lee into my sports coat pocket and allow myself another smile. With a little luck, maybe I'll get the chance to tell Jupe that he's named for a god, not after Grandfather's old horse.

In the car, memories become passengers with me on the dull, dark drive to Wrenton. I can't summon many; we didn't spend much time together, Jupe and I, but that seemed to develop out of mutual accommodation. We found parts of each other distasteful, parts delightful, to use one of Miss Lee's words. As father and son, we loved each other. Still do. The thing is, I never did trust him, even as a child. Still don't. Like the sign tacked on the wall at Winchell's Café, HIRE A TEENAGER WHILE THEY'RE STILL SMARTER THAN YOU, an echo of Mark Twain, I've *always* believed I was smarter than my father—at least, more knowledgeable.

Still, you'd never meet a crazier, funnier, wilder man than Edward Jupiter Duncan. He made life's sensual pleasures a priority, above intellectual pursuits, without giving any thought to the consequences. Sure, I had my hedonistic days, too, but not with the same abandon. Maybe I just had an innate fear, a set of psychological brakes that Jupe never had. And now that I sit in a chair, my choices are limited. I don't think he ever gave me much credit for adapting. On the other hand, I never did give him credit for being a survivor. Still, the thing I love most about my dad is that he never meddled in my adult life, never made my business his. He expected the same from me. Perhaps, now in hindsight's irony, we should have been more involved in each other's lives. But when does a father's intrusion becomes a son's burden? I wonder if Jesus asked the same question at the end.

I also wonder if the craziness is over—at least for Jupe.

The longest time Dad, Jerod, and I spent together were the two years he was stationed in Germany. I was fourteen years old then, Eddie's age, and Jerod was seven. None of us was living with a mother by then—Jerod's had died and mine had run off. Grandmother later told me that she pleaded with her son to let us stay with them for the duration of his overseas tour.

Jupe would hear nothing of it.

"This is a great opportunity for the boys," my father told her. "They'll get to see some of the world, just like I did."

Off we went.

We might as well have been living in one of New Cumbria's subsidized housing projects. The population of the U.S. military in Mannheim, where Jupe's orders sent us, exceeded our home-town county's population by four thousand people. We lived in Benjamin Franklin Village, hence the beginning of my interest in the wise and witty statesman. Ol' Ben would have been appalled at the living conditions. The mottled white, three-story, thin-walled apartment buildings housed hives of young Americans who had no concept of Germany, let alone Europe. While my father no doubt rearranged the military's inventory in creative ways, and the German black market enjoyed its most prosperous season, Jerod and I plundered our newfound, absolute freedom.

With no supervision outside school, Jerod and I had ready access to cheap bowling and cheap movies, a decent school with instant friends, *Schwimmbade*—the deluxe German swimming parks where girls got naked in public, changing from bikinis to regular clothes, just like that!—and, best of all, beer. Anyone of any age can drink beer in Germany. I loved German beer.

Several mornings I just couldn't make it to school, home of the best American football team in the Department of Defense European high school league. After school, friends and I would wander off post to the *Gasthaus,* and the bigger guys, the seniors on the football or soccer teams, would pick up some Eichbaum, the delectable local brew. I'd eventually stumble home, pop a pair of TV dinners into the oven for Jerod and me, then fall into bed.

Even Dad, who was busy with the United States Army and whatever extracurricular projects that afforded him, began to notice my unusual health issues. Maybe that's when Jupe and Jerod began forging their bond, while I was passed out in bed.

One night, Jupe, apparently aware of my shenanigans, had had enough. We left Jerod with his homework.

Off we went to a *Gasthaus,* where, unfortunately, the proprietor thought he recognized me. We dined on a sumptuous *Jägerschnitzel,* perfectly sautéed veal cutlet with the richest dark mushroom gravy I had ever tasted, along with *pommes frites* and red cabbage. Then my father proceeded to get me so drunk I'm surprised I didn't die.

With my legs unable to function, Jupe dragged me out of the restaurant and into the ancient Mercedes he had conned out of some lieutenant, a diesel that rattled like a World War II motorcycle. For the next hour, he raced up the autobahn at speeds designed to purge the alcohol from my system, either through fear, tears, sweat, or vomit.

Next, he whipped through the winding cobbled streets of Worms.

As we were flying down a two-lane road designed for barely one car and bouncing up and down, my stomach with it, my head and body were about to explode.

"Where are we going?" I spit out, fearing I would throw up all over the dashboard.

"Isn't this great? Some father-son time? Dinner, drinks, a trip through *living* European history?"

"It's dark."

"We don't get to spend time together, you and me. Yeah, it's dark, but you're so busy with school, I'm so busy with soldiering, fighting for my country"—that was a load of crap, but I was in no position to argue—"I thought we should go out, man to man, have some fucking fun!"

I'd heard him cuss before, but not in casual conversation with *me*. "Can't we just go home? And can't you slow down?"

"Ix-nay on ow-slay, pardner. Hang on for the treat I have in store for you!"

We sailed through the tiny farming village of Eich, a kilometer or so from the Rhine. It was so dark that I could make out only a few stucco-and-cinder-block homes. The air was putrid, rank with manure and God knows what else.

"There's a poultry farm a few klicks from here," Jupe said. "Chickens. Man, they shit and piss at the same time. Explains why it stinks to high heaven. Quaint as hell, ain't it?"

I had never heard my father sound like this. I wonder what Grandfather would have thought. Jupe had enlisted almost fifteen years before, when he couldn't find gainful employment. I imagine he was ashamed that his staff sergeant's stripes would never match up to his father's full bird. What Jupe never understood was that Grandfather took enormous pride in the fact that his son wore a uniform at all. I know, because Grandfather told me, even if he never told Jupe. Come to think of it, Grandfather would have approved one hundred percent of Jupe's method of torture, too—he'd used a similar technique on his own son years before in the Great Rickshaw Episode.

Jupe drove me to the banks of the Rhine River.

While I bent over the waving riparian weeds and heaved up my entire meal between gulps of misery and humiliation, I vowed to myself and to him that I would never drink again, a promise that didn't last much longer than the following week.

"Randol, let me tell you something." Jupe stood behind me. "Several miles upstream from this very spot, your grandfather nearly got blown to bits walking across the Ludendorff Bridge at Remagen. The shit wasn't just hitting the fan, it was flying everywhere. Blood, bodies, steel, bullets, you name it." He stopped and looked across the India-ink current that moved faster than he could talk. We were watching history flow by. "Your grandfather and his regiment, they were on the other side of the Rhine, one of the first units to get across. And y'know what his crazy sumbitches did? They blew up the motherfuckin' bridge."

My gut churned, my head felt like a balloon on the verge of bursting, and the taste in my mouth made me want to vomit all over again. But I struggled to understand what my father was saying. I wanted to believe he was telling one of his Vietnam war stories as if it belonged to Grandfather instead—or maybe the other way around.

"So, now your grandfather and his doughs had no way to escape. They were trapped on the other side of *this* river, this very *same* fucking river, the one you're looking at *right here*, Randol, stuck *over there*"—he pointed to the opposite bank—"with the enemy they either had to destroy or die trying. There was no other way home."

"Speaking of home . . ." I lifted my head and pulled myself up and wobbled back to the car.

Of course, I didn't know until much later that I'd mangled most of the facts, but at the time, he was on a roll and I wasn't feeling too good myself.

"They were real enemies, the Nazis, and yet we had no fear. We didn't make up enemies, and we didn't make up fear. Your grandfather fought them, chased them, no turning back—and that's the way your grandfather has always lived his life. He's always lived his life with a goal, a purpose, a mission. Find yours, without fear, and don't fuck it up."

We got back in the car and Jupe drove, slowly this time, back past Eich to the edge of a sugar-beet field. Jupe pulled off into the field, destroying some farmer's crops, and turned off the ignition. The plants were low and green, cool and wet from the night. I wanted to lie down in them.

In the darkness, Jupe began again: "This is the Cold War, Randol, completely different from your grandfather's war. Maybe you'll never wear a uniform. But you'll still have to pick your fights."

He got out of the car.

I followed his lead but leaned against the hood, still weak and shaky, confused about why we had stopped and what we were doing and why. Sweat chilled my forehead. I felt blanched and empty.

Soon, rolling thunder enveloped us, relentless rumbles that seemed to be dropping from the heavens, but the sky was clear.

The ground was shaking.

The low bellow neared.

"Dad?" My feet wouldn't move.

Soon, a light shot at us. I thought it was the face of God. The white glare bounced on the road.

The thunder roared stronger, mechanical *booms* churning up the road.

Fear . . . evolved . . . into . . . a . . . slow . . . cold . . . dread.

From the bass rumbles shot high-pitched squeals and crushing sounds. The light grew impossibly brighter, and I shaded my eyes with my hand.

At last, through the brilliance, I saw a column of American tanks.

"Forty-six short tons of death and destruction," Dad shouted with martial pride. "Twelve Sheridans headed for the Rhine. Nighttime pontoon-bridge exercises."

Tank treads chewed the asphalt like an aerator machine punching through a lawn.

I couldn't imagine the Germans would be too thrilled about having to plow thousands of deutsche marks into replacing the entire road or having to drive on a washboard until the repaving was done.

The din hammered through us until the column passed, but the earth rumbled until the tanks followed their glaring lamps into the darkness.

"Imagine hearing that night and day. Imagine the sky flaring up with lights and smoke. Imagine the *pat-pat-pat*"—he tapped the top of the Mercedes with his forefinger—"of machine guns and automatic weapons all around you. Endlessly. Hell, no need to imagine, right, Randol? You just heard a little bit of what your grandfather lived through for most of two years. What he gave his life to."

I was too sick to talk, too miserable to think, too sick to be miserable. I don't remember the drive home, walking inside our apartment, or falling into bed.

But Jupe woke me up the next morning with a splash of ice water on my face, a Bloody Mary for breakfast (so much for my pledge), red-hot cinnamon gum to cover the vodka smell, and a suggestion to "run like a hound dog in heat" during gym class to sweat out the cocktail from breakfast and the poison from the night before.

"Welcome to the Fraternal Order of Manhood, son." He pounded me on the back. "If we were Jewish, I guess we'd have had a bar mitzvah. As it is, you passed Jupe's basic training, and you did all right. Now." He held my shoulders with both hands. "Get your ass to school."

More than two decades later, I'm driving into a hospital parking lot with memories of that evening in Germany thundering back like the tanks on that dark farm road. And I feel the same rumbling fear.

No one pays much attention to me when I roll past the front desk. Not that I need information or directions. I know my way around this place, and I'd already called to confirm that Jupe is in the second-floor intensive-care unit.

Without bothering to check visiting hours, I push the automatic-door openers into the ICU and wheel into the ward of patients and machines, nurses and doctors, all fighting for the same thing. Man and machine alike are too busy to notice anyone in a wheelchair.

I like to think I've prepared myself for what I might see. I haven't.

Jupe lies in the third bed to my right, his bed flat, his eyes closed, an oxygen tube in his nose. He is breathing on his own, thank God, no tubes jammed down his throat. Intravenous fluid drips from a clear bag hanging over his shoulder. Monitors beep his heart rate, blood pressure, and other vital functions. A bag of urine, like mine, hangs from the bed, already half full. They have pumped him full of blood thinners and who knows what else to entice his body and brain back from the stroke.

He doesn't look much different than he did at Central Prison.

I clasp his hands, and the tips of his fingers, with a touch soft as butterflies, respond to mine. He groans through slack, dry lips, his eyes still closed. I believe he knows me, and I hope he knows me as Randol, as Esau, the blessed son, not the deceitful one.

"Hey, Jupe." He tries to open one eye to a narrow slit.

"Stroke of bad luck, huh?" My eyes sting. I never expected to feel this way seeing my father like this. "Or is that kind of humor in particularly bad taste?"

He wants to speak, but can only drool. I wish I could hear him say something, a smart-ass remark, anything.

A doctor approaches. "Can I help you?"

"I'm not sure I'm the one who needs the help," I say, immediately regretting my foolish retort. "But it looks like you've got my old man under control here."

"Your father?"

I nod. I know he sees how red my eyes are now.

"He's a feisty one, your dad." The doctor flips open a steel chart. "Duncan, Edward. J. Small-vessel ischemic stroke believed caused by microatheromata of unknown origin that occluded the orifice of penetrating arteries. Treatment with heavy doses of heparin and warfarin, still NPO . . ."

"Correct me if I'm wrong, Doc, but I believe you just said, 'Insert Tab A into Slot B. May require additional assembly, batteries not included. And . . . shown actual size.'"

"I *thought* I recognized you from med school." He offers his hand. "Chris Nguyen."

"Right, I saw your name tag, just never knew how to pronounce the name. Vietnamese, right?"

"American. Vietnamese father, American mother, second generation."

I nod. "Right. I got my degree from Saigon Medical University, specialized in knee-bone-connected-to-the-thigh-bone."

"University of Chicago." His smile vanishes. "Your father's lucky. If we hadn't gotten him when we did—"

"How bad is it? Really?"

"No stroke's a good stroke, Mr., um . . ."

"Duncan, Randol Duncan. Please, call me Randol."

"Right." He purses his lips and pushes his glasses against his eyes. "Something, an embolism, floated into a brain artery, stopped the flow of blood in a portion of his brain, and caused the stroke. Anything could have caused the embolus, but the leading causes of this kind of ischemic stroke, especially in men like your dad, are hypertension, cigarettes, drug use, lipids, or fats, though your father doesn't look like that kind of candidate, and his cholesterol counts are remarkably low."

"What are his chances?"

"Of walking out of here? Good. But his convalescence is going to take time, and he'll need plenty of physical therapy, a lot of help." He looks at the wheelchair instead of at me. "You know all about that."

"What about the short term?"

"He'll be in the hospital for another week or so, at least, until he's stabilized. Then you can take him home or to a rehabilitation facility, wherever you think he can get the best care."

Volusia's the answer there. And it's a good thing, after all, that I decided to leave Grandfather's room more or less as it was. Jupe may not like living there, but in his condition, he won't be able to put up much of a fuss.

"I'll give you another few minutes with him, Mr. Duncan, but then you really do have to let him rest."

I nod again, but before I go, I pull out Harper Lee's letter and whisper its contents to my father. I'm certain he hears me—god that he is.

My body warns me that I need to be careful. It's nearly one A.M., and I'm physically and emotionally spent. I can't drive home. If I push myself now, I will be in agony, and, like an idiot, I didn't bring any pills.

Where's Jerod? He should be here. He should be around to take care of Dad, to help take care of *me*.

I punch in his number on my cell phone.

" 'Lo?"

"Jupe's had a stroke."

"What?"

"He's lying here, half dead, at Wrenton Memorial. Where are you?"

"You're calling to say our father's had a stroke, and you want to make this about me?"

"Sure, Jerod, why not?" It astonishes me that my self-absorbed brother can't see that he *wants* everything to be about him—even our father's stroke. I sigh for dramatic effect, a pause that I hope earns a little sympathy. Getting none, I give in and start over. "Okay, he's in ICU, and it looks like he's going to be okay, but he also looks like a dried-up apricot."

"Charming. You always did have a way of making things sound better even at the most inappropriate times."

"Look, Jerod, I don't know much. Recuperation's going to take a long time, and he might never be quite the same again, and I'm stuck here in Wrenton in the middle of the night, too tired to drive—"

"What do you want *me* to do about it?"

"Honestly, I don't much care what you do, but I sure as hell would like you to offer to do *something*."

"Listen, I happen to be in Newark waiting for a flight to Charlotte. My connection to Wrenton isn't until tomorrow, so unless I rent a car . . ."

I tune him out as if he's one of those self-indulgent radio talk shows.

Damn him. Damn me for even thinking about wanting his help. No point in even asking what Jerod was doing in Newark.

He'd just lie to me. Besides, I'm certain that the less I know about Jerod, the better. Kind of like Jupe all these years.

"Y'know, Jerod, perhaps you could summon just enough decency to at least visit your father. He may be barely conscious, but he knows what's going on, and since you happen to be his favorite, which mystifies the hell out of me, he might actually get some comfort from you if you managed to take a few minutes out of your busy entrepreneurial schedule to visit the poor son of a bitch."

"Wow, Randol, I'm impressed." So am I. He almost passes for sincere. "That's the first time I've heard you say what you mean without making some kind of stupid joke."

"Okay, then, why don't you impress the rest of us by doing something selfless for the old coot?"

"You don't even know the half of it, Randol."

"What the hell does *that* mean?" I say, though I know he's referring to the half I haven't known since he was seven years old in Benjamin Franklin Village in Germany.

"I'd better go; they're calling my row at the gate."

He shuts me down just that fast.

Anger, frustration, and confusion surge through me as hot as the airplane fuel that's about to bring Jerod home—or maybe not. A bed somewhere, a motel, some aspirin can wait a few hours, though I may pay the price in pain. I need to find out what the hell is going on, and I know just the place to start.

The Jupe Box squats against a stand of bamboo and palmetto trees about a thousand yards from Wrenton's Downtown Executive Airport. A halogen streetlamp splits its light between the bar and the airfield's concertina-wired entrance. The two-story control tower sits empty, its red lights blinking time with the katydids and cicadas. The airport's apron, lined with white lights, waits for anyone to fly in any time. The bar has had three additions over the years: a beige Quonset hut on the left, a dark blue cinder-block structure on the right, and a satellite-TV dish on the roof that points toward Jupiter. Three older-model American-made cars and a beat-up Ford pickup with an empty gun rack sit in the weedy parking lot.

Pulling as close to the door as possible so I don't have to navigate my wheelchair through gravel, I work my way into the bar. Smoke drapes the wood-paneled room like a parachute, and the smell burns my eyes and lungs. A South Vietnamese flag (three red stripes against a gold field) covers the wall beyond two regulation pool tables. Two men in black leather vests, denim shirts, gray beards, and red bandannas play at one of the tables. The walls are filled with street signs, license plates—IMAVET, GR8-RYD—and the occasional trophy buck and bass. Lynyrd Skynyrd—who else?—rocks the Wurlitzer that pulses with liquid colors between the bar and the bathrooms.

The doors leading to the building's additions are closed. Every now and then, an old black man shuffles through the left-hand door. On the right-hand side, a barrel of a man stands guard in a T-shirt with a Confederate flag that reads DON'T SCREW WITH DIXIE. He would get thrown off Ari Manios's high school campus.

My father owns this place, along with a pair of convenience stores and a trailer park. As Led Zeppelin would also sing from the jukebox: "And it makes me wonder."

The bar's lustrous oak finish and fine curves shine among the battered tables and chairs. I feel equally out of place.

I roll to one side so the bartender doesn't have to lean over to see me. "Gunny."

"Thassright."

He looks as crusty as my father, though he's probably not even half Jupe's age. Hard to tell on a man with more miles on him than years. His gray-streaked hair hangs to his shoulders. His brown eyes look black and seem as hollow as his cheeks. Behind his rusted goatee are a few scars around his throat; apparently he has needed help breathing. The tattoos on his arm are colorful, unreadable stories of a life too brutal to contemplate.

I introduce myself.

"The sarge's kid."

"Thassright." It's probably not too bright to mimic a man like Gunny. "He'll be okay. He'll be in the hospital a while, but he'll be all right."

"Then back here." He taps out a cigarette and offers me one. I shake my head.

"Doubt it. No time soon; maybe never."

"Wouldn't put money on that."

"Gunny. So . . . you were a Marine gunnery sergeant."

"Thassright." He blows a full cumulus cloud over my head.

"Iraq?"

He shakes his head and takes another long drag, then reaches into the cooler. A man appears behind me and asks for a Budweiser. "Make that two, Gunny. And just stick 'em on my tab."

Gunny pulls out three beers. He glances at me, and I shake my head again. The longneck bottles are tempting in the bar's dry, smoky heat.

"How's it going back there?" Gunny asks into the air above my head.

"Done. All good."

My curiosity rises like a fever, but I resist the temptation to twist around and see what's going on behind me.

"That Iraq thing." Gunny kisses the longneck and suckles the beer. A few drops fall on his shirt and he wipes them away without a thought. "Guess they're going to have to build another one of them black marble walls."

"What time you fellas close?"

"City says two"—he smiles at me—"but we pretty much close when we're done. We're hardly ever done."

I'm surprised at his openness, but I guess it's because I'm the son of "Sarge." Little does he know that "Sarge" would never cough up half as many details to anyone. I've never heard anyone call my father that. Jupe left the service after we returned from Germany to the World—that's what we called the States. He came straight back to Wrenton, and I stayed as far from home as I could. PeeCee helped me enroll in Columbia Prep School in New York for my senior year. She paid my tuition, too.

"The sarge asked me if I would gather up a few things in the office."

He squints at me. "He don't like nobody going in there. 'Cept me. Tell me what he's after, and I'll fetch it."

I'm afraid the fresh sprouts of sweat on my forehead will betray my ruse. "Gunny, honestly, I'm not going to know what it is until I see it."

His eyebrows rise, not a good sign on a face so violently impassive—or so passively violent.

"Ah, c'mon, Gunny. The sarge is in bad shape, and worrying about his papers and stuff, well, that's just making things worse." He looks as if he may be relaxing some. "Listen, my dad just told me to take everything I can to Jerod." For the first time tonight, Gunny's eyes shift from dark to light.

I'm not *on* my feet, but I still feel good about being *quick* on them.

Gunny inhales the last of his cigarette and blows another

mighty billow. He tamps the butt into a brass shell-casing ash-tray, then leads me to the cinder-block addition and unlocks the dead bolt.

A half dozen men mill around a large oval table, nearly in-visible under a curtain of cigar, cigarette, and pot smoke. I gather they've been playing cards, but the deck is nowhere in sight. Three illegal video poker machines sit in the corner; they're un-plugged. They probably got that way the moment Gunny turned the dead bolt.

"You boys don't mind giving us a little privacy, do ya?" Gunny asks. The men oblige with a grumble here, a slap on the back there, and a general agreement that maybe it *is* time to go home.

He snaps on a lamp at a desk in an otherwise empty corner of the room. Papers are strewn on top: scribbled notes, bar invoices, receipts, along with beer coasters, coffee mugs, overflowing ash-trays, some butts smeared with lipstick. Not a single photograph of friends or family.

Gunny waits for me to get what I need.

"Yo, Gunny, I'll bet you have a customer or two." I am the old man's son, after all, and I hope that earns me the right to be alone with his stuff. "My guess is that those guys just finished a round of faceup poker and that one of 'em's got about a grand in his pocket. I bet he's itching to buy a round for the house. Which means a big-ass tip for you."

Gunny may not like being manipulated but decides to leave me by myself, anyway—at least for a moment.

I roll around to the other side of the desk. The drawers are locked. Jupe doesn't have a computer. Even if he knew what to do with one, to own one would be insane. E-mail? Forget about it. You can *always* lose a paper trail—Eddie has that much sense.

Pulling out my car keys, I fidget with the pocketknife tool kit I use for minor repairs on my wheelchair. As quickly as I can, I worry the locks on the gray metal government-issue desk, and in no time, the left-hand drawer snaps open. Then the right one.

In the left side I find a small three-ring binder and flip it open. Incomprehensible scribbles fill two dozen or so loose-leaf pages of accounting paper. At the bottom of the other drawer, wrapped in a purple Crown Royal pouch, is a two-megabyte computer jump drive the size of a disposable cigarette lighter. Maybe Jupe does have a computer squirreled away somewhere. I guess I'm about to find out.

I stuff the binder and the jump drive behind my back and ease the drawers closed a second before Gunny steps back into the office.

"Damn chair." I lean into the right wheel and pretend to tighten some spokes with my tool. "You'd never believe how often these spokes pop right out."

"Guess we're gonna lock up for the night."

"All right." I don't want to argue with him that just a few minutes before, he had told me that the goings-on at the Jupe Box are "never done." I just roll out of the office as he switches off the lights. "Thanks. I know my father is going to appreciate your help."

"Tell the old man we're all pulling for him."

I nod, doing my best to look grim. That's not much of a stretch. After all, I suspect my father has far more troubles than the ones that put him in a hospital bed a few hours ago.

CHAPTER ELEVEN

RATHER THAN risk slamming into another wall of agony, I pull myself, my chair, and the booty from Jupe's office into my car and into the parking lot of a Motel 6 less than a half mile from the bar. The OxyContin in my medicine cabinet calls to me, and while Eddie and Volusia will be worried sick about me in the morning, I owe it to them—Eddie especially—not to risk the dark South Carolina highways that took my legs two years ago. Besides, one quick credit card transaction with the gum-snapping night clerk, reasonably clean sheets, and a pillow are all I need for a few hours of restorative rest.

Before dawn, the motel's air conditioner kicks on and wakes me up with a noise that sounds like an old Volkswagen. Three pain-free hours of sleep were well worth the money, though some residual discomfort chews my insides.

I return home to my good drugs and my son before any alarms have sounded that I've gone missing—in spite of that fact that Eddie's already awake in the SQ.

After the night I just spent with my father, a searing lump of emotion chars my throat when I see Eddie.

He's hunched over his computer, probably blogging his life for the world to see. They want their privacy, these kids, so they tell millions of people their secrets. But those people don't count, those anonymous cyber people. We've all become anonymous. Makes it easier to start wars that way.

I'm too emotional to get into anything with Eddie, too raw. But my body is raring to keep me in the fight. I hear its bell taunting me to go another round—*ding ding*!

"You know what would be awesome?" I bump across the threshold, startling Eddie from his Web.

"Huh?" He's still in boxer shorts and a white T-shirt three times too big for him, streaked with soft-drink and junk-food stains.

"It would be so cool if you could type 'breakfast' into that thing and have it ready, poof!, just like that." I snap my fingers.

He looks around, clearing his morning daze and his deep concentration. He glances at his wrist as if he is wearing a watch. "Dad, is everything . . . what's going on?"

An image of Jupe snaps into my mind's eye. I rub my face and mumble that my father's going to be okay.

"Hey, Eddie, how about making your old man a pot of coffee and getting yourself ready for school, bowl of cereal, all that."

Eddie says over the clatter while I start the coffee myself, "So, Dad, seriously, what *about* Grandpa? What happened with you last night?"

I tell him about Jupe, the stroke, the prognosis. His face falls when he hears that his grandfather could be joining us—at least in the HQ, the big house.

"He's going to need us, Eddie, all of us, a lot of help."

He sighs, as if I'd just told him his summer was canceled. He pours a bowl of his sugar-coated cereal in silence.

"Would you rather have me move him to the old folks' home down the street?" Eddie used to walk past Magnolia Living Center on his way to elementary school, and Volusia has friends who work as orderlies there, but Jupe would rather die than slide one foot inside the place.

He dives into his cereal and considers what options, concerning my father, might work best for him.

"Hey, Eddie, did I ever tell you about the time your grandfather caught me drunk and, as punishment, made me drink so much that I puked my guts into the Rhine River?"

Eddie slurps the syrupy-sweet milk from his bowl and pushes the bowl away, then leans back against his chair. He smiles at me to continue.

"And did Uncle Jerod ever tell you about the time he 'borrowed' the rickshaw from the China Room and used it to carry a date up Buncombe Boulevard?" We glance toward the big house. "They almost got run over by a little ol' lady."

"Seriously?" Eddie laughs at the gauzy image.

"It's funny *now*." I pour myself a cup of coffee, preferring Volusia's. I figure she's up at the HQ already.

"Tell me."

"Time for school. Only a couple of days to go before summer."

"I've got time," he insists.

"Okay, so, Jerod was on a date. He'd asked out the prettiest girl at New Cumbria, of course. Bitsy Sherwood. She was more than just the head cheerleader, she was homecoming queen—Miss South Carolina material. But, see, in those days your uncle Jerod wasn't as smooth as he is today. So, in a sense, by asking her out, he kind of screwed up."

"How so?" Eddie leans toward me, his grandfather forgotten, at least for the moment.

"Well. Now that the prettiest girl in school had agreed to go on a date with him, he didn't have a clue what to do with her. In New Cumbria."

"Word."

"Word is right. I mean, right? On a Friday night in this town, there's football—and it wasn't even football season. You could sneak cigarettes or go to the only movie in town—lame—or hang out at the Dairy Bar and try to figure out how to get in a girl's pants. In Bitsy Sherwood's case, *that* was never going to happen."

He shrugs in disbelief, his powerful faith in his uncle's charms transcending time.

"Oh, no, not Bitsy." I roll toward my room, the pills beckoning me. "Anyhoo. Our Casanova-cum-genius decides that Spectacle is the best way to impress a woman of Bitsy Sherwood's caliber. Clever son-of-a-gun that your uncle Jerod was—and is—he picks a night when he knows Grandmother and Grandfather will be out for one of their myriad social engagements and asks Bitsy for drinks and dinner."

"Drinks? Wasn't he still in high school?"

"As if that ever stopped anyone."

He lights up again. (Note to self: Discretion is the better part of being a father.)

"A Chinese restaurant had just opened a few months before near the black section of town, not too far from Volusia's house. Jerod had heard they had these fabulous frozen drinks served in real coconut shells with tiny paper parasols."

I edge into my bedroom. Eddie follows me.

"Jerod has everything planned. Grandmother and Grandfather take off for their party. And Jerod shows up with a truck he's borrowed."

"Is he even allowed to drive?"

"Oh, yeah, he's seventeen."

"Okay, okay . . ."

"So he hauls the rickshaw, lock, stock, and barrel, out of the China Room and into the pickup and drives it to McDavits Court." I wave in the direction that the Sherwoods live. "And, wearing—I am not kidding here—your grandfather's tuxedo and bowling shoes—."

Eddie's laughter interrupts me, becomes contagious and brings tears to my eyes.

"He knocks on the Sherwoods' door, hands Bitsy an orchid corsage, escorts her gallantly to the rickshaw, and whisks her to the Chinese restaurant."

His laughter rolls on. "In a tux and bowling shoes?"

"Oh, yeah." I wipe my eyes. "He'd lifted a pair of size tens from the Brunswick Bowl, said they made great dancing shoes. Guess they were great for running a rickshaw, too."

Eddie throws himself onto my bed and holds his gut in hysterics, laughing so hard he's wheezing. I've made Jerod a hero again.

"Oh, but that's not the best part."

He sits up. It *can't* get any better, but he looks at me with anticipation.

"Turn off the computer and get ready for school. Three days left until summer starts, the concert on Friday, and you haven't been late for school once since February. Don't blow it now."

"But . . . wait!"

"Wait for me to get cranky? Not a good idea. I need rest. Now. Please."

"No, I mean, what happened?"

"Whaddya mean, what happened?" I level a gaze at him. My eyes tingle. I think I could faint if I don't get horizontal soon. I fetch my pills and throw back a pair of OxyContin. Eddie and my pain will be fuzzy memories soon. "Grandfather, of course, finds out about Jerod's hijinks because Jerod nearly got himself, Bitsy, and the rickshaw smashed to bits when ol' Miss Farraway almost ran them over."

I pause. Eddie looks at me as if I'm being my usual drama-queen self. "Seriously, she damn near killed them."

He nods. "Okay, I get that."

"So, as punishment, Grandfather enters Jerod in the New Cumbria homecoming parade. Dresses him up in a coolie costume he saved from China. It was tight, but it almost fit, including the most garish hot pink slippers you've ever seen.

"'Son,' your great-grandfather said, 'you evidently need practice driving that rickshaw, and I can't think of a better place than this parade.' Jerod starts at the football field, pulls the contraption once around the track, all the way up Buncombe to Main—and then has to roll it back home and put it back in its place. And it was cold as hell that day, too."

"You guys like to teach lessons that way, don't you?"

I wink at him. "Kind of fun, isn't it? When you get to be a father, you can come up with creative ideas of your own. Give me a call when you try 'em out."

Maybe it's the pain, but I'm not real hopeful I'll be around for that day. People with severe spinal cord injuries—SCI's, like me—generally live about fifteen years after their accidents.

"Hey, Eddie," I say through the wall. He has gone back to clicking away on his computer keyboard. "Shut that thing off and get dressed for school. Boxer shorts are a clear violation of the dress code."

"Almost done."

"If you people didn't hide behind e-mails and instant messaging, you might learn to respect each other."

"Don't preach, shithead"—a version of what I call my own father.

"Watch it, mister, your odds of making it to that concert may get a lot slimmer."

Lying awake waiting for my pills to take effect, I realize that it's not just kids who hide behind technology. The only stories adults tell anymore are on television; family lore isn't the parlor game it used to be. Which compels me to share more of my family's rich history with my son.

Take my grandmother, for instance. Eddie knows almost nothing about Pearl Clementine Duncan, beyond her furniture. I've never experienced any couple like my grandparents. Their passion extended fifty-seven years, until PeeCee died and left Grandfather heartbroken. Yet even until the day he passed away, he was stronger for the experience of having loved her.

"Come in here a second, buddy, sit on the bed here with me for a minute. I think we should have a little history period before school starts."

Eddie slinks into the room and, considering that I've been nagging him for an hour to hurry up, looks at me as if I've lost my last marble.

So I tell him a story Grandmother told me when I was home from college one summer, complete with an old newspaper society-column clipping that showed a picture of her in a black satin dress, décolleté with white lace ruffles falling just off her ivory shoulders.

Annie Harkin has nothing on my grandmother.

A Royal Navy petty officer was leading the British Legation's Rin Tin Tientsin Orchestra through a dreamy rendition of "Shadow Waltz" when PeeCee and her husband settled into their seats.

"And here's a new tune dedicated to the young American officer and his elegant bride, Captain and Mrs. Edward R. Duncan," the cherry-cheeked bandleader, Danny Lynton, clucked. "We welcome you to your Fifteenth Infantry Regiment, to Tientsin, and to China, where you'll find the summer heat as loathsome as the rickshaw drivers, each in no particular hurry to move anywhere."

Sparse laughter rippled across the sea of white tablecloths and through the dense cigar and cigarette smoke in the British Club, the grand colonial hall on Victoria Road. The evening's dance was held there rather than in Gordon Hall or at the Astor Hotel because only a handful of officers among the 890 Americans in the entire U.S. Army garrison would attend. Why bother with a bigger venue?

The sixteen-piece band was doing quite well, indeed; in fact, Lynton had gotten hold of hot new charts fresh from Jack Hylton, Jay Wilbur, and even Harry Warren himself. So the orchestra struck up "When a Lady Meets a Gentleman Down South."

Then they walk along where magnolias grow
Two hearts sing a song that was written long ago
If that's not sweet romance, then hush my mouth
When a lady meets a gentleman
A very polished gentleman
When a lady meets a gentleman down South

Having been in China barely three weeks, the dashing young captain had already availed himself of Ching Chong Gentleman's Tailor & Woollen Cotton Merchant. There, he purchased a custom-fitted tuxedo, the first he had ever owned. "In China," the regimental commander's booklet had advised, "the tuxedo is worn during the winter months at the social functions in the evening."

They looked like new lovers on the most exotic of honeymoons, the junior captain with his bushy walrus mustache and already silver hair, and his bride with her perfect chestnut coif and amber eyes reflecting the dazzling crystal chandeliers. On the dance floor, they cut an exuberant hop around delighted British colleagues. In politic humility, they dialed down their agility when they moved close to American field-grade and flag officers.

As the Rin Tin Tientsiners slowed to a waltz, a most imposing figure approached the couple.

He looked a bit like a West Point cadet, only Chinese and with more feathers. His lighter-than-normal black hair was slicked back with pomade from his prominent forehead. His eyes were steady, intense, careful, and alive with intelligence. His face, not quite round, was a shade lighter than a pecan, his complexion so smooth that PeeCee wanted to touch him to see if he ever needed to shave. He wore a cutaway swallow-tailed coat in the same design as a West Pointer's, with knobby gilt buttons. The navy blue wool was embroidered with corn sheaves. Across his chest draped a sash signifying the Star of the Precious Brilliant Golden Grain of the Republic of China.

PeeCee recognized him. For one year the previous decade, he had been this war-riddled country's president, though he lacked the thin lips her husband always joked were required of true leadership.

Tonight, he looked as if he could use a smile. Despite his stern, almost morose demeanor, she could sense his humor.

"Dr. Wellington, I presume," PeeCee said, and smiled with her trademark Southern coquettishness.

He laughed. "I like to think I'm no explorer in my own country," he said, catching her sly reference to the British explorer Dr. John Livingston, "though, heaven knows, every nation needs its healers, I dare say."

She had heard that his English was impeccable. After all, he had attended Columbia University, then went on to earn his doctorate there.

"It can't be true what they say you told that poor woman at the Washington Conference in 'twenty-one, is it, sir?" PeeCee asked.

With utmost discretion, Captain Duncan raised his eyebrow; he knew little of the elegant statesman.

"Indeed I did, madam. After she asked me if I, and I quote, 'Likee soupee?', I delivered a most eloquent speech in what I have to say is fairly serviceable New York English. I simply felt the young lady needed a mild upbraiding."

PeeCee covered her mouth and laughed. "But when you sat back down next to her and said, 'Likee speechee?, now, Dr. Wellington . . .'"

The young Captain Duncan laughed so hard the band almost stopped playing.

"Your wife, I presume?" Wellington Koo turned to the officer, who nodded. "I am charmed indeed, sir, but with all due respect she doesn't fit the mold of American military wives. You will find that serves you both well, Captain Duncan, as I'm certain you are most aware."

The American bowed. Dr. Wellington took PeeCee's hand.

"Do you mind, sir, if I have this next dance?" the Chinese

man asked, glancing toward his own wife, a tiny woman who looked forlorn without her husband.

Captain Duncan knew how to take a cue. Within seconds, on opposite ends of the floor, the couples shared the slow and heady "Shadow Waltz."

Silhouettes in blue,
Dancing in the dew;
Here am I,
Where are you?

Next, the band bounded into a rollicking version of "In a Shanty in Old Shanty Town." Halfway through, the two couples, as if in long-rehearsed choreography, twirled to exchange partners.

I'd give up a palace if I were a king.
It's more than a palace, it's my everything.
There's a queen waiting there with a silvery crown
In a shanty in old Shanty Town

Young, alive, filled with the exotic and glamorous, the Duncans sat and quaffed Pimm's Cup. Captain Duncan puffed on a Cuban cigar, a gift from a British rear admiral, though he rarely smoked.

At a table behind them sat another Chinese dignitary, Lin Yutang, looking quite the intellectual, with his black hair brushed back, his big pipe puffing plumes. He had big ears, big round glasses, and a vast smile. Holding court at his table, he chattered away with the British officers and flirted with the ladies.

"Would you mind terribly, dear?" PeeCee turned to her husband, whose astonishment by now had evaporated.

She approached the writer and leaned into him. "Would you care to dance, Dr. Lin?"

"Dancing is for butterflies, madam, and while you flutter among the prettiest, I am but a moth, and I fear I would but burn in your flame." His smile was such a chasm she thought she would fall in it. "I am impressed, once again, by your American, shall I say, joie de vivre. Your people certainly do have an effervescent lack of restraint."

A mousy woman sitting next to him—also an American officer's wife—inched away from PeeCee, clearly clueless about the great man's giant intellect. So PeeCee pulled a chair from another table, wedged it between the woman and Dr. Lin, and gazed into the writer's eyes.

"I remember a passage from your new book, *My Country and My People*." PeeCee recited: "'The difference between China and the West seems to be that the Westerners have a greater capacity for getting and making more things and a lesser ability to enjoy, while the Chinese have a greater determination and capacity to enjoy the few things they have.' No truer words, in my opinion, have ever been written, but I'm not sure they apply only to the Chinese."

"The American officer's wife has the memory of an elephant, the beauty of a lotus flower, and the playfulness of a panda cub. . . . And you would be?"

"My name is Pearl Clementine Duncan." She looked toward her husband. "We've just been stationed here. On behalf of Captain Edward R. Duncan, we are at your service, sir."

"Pearl." He puffed on his pipe. "I imagine you've read your own Pearl S. Buck? Same name, after all."

She smiled. "Of course. A Southern girl like myself, though she is far more accomplished." She fluttered her eyelids in sincere humility. "My friends call me PeeCee."

"Well, yes. My dear friend Mrs. Buck insisted I write the very book you just quoted."

Thus they launched into a lively discussion of Tientsin and what the young Duncans could expect of their new post. Lin told her of the hazards facing the captain, especially dealing with his bored young enlistees, who threw their paychecks away on the girls in the Chin-wang-tao brothels; dice, card games, and matchstick gambling in the barracks; and fights with the sailors on the Hao River.

He also told her of the letter that "everyone here knew about," the one General George C. Marshall Jr. wrote to Black Jack Pershing on January 30, 1925, saying, "Today is 'pay day' and we are up against the problem of cheap liquor and cheaper women—Chinese, Japanese, Russian and Korean. I am relearning about the practical side of handling men, but it seems much the same old problem."

She looked at him now not so much as a student but as a colleague, and she knew he was charmed. "Handling men really isn't the problem, Dr. Lin."

"Oh?"

"Simply read Aristophanes and his *Lysistrata*. If the gun, let's just say for argument's sake, were the extension of the"—she coughed with discretion into her white-gloved hand—"I would have to argue that if the girls of Chin-wang-tao closed up shop until all the soldiers destroyed all their guns . . . or . . ." She stopped and looked into the chandelier's crystals for inspiration.

He chuckled at her naïveté.

"Better yet, Dr. Lin, women should wear the breeches and command the troops."

"Then, I recommend you forgo your afternoons of bridge and reading, supervising your Number One Boy and his coolie staff, and watching your husband play polo, which I understand he does with remarkable skill, and throw yourself into more political or artistic pursuits. Much like my friend Miss Buck."

PeeCee knew a slap when she heard one. "Let me quote a charming and brilliant Chinese writer on one point that I have learned perfectly well in this perfectly fascinating country, Dr. Lin: 'If you can spend a perfectly useless afternoon in a perfectly useless manner, you have learned how to live.' We in the American South, sir, have honed to an idyll the art of fine living, as you yourself define it, and I daresay all that remains for me is a challenging book and the continued pleasure of my husband's company."

She stood and stuck a gloved hand in his face.

He shook it.

"It's been my treat, Dr. Lin. Good evening."

His laughter exploded, and the entire room stopped to look at him.

After dinner, Captain Duncan and his wife strolled up the broad Victoria Avenue in the cool, if malodorous, Tientsin evening.

Along the way, they saw a wizened Chinese man with a rickshaw and, in pidgin sign language, Edward asked if he could buy the man's mode of conveyance—and income.

"You can't be serious, Edward!" PeeCee said.

"Darling," he said, "you have shopped for more than a thousand pounds of furniture, rugs, lamps, mother-of-pearl screens, clothing, and we've barely been here three weeks. I begrudge you nothing, of course. We couldn't afford any of this stuff anywhere else. So, please, let me get away with this one indulgence."

The flummoxed rickshaw driver, who had been waiting under the honey glow of a streetlight for a lonely Turk or Russian bachelor to wander by, looked at the American as if he had lost his mind.

The officer flipped open his brown leather wallet and pulled out a few bills. "Fifty dollars Mex?" That was about twenty dollars American. Considering the average rate for a rickshaw ride was forty cents Mex per hour, that translated to more than 312 fares. For that, Captain Duncan probably figured the man could buy a new rickshaw or start his well-deserved retirement. Fifty dollars Mex was a lot of money. Their Number One Boy at home was earning twenty dollars Mex a month, and they had a house staff of ten—about average for a junior captain at the garrison.

The old Chinese man took the money and handed over the rickshaw's poles, offering rudimentary instructions on how the contraption worked. After helping the lady into the seat, he took off running. The coolie undoubtedly believed the insane American would change his mind.

"Whatever are we going to do with a rickshaw, Captain?" she asked her husband, who was now pulling her and walking backward, smiling in victory about his fine souvenir.

"Whatever in the world did you say to the honorable Chinaman at dinner?" he responded.

"*Say* to him? Why, I told him I was a lazy American who adored my gallant husband." She threw him a kiss.

She had never been happier. They had been stationed at Fort Benning, Georgia, and Fort Sam Houston, Texas, before this, two fine posts. Duncan, she knew, had been fortunate, unlike so many young officers stuck in dusty desert posts like Fort Huachuca in Arizona or Fort Robinson, a remote cavalry outpost where they froze in the bitter Nebraska winter. Or they could be stuck in some miserable jungle station like Panama, where military doctors were already having trouble with marijuana and bhang among the soldiers, not that her husband didn't have the same problem here with his troops. After all, their military duties in the garrison ended pretty much by noon, and after that, these hyped-up, testosterone-fueled American boys were on their own, thirteen thousand miles away from home.

She knew it was a fine thing that the United States Army had a man like Edward Randol Duncan. He was low-key, yes, but also dashing, confident, smart, and funny—just the right traits to take him places. He had leadership qualities the brass liked to think they saw in themselves, and the men found him humble and down-to-earth, a charismatic commander who could make a man want to row him upstream on the River Styx if that's what he asked. His rearing served him well, descended as he was from Southern farmers who wore pride like armor and grew cotton while battling droughts and bolls. And their marriage served him well, too. Patience, fortitude, and love kept them together.

The next evening, he told PeeCee about his visit that day with General Joseph W. Stilwell. Captain Duncan had been summoned to the barracks, where Vinegar Joe was visiting from Peiping. A ceiling fan with woven blades as big around as the rickshaw's wheels circled overhead like the buzzards he and Pee-Cee used to see in the vast Texas sky at their last post. The captain could hear the horses on the parade ground outside in the cool morning, massing for review. He could almost smell the hide and tack, the only smell that could mask Tientsin's overwhelming stench of raw, open sewage.

"Yes, sir?" Duncan asked.

"At ease, Ed. Have a seat."

He would be on his mount in a few moments, a much preferred place to this.

The captain remained standing. "Everything all right, sir?" He figured it was. A handful of men had been assigned to observe Communist guerrillas in the Northern provinces, but they were Intelligence officers. Duncan wouldn't protest if that's where the bespectacled GI general needed him to be. "Not to speak out of turn, General, but aren't you serving as military attaché at the moment?"

"I'm a soldier first in this goddamned seventeenth army of the world, then a paper-pusher, and it's men like you, Ed, that turn my wheels." He chewed on his pipe and smiled. "Actually, it's families like yours that make ours the greatest country on Earth. You realize that, don't you, Cap'n Duncan?"

The infantryman knew of the general's salty tongue, but he'd never heard it himself. "So . . . just to be sure . . . things are copacetic?" Duncan asked. "And, General, with all due respect, we haven't had a chance to, excuse me, start a family . . . quite yet."

"Copacetic? Damn right they are!" Uncle Joe laughed. He snapped a piece of onionskin paper across his littered desk toward the startled officer. "Read this."

November 11, 1935
General:

It has come to my attention that the wife of one of our officers, Capt. Edward R. Duncan, by the name of Pearl Clementine Duncan, acquitted herself with uncanny charm at last night's dance at the British Club. It's my opinion you should meet them both, as they are splendid company. As you already know, Capt. Duncan is of the highest caliber, a fine officer with substantial leadership potential.

Regards,
Col. Taylor Osgood, Commanding

Captain Duncan didn't know whether to be proud or embarrassed. His wife's fraternization with the Chinese could, in fact, be troubling. American officers rarely spent time with the Chinese, except those who were their servants.

"General Stilwell, sir, if my wife was unduly forward . . . ."

Stilwell waved away Duncan's distress and handed him Colonel Osgood's memo. "Keep it, Ed. I've got a carbon for your file.

I know I shouldn't be giving stuff like that away, but I thought you'd get a kick out of it. Besides, this wife of yours: sounds like you've met your match, Cap'n. Maybe one day she'll run this spit-and-polish garrison, eh?"

"She's already learning a little Mandarin, sir, and if she were to run the Fifteenth the way she runs our household staff—"

"Well, there you go, Ed. We'll see you both at the country club tonight. Nine o'clock. Looking forward to it." Stilwell winked at him. "Say, Cap'n, you ever been to Jawbone Charlie's?"

"In Chin-wang-tao?" The notorious neighborhood eighty miles north was the troops' paradise. Duncan had warned his doughs that they'd have hell to pay if they didn't get to the infirmary after every visit there. "My wife and her new friends are very much looking forward to what we hear of the beach and leisure at Camp Burrowes during the men's summer target practice, but, Chin-wang-tao proper? No, sir."

"I'd hardly call it 'proper.'" The general laughed, picking up on the captain's impregnable morality.

"Anything else, sir?"

"No, Ed, just get your ass down in that saddle. I hear that's where you do your best soldiering."

Duncan clicked his riding-boot heels, suppressed a smile of enormous pride, and produced a snappy salute.

"Dismissed."

"Thank you, sir. Good day."

"Cool story."

Such is my son's assessment of his great-grandfather's legacy of service, honor, intellect, romance, and history-making vitality. Colonel Duncan would be proud.

"They were cool people."

"Dad?" Eddie asks over his shoulder as he slinks toward the door, finally on his way to school.

"Eddie?"

"Do you think some of that stuff, like the note that General Stilwell actually held in his hands, or a book from one of those Chinese guys, or even Grandfather's tux, might be up in the Plunder Room?"

I say a silent prayer of gratitude. Maybe I'd gotten through after all. "Yeah, I think so, maybe. We just have to figure out a way to get me up there."

"Me and Tyler could . . ."

"We can talk about it later, okay?"

"Thanks, Dad. I'll see you after school."

I'm out cold before he closes the door.

CHAPTER TWELVE

THE MORNING I sleep through has unfurled into another spectacular day. The dew is gone, and the air retains the South's spring perfume, honeyed with rose blossoms that Grandfather planted on each side of the house for PeeCee.

I wouldn't mind another breakfast on the porch, despite the hour and the rising heat, but Hotel Volusia has probably stopped serving. Eddie is at school and, with any luck, wearing appropriate attire, intent on getting to that concert come hell or high decibels, Marnie Jennings notwithstanding.

The only blemish on the start of my day is Jerod's black SUV, which is blocking my route from the driveway to the ramp to the house. So I have to maneuver around his car, which means going up the entire length of the driveway to the sidewalk, where Buncombe Boulevard has no traffic, as usual, and back down the other side of the driveway's U, to get to the ramp. By the time I ascend the porch, I'm swimming in sweat. I suppose I could have called Jerod on my cell phone and asked him to move his car, but I don't feel like asking him for anything. Besides, a little exercise doesn't hurt.

Making my way across the porch, I hear Volusia and Jerod arguing in the back of the house. I wonder if Jerod might have already tasted some soap this morning.

They're toe-to-toe in the hallway when the front door's rattle announces my entrance.

"Mister Jerod, if you ever gave a thought to anyone other than yourself—your father, lying half dead in the hospital, for instance—you wouldn't be flying here and there"—flying the way Volusia's arms are flying every which way—"and doing whatever the *hell* it is you do."

They stop and look at me.

"Afternoon, Mister Randol. 'Bout time you get out of bed; day's almost over." I'm not about to argue with Volusia that I'd been up all night tending to my half-dead father. "I'll see if I can find you something to eat. This ain't no Burger King—you can't have it your way. But at least the coffee's always hot."

"I'm sure Jerod will join me on the porch for a cup."

"Fine. Maybe get some things straightened out round here. Just my opinion."

"One thing she's never had a shortage of," Jerod mumbles.

She wheels around when she hears him. The two of them just can't stay out of each other's way. They're like a pair of fighting cocks, razors attached to their talons, and when you throw those roosters together in the pen and either one of them struts or crows in the other's direction, dust is bound to fly.

"Let me tell you something, mister," Volusia swipes at Jerod, "your grandfather was a heroic man, and you better start understanding that right now. One of the things I learned from him was that every commanding officer had a staff: S-Ones and

G-Threes and whatnot. Your grandfather had people all round him, people he *trusted*."

Jerod's hands fall from his hips. He looks as confused and helpless as I feel.

"I don't know what you're up to, Mister Jerod, but this is a small town. People talk. You may think I'm just some simple nigger living over in Black Town. But that's just 'cause you're not payin' attention. I *am* paying attention, and I don't see you taking responsibility for *nothin'*."

The voltage in the air leaves us both shaken. She turns on me next. "Same goes for you, Mister Randol." She takes a step back, her white shoes squealing once against the wood floor. "Your grandparents used to call me the adjutant in this house. Know what an adjutant is? He—she, in my case—helps the commander with administration. That was me and still is—at least, until you fire me. Your grandmother and me, we kept this house in order."

She begins winding down.

"Know why your grandparents got so much respect in this town? Not because they traveled all over the world and owned this big house, but because of what I just said: They kept their house in order."

She crosses her arms.

"This house has always been in order. All I'm saying is, Mister Jerod, Mister Randol, you damn well better keep it that way."

She turns toward the kitchen. To the pantry, but really to us, she says, "Your food will be out in three minutes."

Stunned, Jerod and I move to the porch.

Outside, the air feels expansive, compared with all the air that just got sucked out inside.

Jerod takes a rocking chair, but doesn't move.

"How was your flight?" I ask, just above a whisper.

"Nothing to it."

We sit in silence for a few minutes until breakfast arrives, and Volusia, wordless, returns to her soap operas and ironing.

"Have you gone to visit Jupe yet?" I ask Jerod.

"'Dipshit'?" He chuckles through a bite of fried eggs.

I laugh, too. Our laughter shatters the stress of the Volusian eruption.

He shakes his head. "Not yet. But I will today." He smacks his lips over his coffee. "I don't know how she does it."

"Mean bean." I laugh again, trying to keep things simple between the two of us, though I know they're not and probably can't be until I figure out what's going on. "It sounded to me like Volusia was hinting at something. That folks around town are 'talking.'"

"Who cares, Randol? And who knows?"

"I guess that's my point. I'm beginning to get a little tired of not knowing."

He drops his head into his breakfast and mops up. If eating were an Olympic sport, the man would be a gold medalist.

Finally, I can't help myself. "I went to the Jupe Box last night after going to see the old man."

He studies me. I can't read his eyes. The gray-blue colors shift, searching for a response.

I prompt him, trying to get my own brother to trust me. "You came back home in February, asking for my help."

"You *did* help; you got Annie a job. If I remember, that was all I asked for."

"School year's about over, isn't it? How'd she do at New Cumbria?"

• 209 •

"Great. They love her, of course. Everybody does."

A silence grows between us, as if we've run out of easy, permissible topics, but if the pause grows any longer, the seasons may change.

"So," Jerod says finally, "how was the Jupe Box?"

"Five-star. First-class. I met my next wife there, CEO of a Fortune Five Hundred company relaxing for cocktails after a two-billion-dollar merger." I hand Jerod my breakfast tray, and he stacks the dishes on the porch next to his chair. "If the place were any more seedy, it would be the world's largest sesame bagel."

The clatter of his breakfast tray rattling onto the porch startles me, but I'm jangled more when he says: "You know what your problem is? You're elitist, aristocratic, arrogant, and spoiled, a total slacker who believes the world owes you a living."

Where did *that* come from? "Doesn't it, Jerod? And don't you believe the same thing? Didn't Jupe teach you that? Didn't Jupe teach you that you can con the world, beat the system, bend the rules, charm people, make anybody do anything you want to get anything you want?"

He wipes his mouth, as if to take back his outburst. "We're a pair, I guess, aren't we?" Then: "So you met Gunny."

"Oh, yeah. If Gunny had both legs blown off in one of our ridiculous wars, he could *still* kick my ass, just by looking at me."

"I 'spose you could call him *Jupe's* adjutant." Jerod says, and I laugh. "Gunny's been working for Dad a long time. He trusts him with everything: his business, his life, even. So I guess I have to trust Gunny, too, is what I'm saying." My palms start to sweat. I can feel something coming. "Gunny told me this morning that he found a couple of things missing from the office."

I swallow hard. I guess he's been working up to asking me about this all morning. Now, believe me, I can usually tell a good story, but straight-out lying is a different kettle of fish. "Dad looked bad last night, really bad," I tell him, "so I just dropped by the bar to pick up a couple of things. I was only there for a few minutes." Jerod's knuckles tighten around the rocking chair. "Maybe we could talk about Dad, helping him out with his stuff, y'know, together."

Silent but angry, wrestling with some unnameable impasse, Jerod glares at me as if he wants to make some sort of threat. Instead, he picks the breakfast trays up off the porch and takes them inside, leaving me alone.

I swear, the weather that is Jerod Duncan can change in a matter of seconds—pleasant disposition one instant, stormy the next. I'm glad he's gone, giving me a little time to think, to decide my next move, to invent some kind of plan. It's a good thing Hurricane Jerod changed course for the moment.

Breathing a blessed sigh of relief, I pull out my cell phone and press my son's speed dial number. Eddie had better not answer; his phone is supposed to be in his locker during school.

Steely Black Steeple's music plays in the background of his message: "If you don't know what to do by now, you're a moron." *Beep.*

"Hey. Listen, I need you to do me a huge favor, not that you owe this particular moron a favor, but think of this particular favor as espionage." *That* should hook him. "The minute you get home, go to my desk, and in the bottom left-hand drawer you'll find a three-ring binder and a computer jump drive. As fast as your geeky little fingers can move, scan all the pages from the binder into my laptop and copy everything from the jump drive onto my laptop, too, then burn all those files onto a compact disc or two. And hurry. *Please!*"

I hear Jerod's Cole Haans snapping toward the door, so I have just enough time to make another phone call, this one to beg a favor from Magnolia Living Center, the nursing home three blocks south on Buncombe Boulevard. Allowing myself a shudder of much-delayed excitement after months of procrastination—not to mention obsessing about Eddie, Annie Harkin, and Jerod—I may get out of this mess with a lot more than just a way to placate my brother.

Jerod returns to the porch.

He is still grim. "I want Dad's stuff back, Randol. Or if you prefer, I could go down to your little bungalow and rip the place apart. You certainly couldn't stop me."

"Volusia would."

Jerod forces a smile—charm fits his purpose better than meanness.

"Listen," I say, "what could be so important? We're talking about a few things from his office—"

"What did you take, exactly, Randol? Gunny mentioned a binder and some computer gear?"

"Right, a single little three-ring binder that probably doesn't contain anything, other than a few meaningless numbers that Jupe made up—"

"Then why don't you just hand it over?"

"Why do you care?" Jerod looks pale. "Okay, then, what *is* in the binder, and what makes *you* the sole heir to its control?"

"You have no idea what you're getting yourself into." He starts pacing.

"Before you start getting all Mafiosa-with-a-Drawl on me, I've got plans for the afternoon that don't involve arguing with you."

His mouth tightens, his pacing slows, he rubs his chin. He's at a loss. He rocks back and forth on his heels and looks at me with enough derision to slice any other man in half, apparently weighing whether he should strangle me or wait me out. He doesn't realize I've got more time than he does—at least fifteen years, anyway.

"Plans?" he says, finally. "What plans, exactly? High tea? Hot date?"

Ridicule me all you want, Jerod, but you're playing into my plans now, I thought. "Actually neither." I nod toward the driveway. "I had more of a treasure hunt in mind."

He already believes I'm nuts, probably having written most of that off to my paraplegia. Now, though, he looks at me as if I'm certifiable.

"When Grandfather died," I begin before he can say anything, "he left me the contents of the Plunder Room. Yes, the Plunder Room—you heard me correctly. And ever since he died and our dear father peed on his trees, I've been trying to figure out how to get up there. But, you see, I've been a little busy, what with rescuing damsels in distress . . ."

Jerod rolls his eyes.

"And rescuing my son from the sins of sloth, angst, bad music, and sartorial devastation."

Jerod sits down and resumes his rocking, but I also know that if I don't speed things up, he will lose his patience again before my help arrives.

"So, anyway, here's the deal. I couldn't have known Dipshit would pick yesterday to keel over half dead and that I would"—I clear my throat in mock drama—"have to rush to his bedside, then commit high intrigue of a familial nature to rescue a few odds and ends from his sorry-ass little dive bar."

Jerod's face turns hot-sauce red. He is through indulging me, and it's way past the time my cavalry was supposed to gallop up the driveway from Buncombe Boulevard and provide the distraction I need.

"The point is, Eddie was never going to get me to the Plunder Room, I wasn't going to levitate on my own, and when I asked Volusia for help hauling me up the staircase, she acted like I was asking her to cross the River Styx for a day trip to hell. Far as she's concerned, the Plunder Room's haunted."

"No shit, it's haunted." He smiles, but only a little. "We always said that room was eerie."

"So," I lied, "I asked Volusia if she could round me up a couple strong fellas . . ."

A current of electric joy shoots through me when I hear the sound of tires on the driveway.

But I look up to see an older-model, sky-blue Volvo pull into the driveway, not the nursing-home van I'd been expecting.

I'm even more surprised to hear Toby Lawson's high, thin voice calling to us on the porch.

With his pie-shaped face, tonsured hair of a fifteenth-century friar, and wire-rimmed glasses, Toby Lawson looks more like a Muppet than a guy about to drill a hole in your skull.

"Hey, Doc." I beckon him up the concrete stairs. "What brings you here?"

Toby looks pale and doughy as a matzo ball. Clearly alarmed. "Have you seen Tyler?"

"He didn't spend the night here, if that's what you mean." I crane my head over my shoulder to see Jerod lurking behind me. "Sorry. Toby, this is my brother, Jerod."

Jerod reaches for Toby's hand, and yet his charm seems to unravel in the face of Toby's anxiety.

"Tyler hasn't been home all night," Toby says.

"That doesn't make any sense, Toby, not for a kid like Tyler." If I could sound any more banal, I'd audition for reality television; I have no fear that Tyler is *somewhere*, somewhere safe, probably with Eddie.

I try calling Eddie on my phone. As expected, he doesn't answer. I don't leave a message.

Dr. Lawson coughs into his fist, then wipes his hand over his sweat-stippled forehead. It's hard to believe this is the man who once served as cantor at Manhattan's glamorous Central Synagogue. I can't imagine the pressure in a place so big, so powerful. Never mind the daily stress of his practice. Still, I admire his faith—he and his wife, Rachel, along with Tyler and their daughters, Sylvia and Lauren, have to drive clear to Wrenton to Temple Beth Am, the closest synagogue, nearly two hours away.

Jerod ushers Toby into the house, then into the China Room, where I wave him to the red-silk davenport.

"Randol," he says, "do you mind if I have a word with you? In private, please?"

Jerod bows out of the room, but I can see him standing just outside of Toby's sight. I hear him tapping on his cell-phone keypad, then the slap of the phone closing. From the corner of my eye, just behind me, I notice Jerod eavesdropping—or perhaps keeping an eye on me.

"When did Tyler go missing?" I ask.

"Well, he came home from school with his sisters, just like he always does, then he went out. We haven't seen him since. Rachel and I turned in early and just assumed that he came in after we went to sleep. But he didn't—his bed wasn't slept in."

"That's *fercockt*. I think we may have a problem." I see Jerod dart to the porch.

Toby drops his head into his hands, and I fear he's about to cry.

"Take a deep breath, Doc. Let me get you some water, something to drink, some coffee."

His smile is too thin to count as a response. He shakes his

head, takes off his glasses, pinches his nose, squeezes his eyes, and replaces his spectacles. In a near whisper, having understood my Yiddish for "all fucked up" and jumping ahead to the contingent crisis, he asks, "What can you tell me about Annie Harkin?"

The question comes like a blow that knocks me speechless.

In the next instant, my brain scrambles for a response.

He must know that Annie is Jerod's consort; everyone in New Cumbria knows that by now. And he must know I was instrumental in getting her the job at the high school. Could he even know about Superintendent Mabry Hollander's call the other day, voicing concerns about Annie's "fraternization" with the kids?

Jerod's cell phone rings out on the porch. He strides back into the China Room, and he's wearing a smile big enough to banish our panic.

"That was Annie. She says Tyler's at school, safe and sound."

Dr. Lawson rises in genteel stoicism. His smile is somewhere between slim and grim. "That's it? No other explanation?"

"She was in the middle of class, Dr. Lawson, I'm sorry."

I don't want to be the middleman, but I glance between Toby and Jerod, finally landing on the former. "I suppose you could, well—" I stop, realizing I have no advice worth giving to a man whose IQ makes mine look like a golf score. "I guess it's mazel tov then, huh, Toby?"

He nods with a hopeful smile, thanks us for our indulgence and concern, moves toward the door and back across the porch, and then hightails it to his Volvo and peels out of the driveway.

Jerod looks at the door as if he's planning a similar escape, all of Jupe's precious articles apparently forgotten.

"Uh-uh, mister," I tell him. "You're not going anywhere."

"What?"

"What was that all about?"

"What?"

"Sit. Down."

"What?"

Jerod skulks back into the China Room and settles into the davenport, reclining as he did in February, feigning ease.

I gaze at him. "Please don't tell me that Annie had anything to do with Tyler Lawson being out all night."

"I wouldn't have the foggiest idea."

"Was she home last night?" My heart thumps, anxious for an answer I don't want to hear.

"At Jessamine Plantation Inn?"

"No, moron, at Tara. What*ever*. Just, for once, give me a straight answer. For crying out freakin' loud."

"Now who's the moron?" he shouts. "You know damned well I was at the airport last night."

I rearrange my face with my hand. "Okay. All right." He's right. I can't believe last night was . . . just last night. "That's true. But all this crap is getting to be"—I look up at the ceiling—"crap."

"Huh?"

"Enough. All of it. The mystery girlfriend. The mystery job. The mystery Jerod." I wish I could pace. I miss pacing. "The mystery dad." I throw my hand up to stop him from speaking, from defending Edward Jupiter Duncan. "I would bet anything that you could tie all these mysteries up into one nifty package."

He smiles. Infuriating.

"Quit being so goddamn smug, because if the other shoe does drop, and the other shoe always does, the one thing you're going to lose is your soul."

"That's funny, Randol. I wish I had your wit." He stands as if to make his exit once and for all.

"But it isn't remotely funny, and you're not leaving. We're not even close to done yet."

He sighs and sits back down, though his posture signals anything but defeat.

I pull the small skeleton key from my shirt pocket and wave it at Jerod. "In just a few minutes, maybe less, I'm expecting a van from Magnolia Living Center to show up with a pair of strong fellas who are going to haul my ass up to the Plunder Room—don't look so inconvenienced."

He looks annoyed, but I'm having none of it.

"Damn, Jerod, it's just like Volusia said. You really *don't* care about me, this house, whatever the hell is upstairs in that room. But I swear on our grandfather's grave, Jerod Barrows Duncan, that I will not allow you and your sorry-ass father, let alone your girlfriend, whoever the hell she is, drag this family's honor through whatever dirt y'all have been conspiring to pile up."

He finally slumps, the shell of his dignity broken.

"You've got until the men get here." I glance toward the door again. "And you're going to tell me about Annie."

He begins his story in a voice that's low and serious, uncharacteristic for him. He starts to tell me about the places he'd been and seen and some things Jupe had told him, tales of exotica and iniquity. His tone alone tells me what I had already guessed—that Jerod's travels abroad are more than "business trips" and that Jupe runs more than a simple garden-variety enterprise that includes a tavern, a trailer park, and God knows what else.

Annie came into Jerod's life about a year ago, by way of Hong Kong.

Jerod was living in a West Village town house that was far more expensive than his holy-aromatherapy enterprise could afford him, given its shaky financial standing. But he wasn't spending much time in Manhattan, anyway, thanks to women and trips, many of them overseas. About the time Jupe started calling him to move back to Wrenton, Jerod also got a call from Barry Stemple, a former classmate from NYU. Stemple, a hotshot commodities trader at Chicago's Mercantile Exchange, was on the verge of being busted for securities fraud. He proposed a trip to Vietnam.

"Why?" Jerod asked.

"Because it's there, dumb-ass. The country's overrun with trade opportunities: coffee, shrimp, maybe oil. We could also take a little side trip to Bangkok, a paradise packed with golf, women."

The exotic lure of Thailand persuaded Jerod to make the trip, just as it had lured Jupe. My father was always full of stories, most of them too outlandish to be believed, about his fellow GIs, who took their R&R in Thailand's free-for-all sex-and-beaches playground, gorging themselves on the smorgasbord of beautiful Thai girls. And squeezed between what is now a 7-Eleven store and the seamy Embassy Motel on Pradiphat Road, just north-west of downtown Bangkok, Jupe began all those years ago to funnel untold sums of cash, from untold sources, into a financial institution he helped found: the Pradiphat Trust Bank.

Jerod and Stemple wouldn't be flying straight into Vietnam or even to Bangkok.

"Deal is," Stemple told him, "we're flying through Hong Kong. It's easier to snap up visas there."

Before two weeks were out, they were aboard a 747 flying past towering tenements stitched alongside Hong Kong's old air-port runways.

Turned out neither Stemple nor Jerod had much cash to spare for a luxury stay.

So, in Kowloon, after sixteen hours in a humming silver tube, Stemple found a twelve-story hostel that was part brothel, part roach motel, part tourist trap, and part campground for every Euro-snail with a backpack. Each suite of rooms in the gray-mottled concrete tower was owned by a different proprietor— leather-faced men in filthy clothes chewing betel, tobacco, and opium and advertising their rooms with handbills in the sweat-rank humidity outside. All offered "best rooms, best price, best view." Some offered private rooms. Some offered rack rooms. Some offered rooms with private bathrooms. Some offered rooms with girls.

My brother and his friend paid a premium for a tenth-floor, private, two-bedroom suite. After tossing their bags, Stemple dragged Jerod into the night.

Tsim Sha Tsui, the southernmost part of Kowloon, was old Forty-second Street New York magnified a thousand times—more porn shops, more crack houses, more shooting galleries, and more people, even at two o'clock in the morning. An olfactory jungle of incense, cigarettes, hashish, sweat, barbecuing meat, and laundry. Rudyard Kipling was right: You knew a country by its smell.

In a stupor, Jerod and Stemple wobbled into a pallid court-yard ghetto with decaying balconies and helter-skelter lines of multihued laundry draped like navy signal flags on lines and railings. Chinese lanterns dangled from electric cables. Sliding-glass doors and windows were open, men and women hanging out of them, chattering in gurgling Mandarin.

The young men sat at a table in the courtyard under the tow-ering outline of a neon Vargas girl in purple, red, green, and white lights. She was smoking a luminous cigarette with electric-blue smoke. Their first Tsingtao beer was cold, then it was gone. Cheap whiskey was next, warm and gone. Another beer went just as fast.

Then Stemple pulled Jerod into the doorway between the neon sign's two-story legs.

Real girls in loin cloths slithered through a dark labyrinth of leather sofas, cold tile floors, and amber mood lights. They had black hair. Glazed breasts. Almond eyes. Ruby lips. Without a word, one of them handed Jerod a towel and flip-flops.

He showered, then wandered back into the darkened lobby, where Stemple stood in a towel, too. They looked at each other, the happiest idiots on Earth, and Jerod understood how Jupe came to love the hedonism of his Asian experience, how his father wanted to draw him into this world.

Two girls of indeterminate age, one of them pretty and one not, pulled them by the wrists into another room with four massage tables. The less attractive of the two girls eased Jerod onto his abdomen and proceeded to rub him down with oil.

Her hands were at turns butterflies and vise grips. They fluttered and attacked, tippled and bore deep into muscles he didn't know he had. In an hour, Stemple and Jerod were out the door, returned to the fetid humidity and squalor.

Back in their half-star resort, Jerod could have been pronounced clinically dead the moment he hit the pillow.

The next morning, he awoke to a dazzling view of Hong Kong Island. Sampans, junks, and modern two- and three-masted fishing vessels bobbed in the white-cresting waters. Hong Kong looked Oz-like, a glistening jewel, the place where the buck really did stop, the repository of all the world's money. He was intoxicated anew, ready to plunder everything this place had to offer.

Stemple was gone. At least he had left a note:

Went back for more last night and scored a hummer, so I'm out hunting again! No, for real, I'm out running our passports and payola over to the Vietnamese Consulate. Meet me for dim sum at the Jade Palace.

Jerod swallowed a few aspirin, drank a bottle of water that Stemple had left, got dressed, and went downstairs to dive into Kowloon. Pushing aside the aromatic old men chewing their betel and thrusting handbills for their rooms upstairs, Jerod made his way into the pandemonium. The flood of human traffic made Manhattan seem like a smaller town by comparison, and he fell in love all over again. He felt the thrill of potential as he threw himself into the rush of smells from the people, the culinary oddities blowing from storefronts, and the traffic and stinging smog and brine from the nearby channel. He drank in the hustle, the colors and cacophony of unreadable signs and unknowable people.

After an epic lunch at the Jade Palace—dumplings, squid, multiple varieties of noodles, dim sum, spring rolls—Jerod and Stemple rode the Star Ferry to Hong Kong's main island. Jerod moved to the bow, where, like a dog that sticks his snout out the car window, he breathed in everything he could.

A Caucasian woman stood next to him at the front of the boat. She seemed to mimic Jerod's every move, to watch what he was doing and do what he was doing, to enjoy what he was enjoying.

She wore Italian linens, off-white, that billowed in the wind. He could just about see her legs through the fine fabric. Her emerald, green, and burgundy scarf fluttered around the loveliest face Jerod had ever seen. Her cascading sandy-blond hair framed azure blue eyes and brilliant white teeth, and her body . . . she had a figure only Michelangelo could have carved.

"Man, is she hot or what," Stemple panted into Jerod's ear. "Ten bucks says I get her phone number in ten minutes."

"That's only a dollar a minute, Stumpy." Jerod pounded the railing and laughed hard enough at his own joke to catch the woman's attention. He turned and faced Stemple instead. "What in the world makes you think a hot, rich babe like her would even make *eye contact* with a runt like you?"

"Because I am a world-class stud."

"You're a world-class idiot." Jerod turned back to face the approaching island, where the ferry would land in minutes. Then he leaned toward the woman and nodded toward Stemple. "Excuse me, but if this chump's annoying you, I'd be happy to beat the shit out of him."

She smiled and told him her name. "Annie Harkin."

"What brings you to Hong Kong?" he asked.

"A dream." She smiled. "I plan on doing whatever I need to do to be wealthy enough to live here forever."

The ferry bumped to a landing. After introducing his old friend to his newest friend, Jerod communicated through nods, grunts, and a discreet kick in the shin that Stemple's company was no longer necessary.

Jerod never did make it to Vietnam or Thailand.

He did return to Kowloon, but this time he stayed in a luxurious hotel. The seven-thousand-square-foot suite had five bedrooms with a jaw-dropping view of the main island. The largest room had a TV as big as a windshield, its own swimming pool, and more state-of-the-art gadgets than anyone could ever learn to use.

He stayed three days with Annie, never bothering to find out what she really *was* doing in Hong Kong. He never once wondered how a woman no older than twenty-six could afford a hotel bill that rang up to $18,356.46. And that was after a substantial discount.

"My God, Jerod, didn't you see enough red flags around Annie Harkin to make you think you were in a Chinese Army parade?"

He laughs and shakes his head. "Are you kidding? That whole thing? I felt like I was Bond. James Bond. Complete with the ultimate Bond girl."

The penis is a magnificent brain: The one we have in our skulls weighs a scant three pounds, but the one we have in our pants can add a hundred or so pounds in less than thirty seconds.

Before I can grill my brother further about Jupe and Bangkok, Annie and Hong Kong, with the questions filling my brain like air filling a balloon about to burst, I finally hear wheels crush the gravel driveway.

The men from Magnolia Living Center have finally arrived.

I move toward the bottom of the grand staircase.

When the two orderlies walk into the house wearing their starched white uniforms, I feel a bit like Randle Patrick McMurphy from *One Flew Over the Cuckoo's Nest*. Maybe, after everything I just heard from Jerod, they *should* take me away, get me a little electroshock therapy. Couldn't leave my brain any more scrambled than it already is.

Jerod looks at me as if he just had a little jolt himself. "What's with these guys?"

They introduce themselves as Gerald and Tremaine. They apologize for being late, but I cut them off before they can divulge that I'd called hours, rather than days, before.

"It's not like I can fly up the stairs," I tell my brother. "Otherwise I would have done that months ago." I nod toward the two silent hulks, then toward the grand staircase. "These fellas are friends of Volusia's son, and they can bench-press—well, me and my chair. So take a deep breath and pray they don't drop me."

Nineteen stairs with a landing in the middle makes for a climb of about thirteen vertical feet. Pulling a 187-pound man in a 29-pound chair—216 pounds of dead weight—is not exactly elegant.

Amid the racket, Volusia pops out of the kitchen and looks up at the landing, where we're parked so Gerald and Tremaine can reorient my chair. She looks terrified, horrified, and, at the very least, annoyed.

"Hello, Miss Volusia," Gerald says. Neither man has even broken so much as a sweat.

"Well, hello there, Gerald. Make sure that man you're carrying gives you a nice, fat tip for your services."

"Jerod's got that covered," I call to Volusia. "Isn't that right, big guy?" I ask my brother, who remains two steps below Tremaine, who is bringing up my feet.

"If you drop him, Tremaine, please don't bust up the banisters."

"No problem, Miss V." His laugh is good-natured.

"Tremaine, Gerald, when you finish taking them upstairs, come on in the kitchen for some lunch. You can just leave 'im upstairs, we'll figure out a way to get 'im back down. And Mr. Randol, Mr. Jerod, I don't want to hear no screamin'—about no dead bodies, no ghosts, none of that."

"Why don't we fire her, Randol?"

"I heard that, Mister Jerod." Volusia's voice fades into the pantry. "You go right on ahead and fire me. Then see how your brother likes to make his own meals and maybe *you* can come do his laundry . . ."

Gerald and Tremaine chuckle their way up the rest of the staircase.

CHAPTER THIRTEEN

JEROD PAYS the two orderlies for hoisting me upstairs, and the men thump back down to the kitchen, whence smells of greens and fatback begin rising toward the Plunder Room.

My brother and I are left alone with the stale air and antiques. The only ghosts in evidence appear to be disguised as dust bunnies.

An Oriental rug that would cost as much as a new luxury car fills most of the floor separating the upstairs bedrooms. Purple lilacs and pink cherry blossoms swirl over the rug's sky-blue background. The colors likely are as rich today as they were when my grandmother bought the masterpiece in some Tientsin or Beijing market. Too bad it sits up here, but it's simply too big to fit in the China Room. A petit-point davenport sits over the far tassels, and in front of that is a coffee table with two drawers.

The air lolls thick and close, like in a musty old library. The doors to the four bedrooms are shut tight, as are their windows. That can't be healthy for the antiques: the four-poster beds and the chests, armoires, and sideboards that Grandmother and Grandfather collected from post to post during his thirty years of service to the American people.

Jerod flips the switch to the gigantic attic fan, which heaves into action like a World War I propeller plane. Next comes the mesmeric roar we slept to as boys.

Grinning as he skips from bedroom to bedroom, Jerod says, "Time to open this haunted house." It's good to see him lighten up, but the murky stories he has just told still trouble me.

A coat of dust aside, the rooms are tidy, as if ready for a quarters inspection. The beds are made, the chenille covers pulled tight. The sheers over the windows are yellowed. A dust bunny skitters down the hall, now that the air is stirring.

I roll over to the coffee table on the Oriental rug. Months ago I remembered that the table had two small, lockable drawers, so it only made sense to me that Grandfather's small key would fit them. I pull out the tiny key I've been carrying around and wiggle it into the left-hand drawer and it opens. It's empty. The right-hand drawer is next. Inside is a skeleton key as long as my index finger.

I roll to the Plunder Room door. The hole that we used to look through when we were kids takes the skeleton key just like it's supposed to.

Jittery, I glance at Jerod, who offers a sly smile.

"Well," I say, "here goes everything."

The lock gives with an easy *th'plunk*.

The door swings open, as if a ghostly docent has been waiting all these years to welcome us.

For a moment, Jerod and I don't move. My heart thuds like

the muffled artillery that rocked my grandfather to sleep for nearly two years.

"You first," I tell my brother, looking at him as if I'm ten years old again, which would make him three—and much braver.

He walks into the room, which is as big as a two-car garage. The air is as old and heavy as its contents. The rose-print wallpaper has faded to ochre. A brown mold stain the shape of Brazil has grown from the left-hand corner of the ceiling. Under the spot where Rio de Janeiro would be sits a faded U.S. Army field cot, along with a small pile of khaki and olive-drab clothing, likely Grandfather's uniforms. History's perfume—worn cotton and wool, gun grease and linseed oil, equestrian leather, Brasso and ink—swills around my head like a shot of officer's hooch.

Near the center of the room, three military footlockers sit like coffins. Two are olive drab, one's painted black. They're made of wood, reinforced with rivets, the metal rusting. One trunk still has its leather straps; the black footlocker has wooden handles. Grandfather's name is stenciled on each; the black one reads "Capt.," the other two "Col." The shipment tags, all torn and yellowed, hang pasted and taped to the sides.

Padlocks secure all three.

"Son. Of. A. Bitch." Jerod collapses on the cot. "First, he keeps a key to the room in a drawer with a key, then he has all the trunks bolted. It's like Fort freakin' Knox up here."

He starts fingering the pile of uniforms, his interest growing.

I've rolled over to the trunks to see if I can figure out how to get the locks open.

Next thing I know, Jerod's standing over me and looking like a younger version of my grandfather. He's wearing Grandfather's officer's pinks: an army uniform of light elastique wool riding breeches and a long-sleeved wool blouse with epaulets in a light reddish hue. The clothes are ironed to a razor crease as if Grand-father were about to head to the parade field.

"These things feel good." He grins, still wearing his black socks and looking ludicrous. "Makes you feel kind of like a god."

"They *were* in those days. They didn't call it the Grand Old Army for nothing."

Jerod finds Grandfather's riding crop under some more clothes: another pair of breeches, some jodhpurs, a full-dress uniform, khakis, and an olive officer's tunic, all stripped of Grandfather's ribbons and medals. At the end of the cot are two pairs of old-fashioned leggings, or puttees, that the GIs used to wear around their combat boots, one pair leather, another canvas. A large blood stain smears the cloth puttees, and I wonder if that's where the word *am putee* comes from; a phantom tingle runs up my legs. I'd never heard that Grandfather had sustained a combat injury.

Jerod slaps his thigh with the leather swagger stick, then snaps it under his armpit. *"Ten-hut!"* He struts around the room, playing soldier.

I bristle, as if he's trivializing our grandfather. He probably isn't, but I snap at him just the same, "Give me that!"

"It's not your turn to play with it." He smiles, but hands me the crop.

I thread the rippled leather dowel through the lock and use it as leverage to lift the trunk, raising the opposite side of it about six inches off the floor.

"Geez, Randol, you're as strong as you smell."

"And you're as funny as you look."

Jerod falls to his knees and looks under the locker. "Hold on a sec; I think I see something." He feels around the base until I start to wobble with it, threatening to drop it on his hand, which he snatches away. "Try lifting it again."

I put more weight behind my crop-leverage, this time pulling the trunk up over my numb feet and onto my shins. After all, I don't feel anything but pressure, and while the trunk *is* heavy, I can hold it this way indefinitely.

Jerod examines the bottom of the footlocker. "Well, I'll be damned."

"I've been telling you that for years, Jerod."

I hear the sound of ripping tape.

Jerod looks up. "You can drop the trunk now."

So I do, with a thud. In my head I hear the ghost of a dead Jerry complain from inside the footlocker, *"Seien Sie ein wenig vorsichtiger, Dummkopf!"* I mumble back. "Yeah, relax, y'Kraut."

"What?" Jerod says, looking at me as if I've finally gone irretrievably mad.

I blush.

"Lookee what we have here." He holds up a key. "He taped 'em to the bottom. Figured us kids, assuming that if we ever got in here, couldn't lift the trunks to get to the keys."

Jerod opens the locker with uncharacteristic exuberance, and as the lid yawns, my brother and I step into a time warp.

My first find is the business card from the whorehouse near Tientsin and the note from Colonel Taylor Osgood, regimental commander of the Fifteenth Infantry Regiment in China. I handle Colonel Osgood's onionskin memo as if it's the rarest piece of blown glass in history and put the glossy card on my lap.

Jerod begins excavating and unearths a photograph of my grandparents standing with Dr. Wellington Koo and his wife. Under the picture are Grandfather's tuxedo and PeeCee's black satin dress, folded into square perfection as if anxious for another night out.

We take our time emptying the footlocker, poring over maps, brochures, personal papers and correspondence, manuals and books.

When I look up from my reading, Jerod is reading, too, from a novel with a cover depicting a stylized couple in dynastic coitus, opening to a world of ancient Chinese erotica. My grandmother's acquaintance from the British legation dance, Lin Yutang, had translated the book and given it to PeeCee.

Jerod reads the inscription:

> *Enjoy this to bless your marriage, as your marriage appears to be so richly blessed already. May this book challenge you in ways you never dreamed.*
> *Yours sincerely,*
> *Dr. Lin*

"I'd always heard that the colonel and PeeCee were a randy pair," I say, distracted in spite of Jerod's titillating discovery.

"What's wrong? What did you find?"

"Something I've known for a while." I level my gaze at Jerod. "I can't for the life of me figure out what went wrong."

"What went wrong where?"

"They were amazing people."

"And that's a problem because . . ."

"They were smart, incredibly well-read, worldly, well-traveled. They knew who they were, what they meant to each other, what they wanted from life and from each other . . ."

"Again, this is a problem . . ."

"My point is: What happened to *us*?"

"I still don't get it."

"I guess that's *my* point. *We* don't seem to get it. They were such classy people. In every way. And we . . ." I bite my lip, frustrated that I can't find the words. Jerod looks confused. I don't blame him.

Finally I say, "Did you ever know a man named Barrows, a general, a black guy?" I shake my head at my own description. The fact that he's black is irrelevant.

"No, I don't think so."

"Oliver Duncan Barrows. No relation, I don't guess. But he dropped by here after Grandfather's funeral. Distinguished old fella. Fought in Vietnam. Artillery. They called him 'Blast-'Em-Up Barrows.' Long story." I wave my hand. "Anyway, the old man stopped in to pay his respects. And he told me that Grandfather was one of the bravest, toughest soldiers, and the finest, most honorable man he'd ever known. Of course, we already knew all that, but then he went on to say that Grandfather didn't die for his legacy to be forgotten, neglected, or tarnished." I have to stop. My throat stings as I remember Barrows's words. "That kind of shook me up." My eyes begin to sting, too. "Y'know?"

Jerod doesn't move. Am I trying to deliver this information to the wrong address?

"Okay," I try again, "did you ever hear the story about Grandfather getting approached by the pimp in China?" I flip the business card at Jerod that Grandfather got upon his arrival at Chin-wang-tao.

Jerod reads the card and laughs. *"Chu Poon Tang."*

"He turned them down, but"—I try to sound lighthearted, better to open the locked trunk that my brother can be—"back to your story about bedding Annie in the luxury suite overlooking Hong Kong . . ."

His angry squint tells me he doesn't want to go there, doesn't want to return to the discussion he began downstairs, that he would rather, for the moment, at least, remain in the relative safety of our grandparents' glorious past.

"Hey," he says, "let's pop the lock on the next one and see what other goodies are inside."

We do, and Jerod pulls out a Walther P38, one nasty-looking 9mm handgun.

"Any bullets?" He rummages around, and I hear more guns clinking together. He hauls out a Mauser and a pair of Lugers. "Regular freakin' arsenal in here."

"Like I'd let you shoot one of those things even if you did find live ammo."

"Who'd stop me? You and whose army?" He aims the Walther straight at my face.

"Don't point that thing at me, you asshole!"

He unfurls a huge Nazi flag and drapes it across his lap while he continues digging through the footlocker.

The menacing black swastika gives me the shivers. You can hear Aryan youth goose-stepping through cobbled streets, marching under the red, white, and black linen banner. You can see lighted torches and know that Jews like Toby and Rachel, Lauren, Sylvia, and Tyler Lawson have no idea that humanity is nearing collapse.

"Why do you suppose Grandfather never took this stuff out and gave it to a museum?" Jerod asks.

"For the same reason he never thought of himself as a hero." I'm not sure even I know what that means, but it sounds right somehow.

An entirely different kind of memento points up at me from inside the third footlocker.

I pick up a conical hat, the traditional farmer's hat from Vietnam.

"How'd this get in here?" I ask Jerod.

I raise the hat and a delicate purple-ribbon chinstrap floats down from the inside. I remember that purple is the royal color of Hué, the ancient capital of imperial Vietnam. Turning the cone around in the light from the window reveals something special in the hat: A panel of transparent reeds, trimmed and woven into the cone, creates a postcard-sized silhouette of tiny sampans and fishermen.

"Why would any Vietnam stuff be in the Plunder Room?" I ask again, putting on the hat and fishing around in the foot-locker.

I dig out a Polaroid of my father in a pastel guayabera with a watch on his wrist the size of a hockey puck. He looks so young and dark, like Jerod, before life started burying Jupe's natural treasures. He is standing on a smoky terrace somewhere, several stories above unseen streets. You can see the tips of enormous ships, the sky clouded with soot.

"Good-lookin' fella." I hand the snapshot to Jerod. "Any ideas?"

He studies the Polaroid. In the same tone he used to tell me the story about Hong Kong, a knowing tone that tells me he's been there, too, he whispers, "Saigon."

" 'Zat so?"

Jerod sits motionless on the cot, until he leans against the wall, a signal that he has little choice but to surrender, tell me the story I want to hear. Still, I can't help but smile; we must look quite the pair, Jerod in the officer's pinks and me in the Vietnamese farmer's hat.

"Jerod, listen." He peeks at me through the stoic mask he has affected. "Just trust me, okay? Tell me stuff. Tell me about Dad. Tell me what you were about to tell me downstairs. About you, your *real* life. Tell me about Annie. About everything, anything."

"I've worked for him, for Jupe, a couple of years now . . . ," he begins anew.

I admit to myself that my first reaction is jealousy; my father chose Jerod over me. Nevertheless, I can't imagine being involved with my father to the degree that Jerod must be, nor could I imagine my brother's loneliness these last several months. What kind of hell *did* Jerod get himself drawn into, tangled in Jupe's nefarious affairs and mixed up with a woman who seems to have problems with her own moral compass?

I say, a bit more plaintively than I intend, "Just start from where you left off in Hong Kong."

"It's not so much where I left off," he says again, softly, gazing at the snapshot of our father in Saigon. "It's where Dad's story began and, I guess, where my story ultimately intersects his."

On the top floor of the Rex Hotel, Staff Sergeant Jupe Duncan stood on the brown-and-white tile patio and gazed along Nguyen Hué Boulevard toward the Saigon River. Dusk smelled of carbon monoxide from the sooty exhaust of big American cars and Jeeps, sulfur, cargo-ship diesel, jet fumes from nearby Tan Son Nhut, American cologne, cheap perfume, bad beer, Vietnamese vodka that tasted like gasoline, and smoke from his own cut-rate cigar.

Just off the terrace, two Vietnamese men, whom Jupe called Tom 'n' Jerry, stood at microphones and looked like overdressed parrots. They wore polyester leisure suits, Jerry in lime green with a black-and-magenta flowered shirt, Tom in pink with a white-and-navy shirt; Jerry also donned a Panama hat, tipped to his right in the Truman Capote style. They each wore thick rouge and red lipstick, too, and in Vietnamese-smothered English, they crooned their little hearts out, singing Simon & Garfunkel, Everly Brothers, and Roy Orbison hits.

The Five O'Clock Follies briefing would soon let out in one of the hotel rooms below. Jupe was waiting for a couple of guys, who might or might not have had anything to do with the military briefings for the news media downstairs. One was a quartermaster corporal named Bryce Anderson, the other an army warrant officer, WO1 Zane Piccioni.

Jupe wore that baby-blue guayabera and khakis, civvies because he was on leave for a couple of days. He checked his watch. Anderson should have been here by now. Piccioni came and went as he pleased, so he would be late as a matter of course.

Piccioni was one of those freakin' chickenhawks who flew their eggbeaters here, there, and yon—bunch of glorified taxi drivers, really. They airlifted the brass from Firebase BOHICA back to HQ in Danang and then to the Royal Palace hotel in Dalat by nightfall so they could quaff brandy by the fire and chitchat about the wife and kids back at Fort Myer before *shtupping* an army nurse or one of the locals afterward. Piccioni told more than one story about picking up nurses at Tan Son Nhut hospital. The gang would order lobsters from Françoise's, the best restaurant in Nha Trang, then they would fly to Cam Rhan Bay for a beach picnic and some early evening water-skiing behind a commandeered Boston whaler. Jupe had sold him every ounce of hashish for every single one of those parties.

Anderson and Piccioni finally arrived. Together.

Jupe smelled rum on Piccioni's breath, meaning the aviator would be grounded for the next twenty-four hours, at least.

"Good to see you fellas," he said as they pulled up in the rattan chairs.

They ordered mai tais all around from "Steve," the fey waiter. Then got down to business.

"Pitch"—Jupe called Piccioni by the nickname he'd given him—"I'm hearing that some of the flyboys from Air America are looking to cut in on our action in Cholon. First off, I want to be clear about something." He gazed at them with his dead-serious blue eyes. "I'm not doing poppies. To hell with that. They can go bonkers in the Golden Triangle and Laos and all that crap, but that's not my bag." The other two men nodded. "So. No way. We're staying as far away from that horse, I mean literally, that horse*shit* as we can get."

Everyone nodded, sipped cocktails, and twirled little paper umbrellas.

"Thing is, we've got to lay low against the CIA and their Air America wing nuts, who appear to be flying to hell and back with their own shit, so I've got to start thinking of moving product a different way. Not by air, is what I mean, at least not so close to home. So I'm thinkin' we throw the locals a little bit more of a bone, run the organics upriver where Bryce can get to it with a couple borrowed deuce-and-a-halfs and then, Pitch, once we're far enough from everybody's radar, you can pretty much fly it wherever you want."

Bryce leaned into the table. "You sure you want to cut the slants in even more—and even more of 'em?" The corporal was white as Wonder bread, a nineteen-year-old detention-center refugee who decided that enlisting would be better than running up a longer rap sheet in Detroit.

"As if we're not rutting the little fuckers right now, y'numbnuts," Piccioni said.

Jupe bristled, but these were the only two yay-hoos he could find that he could trust. After Fort Lee, Virginia, he had learned the system; in Vietnam, he had all the freedom he needed to fine-tune his own.

After four months in-country, Jupe took two weeks' R&R and six thousand American dollars to Bangkok. At night, he partied with other GIs in the garish neon hedonism of Patpong. But during the day, he convened meetings at various dives along the sleaze strip of Pradiphat Road, not far from the U.S. Army compound where he was staying. In dark bars and stuffy hotel rooms, Jupe hustled together a small group of like-minded would-be financiers: borderline GIs; freelance Air America flyboys; pock-faced Thai "businessmen" who'd been dealing in Mekong Delta rubies and sapphires; refugee Chinese "Black Society" lieutenants; renegade South Vietnamese officers who had deserted with looted bounty; and Golden Triangle opium "investors." With thousands in seed money, entrepreneurial spirit, connections, charm, and skill at government-level bribery, Jupe and his shadowy cartel thus founded the charter branch of the Pradiphat Trust Bank. In effect, a Laundromat for whatever revenues Jupe and Co. felt like depositing there, the bulk of the money wending its way as commercial paper to multinational banks in Hong Kong and points West. He visited Bangkok three times to check on the "bank," which was never open to the general public and, in fact, rarely saw anyone in its rat-hole offices.

One evening before Jupe left Saigon, he and Anderson were hanging out, smoking dope on the stoop of a tiny tin-roofed bar in Cholon. Bryce asked him if he was ever afraid of getting caught; Bryce always got paranoid when he got stoned, especially alfresco.

Jupe smiled and twirled the roach. "Yeah, so, what would they do, throw me out of this beautiful country? Boot me out of the army? Oh, crap, Bryce! Then I'd have to get a real job."

"They say your daddy was a big-league war hero." Jupe grimaced when Bryce added, "Guess he'd be rotating in his grave to see you wrecking this man's army—"

"Let me get something straight. First of all, moron, my father's not dead. Second of all, this man's army has gone to shit in a handbag." The corporal's face fell. "Did you listen to Eisenhower's big speech a few years ago, his harangue about the military-industrial complex?"

Anderson shook his head, looked at Jupe as if he were a Nobel Prize laureate.

"Well, ol' Ike was part of my father's army, the Grand goddamned Old Army, not this go-fight-a-jungle-war-you're-never-gonna-win with a misfit outfit like this one. So, Ike is about to leave the White House, and he tells the American people to keep an eye on the so-called 'military-industrial complex.'" Jupe drew quotations in the humid, opiate air. "I remember exactly what he said, too: He says the military and everything that goes into keeping it going has an economic, political, even spiritual influence on the country. 'Every city, every statehouse, every office of the federal government.' So Ike says there are 'grave implications'"—Jupe clawed quotes into the air again—"if we let the military-industrial complex get away with it."

"'It?' What 'it'?"

"Look around, son. Mass destruction, looting on a grand scale, war on our terms, where we get away with . . ." Jupe winked at him. "You know what I mean. And damned if nobody paid a bit of attention to a single word Ike said."

"So why didn't *you*?"

"Why didn't I *what*?"

"Why didn't *you* stay out of the army-industrial complex?"

Jupe laughed and waved his hands. He flicked the burning butt into the narrow street, hitting a crone wearing a conical hat and dusty black *aoi dai*.

"For the same reason you did, Bryce: I didn't want to find a real job."

"Groovy."

Jupe handed him a roll of bills, two hundred dollars American. "Great." He patted him on the shoulder. "So here's your cut from the latest deal."

A gaggle of girls stampeded past the bar—young, vibrant, and beautiful Vietnamese girls, some dressed in brilliant *aoi dai*, white satiny pantaloons, and shimmering red tunics, and some in shiny red hot pants with pink halter tops.

"Go buy yourself a treat, Anderson."

"No thanks, Sarge, I got a military-industrial complex to get back to at o'dark-thirty tomorrow."

That had been two months before.

Now, at the rooftop of the Rex, Bryce was sporting a new Swiss watch.

"Careful the way you spend your money, Corporal Anderson," Jupe said. "A little too flashy and somebody might catch on that you're making more than the average GI." Jupe took a big puff on his cigar.

The fragrances and pops from steaks on the rooftop grill played havoc with the three men.

"You fellas want some dinner?" Jupe asked.

"I got a date, Sarge," Piccioni said.

"Course you do, Romeo," Jupe said.

"Guy's a regular Italian stallion." Anderson downed his mai tai. "Well, humpers, just so's you know, I'm a double-digit figit."

They all stood, clasped hands and slapped the young Michigander on the back. In less than three months, Bryce Anderson would be returning to the World.

Jupe settled back into his chair and his cocktail. "Guess this means that our little company's going to have to disperse until I find a ground replacement."

"Guess so, Sarge."

"Say, Anderson, what are you going to do with your winnings?" Piccioni asked, "That is, assuming the cheap bastard here greased your palm at least half as good as he did mine."

"Me? Well, I got the GI Bill, and with my little ball of Duncan dough, I'm going to go to college, earn a degree, maybe two, buy me a nice house, find me a beautiful young virgin with round eyes, and make a lot of clean, legitimate money. I've had about enough of this shit. Besides, this is the freakin' Wild West over here. Back in the States, I'm not smart enough, like the Sarge here, to do this crazy crapola and not get caught."

"Gentlemen, I am simply providing goods and services to the men and women of the American Armed Forces, far from home, who need salves, balms, and entertainments under highly stressful conditions, all of which they are more than happy and willing to pay handsome sums to obtain."

Piccioni and Anderson exchanged grins.

Jupe's steak at the Rex Hotel that night was grilled to juicy perfection.

The next afternoon, Piccioni's helicopter crashed, killing everyone on board, including a black lieutenant colonel who was said to be the best hope for a new generation of the military—for everyone from the Fifteenth Field Artillery Regiment to the biggest brass at the Five O'Clock Follies, including a young officer named Oliver Duncan Barrows.

At the Tan Son Nhut gate that evening, an MP friend stopped Jupe to tell him, "They're onto you, Sarge. They found some of your shit in Pitch's flight suit, and it FUBAR'd the whole KIA scene at the crash site. They didn't want any stain on one of their best. So shut it down, man, cut it off. Just a word to the wise."

A pause thickens the air that had been thinning thanks to the attic fan and the open windows.

So what do real men do when they don't know what to say? We eat.

"How 'bout some lunch?" Jerod says with a finality that leaves me alone in a whole new maze of questions.

Without another word, Jerod wraps the handguns in the Nazi flag and rests the bundle atop a gray Waffen-SS uniform.

"What do you think *this* is?" he says, picking a cowhide pouch out of the footlocker and tossing it to me. "I'm going to run downstairs and get Volusia to round up some food. I'll bring it up."

I nod, still trying to process my brother's story but engrossed in the pouch.

The leather is discolored, hard and rough, pale on the inside flap. A smear the size of a Bowie knife looks like blood, faded to light pink against the brushed side of the hide. The bag contains an ID card: Gerhard Stöffel, a twenty-nine-year-old private first class attached to the Third Panzergrenadier Division. The picture shows a man with a classic chiseled chin, eyes as blue and clear as a Berchtesgaden sky, and a tuft of black hair perched atop a narrow head with small ears. His lips are tight and thin, with a smile he probably hadn't used in years. His face offers no sadness or fear, no emotion at all.

A letter folded in quarters hides behind the card. The plain stationery is yellowed with a small burn, probably from a cigarette, in the lower left corner.

Liebe Gertrude,

Dieser Krieg ist verloren. Ich fürchte für das geliebte Vater-
land, für das ich mein Alles gegeben habe, einschließlich, so
weiß ich jetzt, mein Leben. Ich würde alles geben, um wieder
mit Ihnen zusein, und ich hoffe in meiner Seele, daßs ich Sie in
einem entfernten Paradies sehen werde. Ich liebe Sie mehr als ich
je etwas geliebt habe, sogar mehr als meine Heimat. Bitte geben
Sie Erwin und Heidi meine Liebe und sagen Sie ihnen, ich hoffe,
daßich nicht vergeblich gefallen bin.

Mit aller meiner Liebe,

Gerhard

I can read just enough German to get the gist. "Dear Ger-trude," he writes to his wife, "This war is lost. I realize that I will give my life for the Fatherland. I hope to see you in paradise. Give my love to Erwin and Heidi and tell them I hope that I haven't died in vain."

Heartbreaking. In any language.

My cell phone rings, shredding what's left of my nerves. The caller ID says it's my editor, Keith Chen.

"I'm glad you called," I lie. His response is the lack of one. "Listen, Keith, I know why you're calling, and I apologize."

"You sound strange. Where've you been? What's gotten into you?" he asks.

"My son's marijuana. I found it in his condom drawer, we burned it, and I'm stoned."

"Seriously, Randol . . ."

"Before you say anything more, I just want to tell you a couple of things. First, I don't think you're an idiot. I used to think that every boss was an idiot."

"Yeah. Okay. You're freaking me out. If I remember from

your résumé, you never actually ever *had* a boss because I'm pretty certain you never even actually had a *job*, and—"

"And that brings me to the second thing. Thanks for this job. See, there's honor in doing a job, any job, and doing it well."

"Duncan, I swear, I have no idea what medication you're suddenly on. But rather than screwing with my head, you really need to tell me that you can deliver the piece—*pieces*—you promised in the next day or so."

"No prob—"

"The truth is, the last two pieces you wrote generated a decent buzz. Granted, it's not saving the world, but people enjoy what you're writing—or maybe they hate what you're writing—but either way, they're on our site, creating a lot of traffic."

His timing couldn't have been worse, but his comments couldn't have been better.

"I really need to know if you're going to review the Steely Black Steeple show down there this Friday night."

"Matter of fact, my son has a big date, so I thought I'd tag along."

"Good enough. Just don't let me catch their tickets on your expense sheet."

I look at the footlockers and finger the note that the widow Stöffel never received.

"Yeah, sure, Keith. You'll have a concert review first thing Saturday morning." And I flip the cell phone closed.

Keith, accompanied by a faraway Steely Black Steeple sound track, now competes for space in my head with Jerod, Jupe, Annie, Eddie, and my grandparents. With so much of Grandfather's life splayed before me, I wish my grandfather were here. In this room, so warm and close, among his tunics and puttees, guns and banners, files, letters, mementos, and memories, I feel his embrace, even though I know that Grandfather put his arms around only one man; and I finger the Purple Heart that once belonged to the maimed and bloodied Corporal Dahlgren, which now dangles from an armrest on my wheelchair.

For the first time since I buried Grandfather last February, I cry, here alone in the Plunder Room.

CHAPTER FOURTEEN

SCOTT JOPLIN'S "The Entertainer" jingles from my cell phone, pulling me from a macaroni-and-cheese-induced nap, wrought, too, by the dry hangover of hard emotion.

After what my grandparents called dinner and the rest of us call lunch, I pulled myself up into the enormous four-poster bed in the bedroom across the hall and collapsed into a sleep as deep as the ancient mattress, redolent of the odor of mothballs. How many hours later, I have no idea, but I awoke under a canopy of pink-flowered bunting and lace to Eddie's conspiratorial whisper in my phone.

"I did what you told me to do."

"Who's this?" I ask without first clearing my head.

"Who do you think it is—T. J. Wrex?" Even in my daze, I know he's talking about Steely Black Steeple's lead guitarist.

"You only wish. If you were T. J. Wrex . . ." I shake my head. "Never mind. Well?"

"I got the goods."

"Great. Where are you?"

"In the SQ. I'm starving. Where do you want the delivery?"

"Upstairs," I tell him. "And bring my laptop."

"Upstairs? Really? Where?"

"In one of the bedrooms, across from the Plunder Room . . . long story, just—"

"No dice."

" 'Scuse me?"

"I have something you need; you give me something in return."

"Nobody ever talked about a negotiated deal here." I can so see what's coming.

"I surrender the merchandise," he says, without realizing he's doing a fine Edward G. Robinson imitation, "and you let me off the hook with Marnie Jennings."

"I'll tell you what, Mental Wizard, I let you off the hook with Marnie Jennings, and then I'll take those tickets and find my own date. In other words, nothing doing."

He laughs.

"What's so funny?"

"You finding a date."

"You wound me heart and soul, O pitiless cad!" I slide into my chair. "By the way, your uncle J is here."

The line is dead before I flip my phone shut.

I manage to get back into my chair and roll across the vast Oriental rug. Jerod is locking the Plunder Room.

"Done for the day?"

"I've had as much history as I can take," he says. He has changed back into his twills, loafers, and Oxford shirt.

"You look much better as a modern-day con artist than you do as an American officer of the Grand Old Army, I have to say."

He scowls. "How was your nap?"

I nod, a little sleepy still. "Eddie's on his way up."

"Good. He can help me haul your overweight ass and all your heavy hardware downstairs."

"Gravity. It's not just a good idea, it's the law, and this time, it's a law that works in your favor. Or you can push me down the stairs. Suit yourself."

He scowls again. "Everything's funny to you, isn't it?"

"No, not especially. Not after what I learned in there." I glance toward the Plunder Room. I put my hand over my heart and look at Jerod with a seriousness that startles him, "And in here."

I live in a wheelchair; nothing else is particularly serious by comparison. And when bombs and body parts are flying past you and you drag your wife from post to post and you get paid less than a schoolteacher and nobody gives a rat's ass about you, nothing but loving your wife and your family is particularly serious.

Jerod stands with his hands on his hips. His sober look makes me want to explode in laughter that would burst through his absurdity like a German shell. I know what's coming, and I want to say, *"Ihr Krieg ist verloren."* Your war is lost.

"The stuff from Jupe's office—"

"Why do you call him Jupe or, worse, 'Dipshit'?"

I shake my head. Apparently, my brother learned nothing from those footlockers or from the man who left them behind.

"The stuff from *Dad's* office. Eddie's on his way up with it."

"God, you are such a prick, you know that, Randol? A self-satisfied, self-indulgent, lazy, self-absorbed son of a bitch. And you know what else? If you weren't such an arrogant jackass, people would actually take you seriously."

I can't help but consider the genetic reflection looking down at me.

Fishing my cell phone out of my shirt pocket, I push the speed-dial number for Eddie, who picks up on the first ring.

He answers through a mouthful, "I'm in the kitchen."

"Sounds tasty. Got to be a BLT. But I thought you were on your way up here."

"With cheese, extra bacon, and some leftover fried chicken. A man's gotta eat."

"At least you stopped by the mess hall on the way to see your uncle. He's dying to see you, too. So get your butt up here with that stuff I asked for so he can give you a big hug."

Eddie clicks off while Jerod continues to scowl, knowing full well that I'm in the middle of a conspiracy with my son.

"That was the caterer, looking for the mezzanine, Men's Accessor—"

"See that?" Jerod says. "Everything's a joke with you. You're going to raise your kid to be a smart-ass who thinks he's better than everyone else."

"Just so long as he *is* better than everyone else, Jerod, that's fine by me. I'll be sure to work on the part where he's honest, at least. I think he gets that part. Maybe that explains why he likes metal music. Keeps him primal." I look toward the stairs, expecting to see Eddie slinking up them any moment. "Say, wanna go to the show with us on Friday?"

Eddie actually bounds up the stairs. "J-Man!" He throws one arm around his uncle and with the other dumps my computer in my lap. "You buff stallion!"

"You look great, dude. Y'weed, you, growing so fast."

"We don't mention, um, 'weed' around here," I say with a grim half smile. "Well," I add, "why don't you two frat boys run along—"

"Not so fast. We have a few things to discuss," Jerod says.

"Not in front of the children," I say, and Eddie looks around for any real ones. He hates to be considered a child, though fourteen, I have to remind him, is still considered a minor in every state.

Despite the fact that Jerod stands next to me, I am eager to open my laptop and have a look at the files from Jupe's office that, thanks to Eddie, are now copied onto my computer.

"Listen, Jerod, seriously, when you and Eddie are done goofing off, I'll be right here. It's not like I can go anywhere."

Jerod glances at his watch. It's almost four-thirty. He actually looks as if he may be in a hurry now to get somewhere. Dad's nocturnal businesses could need attention, and then, of course, he has Annie . . .

"Okay." He paces, clearly frustrated at the impasse with me and, apparently, with himself. "I'll see you in a few minutes." His voice simmers.

When I flip open the laptop, the CD player whirs. I snap it open to find a disc labeled with Eddie's sloppy handwriting in black Magic Marker: "Fast Eddie's Stolen Property." He also left Jupe's jump drive in the port on the side of my portable computer.

I slide the CD back into the holder. The machine whirs again, and icons begin popping up on the screen, showing all the files Eddie scanned onto the disc.

I can't open each one fast enough.

I can see the handwriting and the lines of the accountant paper. The penmanship is scrunched and scrawled, and it's my father's.

I flip through each page.

In a few minutes, I have a pretty good picture of what's going on.

My father's net worth must be in the millions. Tax-free, I'm sure.

The bookkeeping isn't what a certified public accountant would call reliable, much less audited. And I am certain, too, that forensic accountants from the Internal Revenue Service; Alcohol, Tobacco, Firearms and Explosives; the FBI; and possibly the Immigration and Naturalization Service would be interested and probably amused by the pecuniary dynasty Jupe has created during the last two decades or so.

It's all here in black and white, numbers accompanying the places listed, which I've long known about:

The Jupe Box
Jupiter's Fuel 'n' Go
Jupiter's Fuel 'n' Go Plus
Ganymede's Paradise
Callisto's

But the revenues in the computer files are a lot higher than anything I ever saw during the summer I worked for my father in those days before I lost the use of my legs.

Callisto's may be a strip club, but the joint has become a Wrenton institution. Everyone has been to Callisto's. Even *I* have been to Callisto's, where I drank watered-down beer in twelve-ounce plastic cups and paid double the market price. None of the other patrons, of course, probably realized or cared that Callisto, the name of another Jovian moon, was also the Greek goddess of the hunt. Zeus was so unnerved by the nymph's vow of chastity, as well as her beauty, that he raped her. The unsavory customers in the nightclub as big as an airplane hangar also wouldn't begin to care that nary a one of Jupe's "exotic dancers" would pass as a goddess or a nymph. In fact, the night I was there with D Bag, before he gave his life for his country, we watched a woman with a prosthetic foot and a rose tattoo just above her sternum show off her store-boughts to a near-comatose biker. Still, with every boom of the massive PA system, every pulse of the lights, and every puff of smoke filling the place, Jupe took in another few hundred dollars. He charges men to enter the club; he charges girls to dance. Callisto's has side rooms for lap dances and drug deals, and back rooms for illegal video poker machines; numbers boards; sports betting, complete with part-time bookies; and card games.

According to my quick calculations, Callisto's alone grossed some four and a half million dollars last year. Most, if not all, of that, the tax man will never see. And what about the drug deals? Those ever get recorded anywhere?

I click open the jump drive, and another box appears on my screen, with more virtual folders, only these folders contain dozens of snapshots.

Like the piles of pictures I had seen in the Plunder Room, these, too, tell dozens of stories. Clicking through the images, I feel as if I'm talking with Bryce Anderson and Zane Piccioni. I watch the warrant officer from Hoboken, New Jersey, and Bryce chow down with a bunch of buddies and army nurses at a long table overloaded with lobsters. The jump drive also includes scanned images of postcards from old Saigon, along with numerous snapshots of shirtless GIs in sun-baked firebases. Jupe and friends have written captions to accompany the photos:

> Here's one of Rufus and Toothacher and a few of the Hootch-hitters (that's me, kneeling, in the front row) after pounding the f**k out of the enemy last night when they got too close to the perimeter. Thank god for the Montagnards, the little sapper motherf**kers. They shoot in the dark, just like your pal Pitch with his britches down.
> —Bollweevil

It strikes me as funny that Jupe's digitized scrapbook fits in the palm of my hand, while Grandfather's filled three footlockers. It also unnerves me that my father's memory could be erased in a snap. It would take something violent, like a fire, to destroy what Colonel Duncan had stored and treasured.

I hear Jerod on the stairs, so I close the virtual scrapbook, the virtual folders, the virtual life of my father and brother.

By the time Jerod reaches the staircase landing, I am typing, mouthing the words as I write.

". . . the twin assault of guitars from lead guitarist T. J. Wrex and metal-dominatrix Sara Brill are reminiscent of machine-gun bursts and . . ."

"What are you working on, Randol?" my brother asks, knowing full well that I'm about to lie.

"Getting ready for the Steely Black Steeple show on Friday. I just want to have some boilerplate copy ready so that when I—"

"Yeah, whatever." Jerod strides right past me over the lawn of Oriental rug and plops down on the davenport.

"What'd you do with Eddie?"

"He's hanging with Volusia. Apparently, she wants us to talk 'without the child around,' too."

I nod, closing the computer in my lap. We need to talk about Dad. About these files. But we also need to discuss Dad's future, his recuperation, his care—and who's going to give him that care and where he will live the rest of what are bound to be difficult, lonely, and painful days. We need to talk about Annie. I figure neither of us is eager to delve into any of it.

"So." I finally turn to him and lean back in my chair to avoid seeming aggressive. "You work for Dad."

His smile is so thin it says nothing.

In that instant, I feel a long-trapped bubble rise to the surface of my consciousness—anger, but more than that: profound resentment that these two delinquents have been in their conspiracy . . . for *how* long? My bubble of anger started in Tegucigalpa's Central Prison and never really did pop. Now I feel it getting bigger, and as it rises and grows, I think it may explode. I'm not sure how to handle that.

I scratch my nose, rub my chin, look around the room, and pinch my eyes, all for the sake of trying to figure out what to say next and how to ask questions that might have a remote chance of getting honest answers.

"What are you going to do, Jerod?"

"What do you mean, what am I going to do?"

I can't help but laugh.

"Don't make fun of me, Randol."

"Look at yourself. You're a caricature. You're a phony. You dress in expensive clothes, you talk like you're making a fortune and, well, you probably are. But you're a fraud. Dad's a fraud. You're stealing, Jerod." His face is turning red, and his jaw is starting to work. "Did I tell you about last February? I believe it was February sixteenth, a couple of days after Valentine's Day. Cold, but clear—"

"Stop it, Randol, this is where you get on people's nerves."

My voice rises. I point through the window toward the SQ. "That was the day. Jerod. That I found pot. In Eddie's bedroom."

His face falls.

"You're peddling dope to kids. You sell watery booze to alcoholics drooling over the flesh of the girls you buy. You sell phony dreams to addicted gamblers. At your convenience stores you hand out gallons of milk and give away cartons of cigarettes, when you're not selling them to minors, merchandise that you ring up but never sell. Then you fill your cash drawer with the money you make in your dark little back rooms. And voilà, freshly laundered cash."

"Don't get high-and-mighty with me, mister." He jumps up. "You ignorant little son of a bitch. This is *exactly* why Dad came to me. Because he knew you were arrogant, judgmental—"

"Arrogant, judgmental, *hell*, Jerod, what you people do is illegal! Are you telling me that it's okay for Eddie to score marijuana? I'd even bet that it wasn't too far off your own fucking supply chain."

"Look at you, Randol. Who would be the hypocrite here?"

"What the hell are you talking about, Jerod? I made some bad choices, sure, but I also got a bad break here and there—like winding up in this chair. Is that what you're talking about? You're comparing my bad choices, my bad judgment, my bad luck—you're comparing all *that* to money laundering and peddling drugs to children?" I catch my breath and lower my voice to avoid catching the attention of anyone downstairs, Eddie or Volusia. Good Lord help me. "For once, Jerod, it's *not* about me. And, besides, I'm not even here to argue."

He slumps into the couch and runs his fingers through his hair, trying to control the anger that I know is zinging through his brain.

I whisper to my brother, "The question remains, what are you going to do? I'm afraid for Dad. I don't think he's going to die. At least, not today. But he's had a stroke. Not so good. And he did get busted once, and he was damned lucky. I'm just saying." I shake my head at the memory. "If that little Central American prison episode had happened today, in this world of terror, they would have fried his ass."

"What have the doctors told you?"

I rearrange my body language so that he knows I want him to need me. "I spoke with Dr. Nguyen this morning. He says Dad's out of the woods, but he'll be in the intensive-care unit for three, four days. Then they'll move him to a private room for at least a week, then home, wherever we think that should be, for a couple of months of rehab."

"It's not like he's going to be running the Jupe Box or supervising strippers again anytime soon—"

I put my hands up to stop Jerod. "We've got to be in Wrenton for the concert tomorrow night, but the kids aren't going to want to go see a vegged-out old man before their favorite band blows up the arena. Maybe you and I could go over there first thing Monday, tool around town, visit the Jovian empire."

He apparently doesn't know what "Jovian" means, but he gets my point. Hope drifts across his face, though his eyes look sad, defeated. By any financial measure, I'm certain, my brother is wealthy. By any spiritual standard, well, that isn't my expertise, either.

Eddie stomps up the stairs to let us know that he's invading our space, though I'm certain he has heard our raised voices. He glances at my computer. "You guys downloading any good porn up here?"

"Not since you put the adult filter on my computer, y'ninny," I say.

Jerod stands, then pushes me toward the top of the staircase. The air around us seems lighter, and it's not because of the attic fan.

"Tyler coming over tonight?" I ask. I haven't seen Eddie's best friend in two, maybe three months. "He talked his dad into letting him go to the show tomorrow, right?"

Eddie shakes his head. "Yeah, but he's not coming over."

"What's the deal? You guys break up?"

"No." He looks up at Jerod. "He's been spending a lot of time with Miss Harkin the last couple months."

Eddie looks as if he knows more than we do, which isn't

much of a stretch, because I—and I presume Jerod—know nothing. Eddie's not stupid; kids aren't.

"He says he needs tutoring," Eddie says, his voice speeding, "and since she's the smartest teacher at New Cumbria, he picked her. Well . . . she sort of picked him."

The hair on the back of my neck bristles. Jerod's eyebrows rise, along with his shoulders, like the hackles on a tomcat.

"Beats me," Eddie says, as if trying to talk himself out of trouble he's not in—yet. "But you can ask them about it tomorrow."

"Them?" Jerod and I ask simultaneously.

"Oh, yeah," Eddie says. "Miss Harkin's coming to the show, along with pretty much the entire school. Tomorrow's the last day of class, so it's gonna be a blowout."

"Alrighty, then," Jerod says, anxious now. "Nephew, buddy, let's get your old man down these stairs. He says gravity's working in our favor. Hopefully, it's not working too well."

"Hey, hey, fellas. Give me just a minute. It's taken me a few months to get up here, and God only knows when I'll get back." Eddie backs away; he's not ready for another story, another moment of windy philosophy. "I thought the answers to the mysteries of our universe might be locked in those trunks behind that locked door." I nod toward the Plunder Room, then look into Jerod's eyes, whose sad, silent response knows what I'm trying to say. "We did find some treasures, though, didn't we, Jerod?"

He nods. Eddie seems not to notice.

"Hell, maybe we found some answers, too."

But they both have suffered my foolishness long enough, and my son and my brother stare down at me with the same look: a look that says they would sooner pitch me over the banister than listen to another word.

Before I know it, we're bumping and banging down the stairs—I'm grabbing at my brakes, making them bite into the tires, nearly toppling Jerod and Eddie every other step—until, nineteen steps later, they have me deposited on firm ground.

Eddie's gone before I can settle back into my chair, but Jerod seems hesitant to make the escape he's been hoping for these last few hours.

"Thanks for the ride." I offer my hand.

He takes it. Then he drags his forearm across his brow. "No sweat."

"There's another hot potato for you," I say, trying to keep him around. "What are you going to do about *her*?"

"Damned if I know." He walks to the door, opens it to the warm, perfumed June breeze, and leans against the frame.

"What about Tyler?"

"Tyler was at school, remember? She called. No big deal." He folds his arms.

"Maybe. But are we going to find out where Tyler spent the night?"

His face burns with a new red; I'm about to piss him off again. He simply shakes his head, shrugs his shoulders. After a long pause, during which, presumably, he collects himself and calms down, he predictably looks at his watch again.

Finally, I take a short, apprehensive breath, daring one last stab into yet another unknown.

"Who is she, Jerod?" He looks mystified, as if I'm wondering why the sky is blue or why Volusia's coffee tastes so good.

"Jerod, for pity's sake, you don't even know the woman. You plucked her from God-knows-where and plopped her down in the middle of the most charming, down-on-its-luck old textile town in the South. You're hardly ever around, and, well . . . people, not just me, are asking questions."

Finally, words start spilling from Jerod's mouth, just as they had in the Plunder Room.

"Okay, when Grandfather was so sick, I guess Dad knew he was next in line. Or maybe he saw Grandfather's impending death as a wake-up call and wanted to get his own house in order. I don't know, I never asked him and didn't really care. Anyway, Dad called and asked if I would come back home. I'd been 'involved' with him for a couple of years and, sure, I knew what he'd been doing. I even took a few trips abroad for him, like I told you. So I knew his properties, his worth, his assets, and so forth. But he wanted me around full-time and in Wrenton. That's why he called."

I could only picture Gunny, smoke billowing from a cigarette butt between his lips, toiling side by side with my brother. Tattoos and twills. I nodded and crossed my arms to suppress the amusing image.

"After my trip to Hong Kong, Annie and I were living in New York—I swear, she told me she was a teacher in Brooklyn—and she and I talked about Dad's call. She was . . . Well, I was smitten with the girl. And I thought she was smitten with me.

"Besides, I figured that leaving Manhattan and coming home and getting out of what I was doing, which obviously wasn't working—all that seemed like a good idea."

A lot of that sounds like BS to me. I imagine dollar signs were all it took for Jerod to make his career decision.

"So I sold Annie on the idea of the romantic South, leaving out the parts about intense boredom, the one movie theater in town. She said she wanted to 'get away from it all,' too."

I swear my brother must be color-blind. Bulls can't see the red in the matador's cape, but they know when they're getting the runaround, and they certainly know when the razor-sharp *banderillas* start flying.

"She told me she saw the move as a challenge: the challenge of living in an 'exotic' part of the country, the challenge of teaching here, the challenge of being in a place that didn't offer round-the-clock excitement and—"

"And she also knew she could trap you—or thought she could trap you—into a twenty-four/seven situation where she could get your time and attention and more." I lean back in my chair.

"Guess I hadn't thought about it that way."

Until now, neither had I, frankly—at least, not in those terms and not with such apprehension. "Except she didn't get your time or your attention." I think for a moment of Callisto and the goddesses and nymphs of Olympus who used their beauty for ill-advised gain or for the gods who exploited it.

When Jerod shrugs his usual shrug this time, I can't blame him. For a change, I don't have any answers, either.

"Listen," Jerod says, "I guess I better go."

"Wait a minue, Jerod. That binder and stuff from Dad's office—don't you want to go down to the SQ and get it?"

He returns to my chair, grabs the nape of my neck, and actually plants a kiss on my head. "You're a shit, Randol, but I love you. I'll get the binder and jump drive tomorrow. Don't worry about it."

He turns, leaving me to wonder what in the world just happened.

CHAPTER FIFTEEN

AT GRANDFATHER'S funeral, the Reverend Box Jenkins quoted Jesus: "In my Father's house are many mansions." In *my* father's house are back rooms, a trailer park, a strip club, and a bar.

I just hope Jerod understands that Jupe's house needs a good cleaning. After all, where does one keep a few million dollars? I guess that's a question for another day, most likely tomorrow.

Today I have to attend to Keith Chen's call for the work I've been putting off. And tonight's the Steely Black Steeple show in Wrenton. The thought of a high-octane rock concert is adding some much-needed juice to my battery.

It's raining to drown toads by the time Eddie piles into my car to pick up Marnie Jenkins before heading on to Wrenton. Assuming the weather doesn't snarl interstate traffic, we'll actually make it in time to catch the opening act, the Hi Jax Parade. Actually *seeing* the first band is so déclassé around here, but I've always been under the impression that the price of the concert ticket included the entire evening's entertainment.

Eddie's wearing his de rigueur uniform, the same T-shirt that Ari Manios had evicted from school property and the same chrome-looped jeans that drag through mud puddles. At least he has the sense to wear flip-flops so his feet won't be soaking in drenched socks and sneakers all night. Fortunately, he's forgone his eyeliner, too.

He slides a disc into my car's CD player. In a second, we're assaulted not with the melodic, if heavy, rock of Steely Black Steeple, but with a guitArmageddon of a bigger, even harder band, the Hammord:

> *Who's to say what's right or wrong*
> *Everyone plays by rules*
> *no one follows, Stifling everything*
> *But you will pay the price*
>
> *Our course is skewed by others Who*
> *see the fucking things we do*
> *but now I know In this dark room*
> *That no one's here to save you*
>
> *So watch me play your god*
> *I control what's right or wrong*
> *I control your every breath*
> *and I'll be damned if you take it*

I had reviewed the Hammord's album and front man Matthew Lawrence's raging lyrics for seriousmusic.com when the CD was released:

A cataclysmic orgy of headlong guitars screaming for notice,
with bass and rhythm section competing for brightness where
there should be chest-thumping bravado, and a fresh and dizzy-
ing interplay of pitched vocals—these are what make this band
the superstars they are. While nobody lauds modern-rock lyri-
cists much for their latter-day poetry, what we have here works
only because the music, the melodies behind the words, is bouncy
and, well, redemptive and even somehow happy. The commen-
tary, of course, is typical Teen Angst, plagued with hard rock's
shopworn anger, violence and homicidal hubris. In the case of
this particular album, though, if you listen within the context of
the entire CD or, better yet, see Lawrence & Co. with all their
thrashing energy live, you can't help but feel a pay-for-your-
nihilism message in here somewhere, and that has to be some-
how positive.

"Everyone thought your review was pretty good," Eddie says
over the high-decibel intrusion, "even if it was filled with
big-sounding, self-important words."

"Thanks." I glance at him, then turn back to the flooding
road. The windshield wipers fail to keep time with the attack of
stuttering snare drum and thundering bass. "Say. Didn't you
mention yesterday that Tyler and Miss Harkin were going to the
show?"

"Oh, yeah, a whole convoy's coming from New Cumbria tonight. Most of the kids aren't leaving until later, though."

Of course not. A stampeding herd of them likely will gather
at Ari Manios's grandfather's diner, giving Hero's a week's worth
of business in less than an hour. I'm a little disappointed that
Annie won't be joining us for the hour-plus ride in this miserable weather. At least Marnie Jennings will be with us in a
minute.

"You *could* turn the music down some so we could talk."

"I could. Or we could get jacked up for the show." He pushes himself deeper into his bucket seat, as if to protect himself from the rain spattering on the windshield and from me.

I get it. School's out. Eddie is filled with adrenaline and fantasies, wallowing in an infectious happiness I haven't seen in him for a while. Soon he will be earning a few dollars working around the house, mowing a few lawns. I've got other plans for him, too: helping nurse Jupe back to health, going to summer school to shore up his C-plus grade average, and, maybe, if I can push Jerod in the right direction, cleaning up Jupe's house—his actual house, not his figurative one. Selling Dad's home in west Wrenton could pay for his medical and nursing care, presuming I talk him into moving here. Eddie doesn't know any of this, of course. For the moment, he thinks he has a wide-open, three-month window of freedom. I won't wreck his phantasmagoric view just yet.

"Aren't you the least bit excited about your date with Marnie?" He sniffs at me.

We wind our way about fifteen minutes outside of New Cumbria, with another ten minutes to go before the interstate. The Jenningses live in a new subdivision, a rare and much-needed addition to this town.

As soon as we pull up to the curb, the door swings open, and Marnie, holding an umbrella, races to the car. Eddie doesn't move. I scowl at him in the light that's already dim from the foul weather.

He scowls back, as if to say: *You think* I'm *going to get out of the car and go fetch her and get myself drenched? She saw the car pull up. I don't want to hear about what you did* back in your day.

"Hi, Mr. D!" she squeals when she shakes off her umbrella and nestles into the backseat.

"Hello, Marnie."

Eddie, still wordless, appears thankful that I don't start his date by embarrassing him.

"Hi, Eddie!" She pats him on the shoulder.

The least he can do, the little shit, is to welcome her into the car.

Finally, he says, "Hi, Marnie," sounding about as enthusiastic as if we were going to the family cemetery.

"This is so awesome!" she says. "I've been listening to Steely Black Steeple since I got home from school today. They so totally rock!"

The idea that this sweet young virgin, with perfect skin, long, shaggy blond hair, and clear blue eyes, has allowed those lyrics to inflict themselves . . . Alas, Randol, *you can't help but feel a positive message in there somewhere.* Her hair is wet. Her eyes dazzle with excitement and youth. She wears form-fitting jeans that are a little rained on, so when they dry, they'll be even *more* form-fitting. And her form is thin yet growing into a perfect, perhaps a tad petite, hourglass. Then she shakes out of her Windbreaker. I suspect that her father, Todd, had no idea of her fashion selection, what little there is. She wears a small white halter top just wet enough to offer more views. I had no idea when I visited Ari Manios's office last fall that the young woman had such assets. Gone is, like, the girl, who, y'know, chirped her way through our introduction. Marnie has been replaced by a siren. I am beginning to feel like Humbert Humbert, chaperoning Lolita—while a refugee from *The Lord of the Flies* rides shotgun.

"So." I swallow, keeping my eyes straight ahead and off the rearview mirror. "You're an SBS fan?"

"Ever since Eddie turned me on to them and asked me out. I

think their lyrics suck, but their music is so melodic and complex, you can't help but like them." She cocks her head.

I haven't taken the car out of "Park" yet. The rain's still pouring. The music shreds the air. My palms are sweating.

Eddie clears his throat.

I lean toward him and growl in a half whisper that he might want to get in the back.

He glares at me; I return his glare. Apparently he decides that it must be part of "our deal" from February. He gets out of the car, then jumps into the seat behind me.

Off we go.

By the time we arrive at the arena, smoke from the fog machines and sound from the titanic PA system already are rolling out onto the concourse. Hi Jax Parade has just started playing. The fifteen thousand seats in the concrete oval are about half full, though I've heard the Wrenton Center has sold more than thirteen thousand tickets. Even so, the energy is vibrant, and kids flow down the aisles like a black stream on a beige streambed: black clothes, black hair, and black sentiment.

After Hi Jax's set, the lights go up for about a half hour, then the building darkens again. Hundreds of cigarette lighters and cell phones spark like mating fireflies, and a spontaneous blue cloud floats toward the ceiling carrying a sweet and organic perfume that takes me back to my wilder days—or, at least, back to February.

Onstage, thin, dark figures emerge from the haze amid pulsating lights—dark blues, ambers, reds, and mind-shaking strobes.

Without warning, the band unleashes a wall of sound, not too different from the column of Sheridan tanks heading toward the Rhine.

The war-zone din of the 110-plus decibels that explode

through the coliseum from guitar amplifiers and drums more than wins the war of acoustics, demolishing what might have been lyrics or melody. Their conflict goes on, feverish, unrelenting.

Most of the seats are filled now. On the floor, three or four thousand kids are packed into a heat-soaked pool, smashing into one another like a Roman circus out of control, all the gladiators thrown into one last bloody battle to the death. The pit, hard against the stage, looks like a wave of Art Deco wheat blowing this way and that to the outraged tempo, until a hole opens every now and then. The hole in the crowd often grows as big around as a circus tent; the hole is alive, too, shifting, moving, and re-shaping itself like an amoeba. Inside the circle, moshing starts. Kids bash and flail against one another, shirtless and glistening, bouncing like incensed pinballs until, like some organic thing, the hole closes again. Soon, another opens. I don't see blood, but it has to be there, with so much energy, so much violence.

After a dozen songs, a lanky boy, whom I guess to be about seventeen, tramps up the stairs to our section. Our tickets are off stage right, in line of sight with T. J. Wrex, so we can see perfectly and won't have our heads blasted off by a direct hit from the speakers pointing at the pit and beyond. The boy grips his T-shirt in a tight bundle. The shirt is ripped to shreds and blood-ied. Blood drips from his nose. He falls into a seat a few rows over and tips his head back to stop the trickle.

"Is this fun or *what*?" I scream to Marnie, who sits between Eddie and me.

"Idiot," she says, leaning into my ear.

I notice Eddie has slid his hand onto Marnie's knee, and Marnie grips his hand in return. That's my boy.

By the time the show ended, we still hadn't seen his best friend, Tyler, or Annie Harkin. It's not easy to locate anyone among thirteen thousand–some people, but it's not hard to pick out a man in a wheelchair among a crowd of teenagers, either.

My ears are still ringing when we get home—rather, when *I* get home.

During the drive, Eddie and Marnie started lip exercises in the backseat, I guess to exchange all the "positive messages" they'd gotten from Steely Black Steeple's explosive concert. So when we finally arrived at the Jenningses' house, Eddie asked whether he could stay there.

Though it was already one-thirty in the morning, it wasn't a school night. I told Eddie he had to be home no later than three A.M., handed him a ten-dollar bill, and urged him to call a cab.

"It'd be best," I said to both of them, "if you ask her parents if it's okay that you're here—and you need to call the cab company now."

"Everyone's already asleep," Marnie happily volunteered.

"But seeing as how New Cumbria isn't New York and doesn't have what you'd call an armada of taxicabs prowling the streets at night, especially out here in what you have to admit is the boondocks, it might be wise to call one now and request your ride home." My gaze flickered back and forth between them in the dark. "Summer officially started tonight, Eddie, and with mission accomplished, you—" He waved me away. He knew he had fulfilled all three demands. His slate was clean, and he could keep it that way if he didn't screw up this gift: letting him stay with Marnie. "Super. I guess I don't need to wait up." I smiled at them and turned away when they climbed out of the car.

They were just so damned pretty, and too young to know

how much *trouble* that could get them into. Made me want to cry.

Despite the rain, I rolled down the passenger-side window and yelled across the manicured lawn, "Hey, I had fun tonight. You guys rock. Hope you had a good time."

"Thank you, Mr. D," Marnie screamed.

I know I'll get a thank-you note in the mail within the socially acceptable three days.

Back at the SQ, I drive as close as I can to the door so I won't have to roll through the torrent.

No sooner do I get unpeeled from my wet clothes, fold up my chair, notice that the ringing in my ears has dissipated, stretch out in my bed in dry, warm comfort, and pick up the half-ton *Once an Eagle* than someone pounds on my front door.

I wrap myself in my terry-cloth robe and grab my cell phone.

Throwing myself into my wheelchair, I roll to the frenzied rattle of the door.

I find Jerod blanched. His face looks raw with panic. "Where is she, Randol?"

"Who? Marnie? I would hope she's at home, where I just dropped her off. With Eddie."

"Eddie's not here, either?" He leaps inside to get out of the rain. "He's not with her?"

"Her who?" I'm struck by the lightning of Jerod's distress. "Oh, you mean with *Annie*?"

"Who do you think I mean?" He rakes his palm through his hair, in part to get the rain off his face and in part because of his alarm. His pacing spreads fear like flames across the room, threatening to engulf the entire house in red-hot panic.

"What's going on, Jerod? It's almost two o'cl—"

"Didn't she go to the concert with you? Isn't that what Eddie said, that she was going to the concert with you?" His words zing at me like bullets.

"No. She was going to the concert, and I guess she *did* go to the concert, but nobody said she was actually *going* with us. I thought she might, but—"

"So where is she now?"

"Did you check the Jessamine—"

"Of course I did, Randol. Why do you think I'm here? I've been everywhere." He's screaming now, his breathing short and scary, his voice at terrifying levels.

"Have you heard anything from Tyler?"

"Who the *fuck* is Tyler?"

"C'mon, now, Jerod, you're going to have to think clearly and calm down. You know who Tyler is. Tyler Lawson, Eddie's best friend. The kid who was missing yesterday? *He* was supposed to go with us to the concert, and with Annie. That's the last thing I heard. I thought maybe they all went to Hero's Diner, then to the show, then maybe stayed around Wrenton for a milk shake after the show or something. It's probably nothing."

"What time did the show let out?"

"About two hours ago. She's probably dropping Tyler off at Dr. and Mrs. Lawson's house right about now. I imagine she's heading over to the Jessamine Plantation Inn as we speak."

Jerod drops onto the futon and, for a moment, manages to pull himself together. His elbows fall on his knees and his face into his hands. He keeps running his hands through his hair.

"Better watch it, Jerod, you'll pull all that out, and—"

"Just shut up, asshole!"

I'm alarmed.

Without another word, Jerod gets up and strides into my bedroom.

"Hey, what do you think you're doing in there?" I'm catching his panic like so much influenza. So I fish my cell phone out of my robe and call the Lawsons.

Toby answers. "Who's this?"

"I'm sorry, Dr. Lawson, this is Randol Duncan, and I'm terribly sorry to bother you at this time of night, but is Tyler back yet?"

"Randol, yes, what's wrong?"

"Nothing, I'm fine, but Tyler, is he there?"

"Tyler? Yes, he just got back a few minutes ago. Is everything okay?"

I put my thumb over the tiny microphone. "See there, Jerod. Nothing to worry about. Tyler's at home. Just like I said. So, like I said, I would bet Annie's back at the inn in just a few minutes." Uncovering the speaker, I say to Toby, "Would you mind, Dr. Lawson, if I talked to Tyler for just a second, please?"

"Not at all. Hang on a minute while I get him for you." I hear the doctor's basso bedside-mannered-voice call for his son.

Another line picks up. "This's Tyler."

"Hey, stud. Show kicked ass, didn't it?"

"Who's this?"

"Randol Duncan."

"Oh, yeah, hey, Mr. D, what's up?"

"Have you seen Annie? Um, Miss Harkin? She seems to be missing."

Jerod stalks back into the room with my laptop. The machine is open and flickering. He sits in the chair at my left elbow, glowering.

Tyler says nothing. The pause is discomfiting.

"Tyler?" I prompt him.

"I don't know where she went," he mumbles.

"Where she *went*?"

"I went to the concert with some other kids, Mr. D. I never saw her. That's all I can tell you. Please. I don't want to talk about it anymore."

"Talk about what, Tyler, about *what?*" I fear I'm about to lose him.

Even his pauses sound sullen and panicky.

"Can I tell you something?" he whispers finally. "That you won't tell anyone? You swear?" He sounds like a child who's regressing in years with every word. I wonder whether my grandfather's soldier boys became children again when they were alone and afraid.

"Tyler, listen, whatever it is, it's going to be okay. Just talk to me."

"You can't tell anyone. Do you swear? Do you promise?"

"Just tell me what you can."

"I'm going to call you back on my cell phone."

"No, no. There's nobody on the other line. Just tell me what you're upset about."

He pauses again.

"I swear to God, I will help you with whatever you want to tell me, Tyler."

With that, Tyler begins to sob. Then, in halting heaves: "Annie—Miss Harkin—she . . . asked . . . me . . . to do . . . stuff . . . on a Web site."

"Oh, dear God, Tyler." Where my ears had been ringing just a few minutes before from a rock concert, now they're pounding with the agony I hear in Tyler's voice. Of course, I know what he's telling me is true. "What is the site?"

He whispers the address of an Internet site.

I reach for a pen and a scrap of paper and scribble it down. "Okay. Go slow. I'm an old man, not a geek like you guys."

"Not even Eddie knows the address of the site. Just me, I'm the only one who knows—just me and Annie."

Despite what Tyler has told me, I'm shocked when he calls her by her first name.

"Tyler? Are you okay?" I try as best I can to be discreet, keeping an eye on Jerod, who, I can tell by his scrunched shoulders and scowl, is looking at something on the computer.

I hear Tyler try to choke back tears. "Someone, probably me, is going to get into a shitload of trouble."

"Not from me."

He sighs. Maybe I have reeled him in a little, at least enough so that he can tell me what I need to know.

Jerod shuts my laptop and resumes pacing around me, like a ceiling fan out of control. If he doesn't find out something soon, he'll fly out of his socket.

I grab my laptop from where Jerod left it, and the screen flickers back to life. He has left the screen full of banking information.

"I've got my computer. What do I need to type in, Tyler?"

Jerod stops and stands stock-still.

"Here's the thing," he says. "Eddie doesn't know the Web site address, but I did give him the password, just in case there might be trouble."

Damn, these kids are clever. Adults may think they're in control of the world, but it's the kids who can manipulate it.

"Okay, now, type in this Web address," he says, dictating numbers and letters to me.

The site that pops up is like eleven million others around the world that belong mostly to teenagers. The screen is filled with their favorite music and titillating photos and musings about the travesties of their lives.

"See the very top Web log, the main blog about myself?"

"Yeah, okay."

"Count every third letter in the blog until you have a seven-letter word."

I run my finger across the screen and mouth each letter as I go. "P-E-C-C-A-R-E." I try the word out loud on my tongue. "'*Peccare.*' That's Latin for 'sin.'"

"Correct."

"Have you?" I ask. "Sinned, I mean?"

"That's the user name at another Web site," he says, choking up again. "And that's the site I'm talking about. It's a secured site. Nobody except me and Annie has ever seen it. At least, I hope to God they haven't." He's crying so hard now that he can't speak.

I'm at a loss, helpless in more ways than I can ever remember being. Jerod glares at me with expectation, and I can only stare into my lifeless lap.

"Oh, my God," Tyler blubbers again and again. "Oh . . . oh, my God!"

"Tyler, it's okay." Except that it's not. I wonder if Grandfather felt this powerless when he comforted Corporal Dahlgren—or did Grandfather's medals and decorations provide the young soldier with a sense of hope and wisdom that I cannot?

"I beg you, Mr. Duncan, *please* . . . I beg you with all my life and all my heart, now that I'm about to show this to you—"

"Tyler, it's okay."

He slowly gives me each letter of the second, secured, secret Web address: annie-and-tyler.com.

Jerod moves over my shoulder and watches me type the letters. My brother hasn't heard Tyler's terror and despair, and I resent the anger and curiosity I feel oozing from him.

The computer asks me for a user name and a password. In one box, I type in *p-e-c-c-a-r-e*.

Tyler whispers through an agonized moan, "You have to *swear* to me, promise me—"

"I'll do everything I can. Now tell me the password."

"Promise me!" Tyler hisses.

"I promise. Tell me the password."

"I can't, Mr. D, I just can't. Get it from Eddie. I can't talk anymore." And with that, he hangs up.

"What the *hell* is *this* all about, Randol?"

Ignoring him, I punch Eddie's number into my cell phone. He answers with a groan on the third ring.

"I know, I know, Eddie. Listen, I'm sorry. You knew it was me; you could've just ignored the call."

"No, I figured something was wrong, and besides, I had a great time. So, what's your damage?"

I hear the rustle of bodies untangling and feel a pang of nostalgia. "Listen, I need a favor."

"No can do. I'm kind of in the middle of something."

"Just one quick question, then you can get back to it." I check the time on my laptop. "Until you have to be back here in about, oh, an hour. Have you called the cab company yet? It's going to take them at least that long to send a cab out that way and get you home on time. Do *not*, I repeat, do *not* mess this up."

Jerod, running his hand through his hair for the umpteenth time, looks as if he is seconds away from yanking all of it out.

"Okay." Eddie sighs. "What's your question?"

"I need the password for Tyler's secret, secured Web site."

Long pause. "Dad, nobody even *has* the address for that site."

"I do."

"That just isn't possible."

"Son, give me the password. Now." The seriousness of my

own voice startles even me; I can't imagine what Eddie must be thinking.

"Where'd you get the address?"

"That's not something you need to know right now. So, do you want me to call Mr. Jennings and tell him that it is in his daughter's best interest that he drive you home right now? Or can we have a nice long talk about this over breakfast tomorrow?"

Eddie spits out the password and hangs up. The codeword's heartbreaking irony is lost on the fourteen-year-old: BenFranklin.

I shift the laptop so that my brother and I can both see the screen.

After I type the password into the final box, pictures begin to fill the computer monitor, and I could weep—for my own child and for his friend who listened more than I thought to my stories. And as the images multiply, for the young man, the child, I see exploited before me.

Rather than flick on the stark fluorescent kitchen lights, I have turned on the lamp near Grandfather's old breakfast table. Jerod and I used to spook each other by saying the old yellow lamp shade was made from the skin of dead German soldiers. Dead soldiers or not, the room is filled with a warm glow.

We've spent the better part of two hours talking and raiding the refrigerator, doing serious damage to ham biscuits, pimiento cheese finger sandwiches, cold collard greens, and leftover ambrosia without any fresh, hand-shredded coconut. We've downed cup after cup of coffee, the best we could percolate in Volusia's absence.

At some point, I heard a car pull into the driveway and a door thud. A minute or two later, the front door to the SQ rattled open, then closed, and I looked out the kitchen window to see the lights in Eddie's bedroom go on, then off.

The laptop sits on the breakfast table between us, a technological elephant we can't ignore.

Jerod's rage has subsided to anger, then gloom, then defeat. The same waves will roll again. Then again.

I reach over and click again through page after virtual page. I can't bear to look. I can't bear *not* to look.

The genius of Annie Harkin is more stunning than her looks—not, I suppose, that it takes, genius to create child pornography.

Jerod raises his head, which has been slumped over the kitchen table for the better part of the past half hour. I haven't heard a sob, but his eyes, wet and ringed with red, now land on a picture of Annie, splayed out in centerfold-like glory.

It's too much, even after the Patpong prostitutes in Bangkok and Jupe's strip clubs; perhaps because we know Annie, because Jerod loved her and trusted her, because we trusted her with our children—or maybe because we know that the next picture on the site shows her defiling a child.

Jerod slumps his head back into his arms on the table.

I turn the computer away from him. I am, for a change, unable to choose the right words, or even the wrong ones.

This time, with dawn beginning to throw its fine purple light into my grandparents' warm kitchen, I begin clicking open more pages, the banking sites, although I have looked through them a dozen times and comprehend them about as much as I do the foul plan behind Annie's exploitation of Tyler Lawson—how she seduced the boy and used him to hack into my father's accounts and then documented her exploits in case she needed to blackmail us all.

The numbers are mind-boggling, the accounts labyrinthine.

No one could ever have dreamed she was capable of any of this—no one except possibly Volusia.

Gently, hoping my words come out right, I whisper to my brother: "The bottom line is that we can't go to Terry Magnus with any of this, for obvious reasons."

"No shit," he says, looking up long enough to glare at me, his voice rough. "You mean, we can't go to Chief Magnus and tell him that I've been helping my father, who he's been trying to put in jail for a dozen years or so, that Dad and I have laundered nearly six million dollars and that now—dear God—the most beautiful woman on the planet has exploited a computer-geek teenager to steal most of our money?"

Sometimes I should probably just keep my mouth shut, and maybe this is one of those times, but I say, "That's looking on the bright side, Jerod. She could have taken you mopes for every last penny. But she left you with at least a million and change—or, at least, that's what it looks like to me."

"That's only because Dipshit, as you're so fond of calling him, was sentimental enough to leave a large, unnumbered, secured, inaccessible account open in Bangkok, at the Pradiphat Trust Bank, remember? The one he started back when all this crap began in Vietnam."

I click back through the Web pages, back to the pictures of Annie.

"How'd she do it?" I ask, perhaps a bit too absentmindedly.

"She got into me. I mean, c'mon, Randol. Who would think twice about giving her anything she wants?" He smiles for the first time tonight, a grim, tragic, ruined smile.

I finally remember that comment from Tolstoy, the one I had tried to think of back in February when I first saw Annie Harkin: "What a strange illusion it is to suppose that beauty is goodness."

When he first laid eyes on Annie, Jerod saw an illusion, all right, the same way, as clichéd as it sounds, a man dying of thirst sees the watery mirage of an oasis in the desert.

"What about Tyler?" Jerod asks, pushing himself up from the table and collecting the mess we've made.

"Well." That's all I can offer. I close my laptop with a definitive click, trying hard not to think about that child having . . . and I begin to laugh.

"What could possibly be so . . ." And after all these hours of wretchedness, heartbreak, and disaster, with no possible means of retribution or escape, my brother starts to laugh, too.

The hard plaster walls reverberate with our laughter. We're laughing so hard, I would bet the dead Nazis in the Plunder Room are laughing with us.

"The lucky . . ." I begin, thinking of Tyler and his romps with Annie. But the laughter isn't real.

My heart shreds as I watch my brother move to the kitchen sink and lean into it, retching. He is vomiting up his conscience, I suspect.

I'd give all those trunks upstairs, this house, every one of my pseudointellectual brain cells, even what is left of this mangled body—I would give everything but my son—to be able to stand and take my brother in my arms. At the same time, I feel as if I should be throwing up, too—my own hypocrisy, my own shame, all the regrets I've swallowed with sweet coatings of nihilism and pride through the years.

Rolling toward him, I am without words. I put my hand on the small of his back. And I am silent, at last.

He turns and gazes down at me, the light from the morning sun pouring through the window and coloring his pale, stricken face.

"I caused this, Randol. The truth is, I caused all of it."

He stands, surveying the mess we've made of Grandmother's kitchen. I hand him a dish towel to wipe his face—ensuring severe wrath from Volusia, when she finds it so dirty.

"You were seduced, Jerod. So was Tyler. We all were."

"It's not like you to offer platitudes," Jerod says. "We were all fools, Randol, stupid, that's all."

I cram another ham biscuit into my mouth because I don't know what else to do. "Listen, Jerod, Toby Lawson is a brilliant surgeon. He and his family are a gift to this town. And the fact of the matter is, they're the ones who are going to pay for this."

Jerod looks around the room again. "V's gonna kill us. This place is trashed." He smiles, for real this time.

His lips, thin as Grandfather's leadership lips, are set in the grip of grim resignation. He puts his hand on my shoulder. "Thanks for everything, Randol." I rest my hand on his. "I'm going to take a shower, then head over to the Lawsons.'"

"Maybe they don't have to know," I say, though I know the words sound empty. I manage to whisper, "I'm right here, buddy." And then: "This is home, Jerod, our home. And we're going to make damned sure not to let anything more happen to it regardless of what comes next."

Part Three

LOVES,

LABORS

LOST

CHAPTER SIXTEEN

I TRY to spoon some greenish-brown goop into my father's distorted mouth.

"Honestly, I hate to tell you this, Jupe, but this muck looks and actually smells a little like the stuff that was running through the streets of Tientsin when your father and mother were there."

He smiles, sort of. He can't form words very well, but his hearing is just fine.

"Tasty, huh."

"Like Chinese food," I think he says, or perhaps I just imagine he's trying to say.

"Moo Shoo Poo." I push another spoonful into him. "Yum!"

Volusia squeaks into the China Room. "You boys okay in here? It's hotter'n the hinges on the gates of hell out there." She fans herself with one of Grandmother's old St. Paul's Church fans, with the wooden tongue-depressor handle and a picture of Jesus on one side and a New Cumbria Motors ad on the other. "Can't wait until this August heat wave ends."

"You two're some pair." She laughs. "You're feedin' him like he was a baby, and you stuck in a wheelchair with all the maturity of a kid yourself."

"You'd better have one of those little bars of soap handy for what I want to say right about now." I hand her the accoutrements of Dad's pureed dinner and ask her to bring more coffee.

She squeaks off. All these months, she hasn't asked about Annie Harkin. She knows not to.

And we wouldn't know what to say, really. Nobody knows where Annie has gone.

As best Jerod can figure, Annie managed to wire a bit more than four million dollars from offshore accounts in the names of Edward Jupiter Duncan and Jerod Barrows Duncan into Swiss and Bahamian accounts in her own name, locked and untouchable. As Jerod had said, Annie apparently didn't know about the funds in the Bangkok bank, couldn't figure out how to access the account, or didn't have time. Afterward, she simply vanished, probably by rental car before the concert, then by air at Wrenton International to a major hub like Atlanta or New York—certainly all paid for with cash. My Webzine editor, Keith Chen, did some discreet digging for us through his New York contacts and helped come up with a theory.

Annie could be anywhere, with stolen money and dirty pictures. The Web site, tyler-and-annie.com, disappeared. I'd like to believe the pictures have all been destroyed, but they probably just moved to another address, just as Annie did.

And so she's gone—she tarnished our family's legacy. She couldn't steal our honor.

Tyler Lawson left the day after Annie disappeared. Toby enrolled his son in a prep school in Virginia and told us that the move had been planned all along.

Eddie has taken everything pretty well, though at first he acted like a lion who had lost his male companion. "Look at it this way," I told Eddie. "High school is four years. Lions live only five years, and they spend their last year with their best friends." But Eddie didn't get to spend his "last year" with his best friend. "I'm sure you guys 'talk' on your computers all night, don't you?" He smiled and hunched over his keyboard.

As for my father, well, I try to keep him comfortable. We've moved a brand-new recliner to the China Room in front of the big TV set.

Jerod's still trying to clean up his messes.

I tell Jupe that I think we should write a book about Grandfather, the real story.

He slides his eyes in my direction. He still doesn't have enough strength in his neck muscles to move his head.

"I never did get to describe all the fantastic stuff I found in the Plunder Room," I tell him. "But I imagine you've seen most of it, huh?"

His fingers flicker toward my arm. Taking the hint, I put my hand on his cheek and turn him to face me. His eyes are moist and sad.

I mention a few of the things Jerod and I pulled from the old footlockers.

"What do you think your dad was really like?" I ask. "Do you think he really never went to the whorehouses at Chin-wang-tao? That he never strayed from PeeCee? Never got tempted, the way his boys did?"

Dad curls his lower lip and manages to shake his head. With tremendous difficulty he works his mouth to say the words, and when the words finally do come, they are muffled and wounded: "He . . . was . . . an original. . . . True officer and a . . . genuine"—he stops and takes in several labored breaths— "gentleman." A tear slides down his benumbed cheek.

"So what happened to you, old man?"

He knows the answer and knows that I do, too.

He was weak. The army had become weak, too. Their weaknesses worked well together. I had heard, and everyone knows, that profiteers bloom and flourish in every war, but I wonder, looking at my father, if they're getting craftier, more devious—and wealthier. I have to wonder who they are, too—men a lot more powerful than my father are doing things Jupe could only have dreamed about, but that's a story for another day, and this story's about Jupe and, ultimately, my grandfather.

I suppose Jupe would also say that he envied his father, and that he couldn't live up to his father's example. Maybe he never tried.

"Everything's going to be fine, Jupe." I fluff the pillow behind his head. "You'll be up and around in no time."

Dad tries to ask where Jerod is. I point toward the grand staircase.

Jerod's at work. We made an office for him in one of the bedrooms upstairs, across the big Oriental rug from the Plunder Room. He has everything he needs: wireless Internet, his own phone line, a fax machine—and some things that he doesn't need, like the four-poster bed with the lacy pink canopy.

We have closed down the Jupe Box and Callisto's and hired new management for the convenience stores. Jerod told everyone in Ganymede's Paradise that they will have to leave the trailer park. He even offered each resident a small buyout of their leases. We plan to develop the three and a half acres into a strip-shopping center with reputable tenants.

"Maybe," Jupe mumbles.

"Maybe what, Dad?"

He works to say something about writing his father's story.

I tell him that if Grandfather were alive today, he would still stop and stand in salute every time he heard "Reveille." If his country called him to war, despite his age, he would be first in line.

And I tell Jupe that just before Grandfather died, he said to me, "War is the greatest adventure in the world."

"You know what else he said? The day before he died, he told me, 'A man without honor has no integrity, for to disregard either destroys both.' And he said, 'Leadership, if that's where a man's destiny lies, rests not in power, but in the willingness to die in the name of honor.'" My father looks into my eyes as if he's looking for his own father. "But those weren't his last words. Just before Grandfather died, he reached up to heaven, just like this, as if he were reaching for PeeCee, and he cried out, 'Dear God!'"

Jerod comes down the stairs, rubbing his eyes, which are bright. He is tired, but he seems lighter, too. The expensive shoes, pleated twills, and Oxford shirts are packed away. Instead, he's wearing faded jeans and one of Eddie's death-metal band T-shirts.

In my grandfather, I never did see fatigue. In fact, I never saw any kind of burden—not the way I often did in Jupe and Jerod. Honesty and strong character, I suppose, buy that kind of stamina.

Jerod strolls into the kitchen. I can't hear a thing he and Volusia say to each other, but I hear them laughing.

"You miss Grandfather, don't you?" I ask Jupe.

He nods.

"I do, too, Dad."

I picture Colonel Edward Randol Duncan—his wavy silver hair and huge walrus mustache. He stands outside on the big porch in his officer's pinks and leather puttees. He holds a bouquet of flowers and tells my grandmother that it's time for him to go.

He has another war to fight.

She nods and puts her hands on his cheeks and smiles.

"'I'd give up a palace if I were a king,'" he sings and hands her the flowers. "But I'll be back soon. And I know there's a queen living there."

She tells him she loves him with all her heart and soul. "You're my hero, Edward, darling. Be safe, and I'll be here waiting for you when you get back."

They kiss. Then he says, "To our shanty in old Shanty Town."

ACKNOWLEDGMENTS

Much like the Grand Old Army where Colonel Duncan lived his best, it takes a battalion to create a novel.

For starters, few could live without a family—in my case, no way. My brother, Stephen, gave me his kidney in 1984; I wouldn't be here without him. My sister, Sally, helped raise two hellions. And most of all, my parents gave us opportunities most people never get. My late grandparents; my aunt, Ann Baldwin, a huge fan and reader; my godparents, John Feagin and Martha—all helped in myriad ways tangible and imperceptible (at least, to them). And to Irene Laughlin—always cheering.

Heartfelt thanks to my editor, Ruth Cavin, who capped my quixotic, two-decade odyssey to publication in ways that couldn't possibly have made me happier. Same goes with Toni Plummer, another editorial gem at Thomas Dunne Books. Dream-makers— bless you.

This list is by no means comprehensive, though I wish it

could be: Ashley Warlick, George Wen, Elizabeth Drewry and the Emrys people, Patti and Jim Brown and the others who shared the Algonkian experience. For help in researching the China material, I wish to acknowledge Dr. Elihu Rose, and for help with the lyrics, Matthew Hammond.

I owe deep gratitude to Columbia Journalism School, all the Big Names and the indefatigable, legendary Class of 1986, David Martin, Glen Craney, Beth Nissen, Joyce Shelby, Jim Dwyer, Judith Crist. My thanks also go to Frank Eppes, Will McKibbon, Dr. Bill Lavery, Kathy Greene, and Roger Paul. I owe so much to Loydean Thomas, Karen Haram, John Goodspeed, and so many at the *San Antonio Express-News,* and to Karin Metz and George Joplin. My deep admiration, gratitude, love, thanks, and so much more go to Mary Dedinsky and Carlisle Herbert and to Tim Padgett, who joined the *Chicago Sun-Times* the same day I did, in addition to the entire staff (I wish I could name all of you): Jack Higgins, Tom Brune, Tom McNamee, Andrew Hermann, the most talented and colorful journalists/writers/editors and photogs I've ever been honored to know: Dick Mitchell, Steve Duke, Charlie Dickinson, Ann Henderson, and everybody else there, the Billy Goat and Oprah. Thanks, as well, go to the gems at the *St. Petersburg Times.* Then there's Nancy Faller, Sean LaRoche, dear Margaret, Jay Pitts, John Oudens, Judith Chalmers, John Wilbur, John Bouda, Mark Fowler, Lee Landenberger, Jock Fistick, the Vermont Studio Center, the great writers: Lynn Sharon Schwartz, George Singleton, Scott Gould, Pat Conroy, Mindy Friddle, and many more. And the many, many doctors, Lynn Banowsky, Paraiac Mulgrew, Scott Arnold, Ed Brown, Victor Klimas, Dana Shires, Louis Brady, Christopher Kavolus, Mo Gangai, all the people at Columbia Presbyterian and Walter Reed and Brooke Army medical centers who saved my life. Thanks to the Handlebar and our staff, without whom I couldn't do this, and the fans who support what we work so hard for, all the great music. Thanks to John Mayer, Janis Ian, Joan Baez, Eddie from Ohio, John Hiatt, Dar Williams, Keith Perissi and Ben Friedman and the boys, Corey Smith, Saffire—the Uppity Blues Women and Ann Rabson and the artists and friends who have made our venue venerable, and thanks especially to the ones who have given back. Marty Winsch, Willis Tisdale, Freddie and Kelly Wooten, Bob Ross, Dan Colucci, Bobby Cudd, Brian Hill, Scott Clayton, and Joe Brauner are the best. Thanks to Tommy Brown and Max Shanks for ensuring the computer(s) always worked.

Thanks, as well, to the Hillsborough County Arts Commission in Florida and Greenville, South Carolina's, Metropolitan Arts Council for grants.

Special thanks to Dea Sasso and June. I can't begin to say all that needs to be said. Fortunately, Dea knows what I mean.

And, finally and always, to my wife, Kathy, my best friend, brilliant editor, business partner, counselor, and so much more. How could such a feckless rapscallion as me be any more blessed? I love you *so* much!